The Awa

ALSO BY MATTHEW PEARL

*Save Our Souls: The True Story of a Castaway
Family, Treachery, and Murder*

*The Taking of Jemima Boone: Colonial Settlers, Tribal
Nations, and the Kidnap That Shaped America*

The Dante Chamber

The Last Bookaneer

The Technologists

The Last Dickens

The Poe Shadow

The Dante Club

The Award

A Novel

Matthew Pearl

HARPER
An Imprint of HarperCollins*Publishers*

This is a work of fiction. Names, characters, places, and incidents are products of the author's imagination or are used fictitiously and are not to be construed as real. Any resemblance to actual events, locales, organizations, or persons, living or dead, is entirely coincidental.

Without limiting the exclusive rights of any author, contributor or the publisher of this publication, any unauthorized use of this publication to train generative artificial intelligence (AI) technologies is expressly prohibited. HarperCollins also exercise their rights under Article 4(3) of the Digital Single Market Directive 2019/790 and expressly reserve this publication from the text and data mining exception.

THE AWARD. Copyright © 2025 by Matthew Pearl. All rights reserved. Printed in the United States of America. No part of this book may be used or reproduced in any manner whatsoever without written permission except in the case of brief quotations embodied in critical articles and reviews. For information, address HarperCollins Publishers, 195 Broadway, New York, NY 10007. In Europe, HarperCollins Publishers, Macken House, 39/40 Mayor Street Upper, Dublin 1, D01 C9W8, Ireland.

HarperCollins books may be purchased for educational, business, or sales promotional use. For information, please email the Special Markets Department at SPsales@harpercollins.com.

hc.com

FIRST EDITION

Library of Congress Cataloging-in-Publication Data

Names: Pearl, Matthew, author.
Title: The award: a novel / Matthew Pearl.
Description: First edition. | New York, NY: Harper, 2025.
Identifiers: LCCN 2025007780 | ISBN 9780063445277 (hardcover) | ISBN 9780063445284 (trade paperback) | ISBN 9780063445291 (ebook)
Subjects: LCGFT: Novels.
Classification: LCC PS3616.E25 A97 2025 | DDC 813/.6—dc23/eng/20250224

25 26 27 28 29 LBC 5 4 3 2 1

Writers are dangerous people.
—NIKITA GILL, POET

Author's Note

Some of this happened.

The Award

1

IF HE COULD HAVE KNOWN all the lives that would be wrecked, David still would have agreed to all that was to come, starting that bright, windless day he stood outside 6 Observatory Hill Road, waiting to see the top floor of the three-story Victorian-style house.

The realtor had slowed down as she climbed the front steps. "So tell me what you're looking for."

David and Bonnie trailed behind her.

David tilted his head back to look at the highest windows of the house, defeated by the rays of sun. *Tell me what you're looking for.* The realtor's words snaked into his mind as, roughly, *What are you looking for in life, when at twenty-eight years old you call yourself a writer but you're always trying to finish the same first novel?*

He had been sinking into panic about his prospects lately, which led his mind to wander this way. He knew seven people in his personal orbit who had already published books, though one was with an academic press, and nobody was sure if that counted. Three of the other writers were younger than him, if only by months, and one tiptoed, briefly, onto a best-seller list. David had an MFA—master of fine arts in fiction writing, he'd clarify, most people having no idea what that was—but ultimately his degree dragged him down, merely rendering him self-conscious about his work. He had been grinding out the same manuscript for the last five years. The realtor's question prodded him to mentally grasp for an answer: *I'm looking for my turn.*

That was all. So simple.

Just his turn!

Deep down, though, he feared he could never be good enough. Or that everyone else deserved to reach their goals more than he deserved his.

Bonnie took David's hand, snapping him back to the present. David, who was just above average height when he made an effort to stand up straight, used his free hand to toss his overgrown brown hair from his eyes.

"Two bedrooms would be ideal, in case of family visits, with a bonus room or extra space for David to do his work," Bonnie said. "Wish-list items: at least one and a half baths and a renovated kitchen." Bonnie was not a writer, so she effortlessly sounded like a normal person. Sharon, the realtor, wasn't really listening; she had just been making conversation while sifting through her thicket of keys.

Sharon finally unlocked the door, and they followed her up a narrow, angular stairway that had been added half a century earlier to the side of the house to keep it hidden from the street. Long ago, owners of a Cambridge, Massachusetts, home wouldn't have wanted people to see their servants go in and out, or to know that financially strapped owners rented out the top floor, where David and Bonnie were headed. The stairway was enclosed in flimsy plasterboard. It was dimly lit, and each tread emitted a creak that petered out into a hollow echo.

"Tight squeeze," David commented as the stairwell narrowed even further after another sharp turn, where Bonnie had to take care not to slip in her ballet flats.

They were coming to the third floor, topping the lower floors of the ornate old house, where someone else was living in what must have been a grander fashion.

"Those stairs are a doozy," said Sharon, who had a frizzy red ponytail and a drunken laugh. "You know Cambridge. Everyone is content just to live here."

Her observations could have been sarcastic or sad, hard to tell. After rounding one more odd angle in the stairway, they trailed her into the top floor.

"Ta-da," said Sharon.

Light flooded into the four windows of the vestibule where the stairs let them out. Bonnie's manner and questions to the realtor let on that she liked the place, exactly what a potential tenant wasn't supposed to do, but nothing could convince Bonnie to deceive. The $3,200-a-month price tag was steep, and would be absurd almost anywhere else on earth, but, as the realtor kept making clear, this was Cambridge, Boston's best-educated and haughtiest neighbor. Universities gobbled up real estate, which shrank the supply for desperate renters, which led people with seemingly infinite money from around the world to buy up the remaining properties and further inflate prices. On top of that, there was nowhere new to build housing, because there was nowhere new in Cambridge.

"So few places on the rental market right now," said Sharon. "I helped an assistant professor rent a treehouse earlier this year, and a colleague found a shed for a Tufts graduate student."

Bonnie laughed.

"I'm not kidding," Sharon snapped.

"Sorry," said Bonnie.

"The shed is actually charming, and the lease gives her permission to use the bathroom in the main house, and their kitchen twice a day, as long as she remains in the shed the rest of the time. There's two of you, at least. Two incomes?" Without waiting for an answer, which would have revealed her error, she added, "That's always helpful."

"I have a question, Sharon," David said from the living room, gesturing back at the pitiful staircase that had brought them there. "Is that the only way in and out?"

"I'm afraid so."

"Isn't that a fire hazard?"

The realtor laughed, the same laugh she'd emitted on the stairs, but never denied that a fire here would incinerate anyone inside.

"How would you even move furniture in and out of here?" David persisted. "The three of us barely fit up those stairs. I can't imagine squeezing a couch or a mattress, or—"

"Ah, yes," Sharon said. "That's the catch. Cards on the table, that"—she paused to search her real-estate-friendly vocabulary—"idiosyncratic staircase is the only reason why it's still on the market. Otherwise, poof." She made a hand gesture like a magician making something disappear.

She led them to the hall between the living room and the bedrooms. On the hardwood floor, she pointed out a large rectangular outline: a cutout.

David asked what it was.

"It's the answer to your question. It's a trapdoor over a crawl space, and below that is another trapdoor that opens onto the much larger, wider central stairs running through the two floors of the main house. Your lease gives you the right to use it to move furniture in and out, through the front door of the main house and up their staircase."

The rooms were relatively big and airy, the hardwood floors shiny and clean. Even that convoluted clause in the lease couldn't dampen Bonnie's enthusiasm. "That's handy, to have the landlords downstairs, in case there's any problems," she said. "I'm sure they're very nice." Bonnie always assumed the best in people, without evidence, which left her irritated when it was proven otherwise. Her upbeat vibes would have served her in countless lucrative career paths;

maybe she could even have been a realtor herself, though a vague guilt-driven suspicion about the morality of most fields had led her to her job with a nonprofit, where she helped match underserved families with needed services.

"Oh, those won't be your landlords if you rent here," Sharon corrected her. "Many years ago, this all used to be a single-family house. Then the first two floors sold to one owner, and this top floor sold to a different owner, who added the stairs on the side of the house where we came up, and created the crawl space between them." She pointed again to the cutout in the floor.

"Then if the downstairs neighbors aren't the landlords—" David began.

"The current owners of this top floor are a young couple, like you. They moved to the suburbs—I believe they wanted space to start a family. The couple initially placed this unit on the market to sell, but when potential buyers were put off by those stairs, they recently decided to try to rent it out. *They*'d be your landlords, not the people downstairs. Technically this is a condo association made up of two units."

"Hopefully the neighbors downstairs appreciate strangers dragging their furniture up through their house," David muttered.

As the realtor flipped through her notes, Bonnie beckoned David over to show him a few possible spots to set up his desk. Even though it only generated debt, Bonnie took David's writing as seriously as he did. David loved that about her, but it had the unintended effect of making him more nervous than ever that he'd fall short. Now that sinking feeling overtook him again, the feeling that he would never meet expectations, his or hers, a pessimism that in turn always upset Bonnie. His greatest fear was not about the writing itself. He had decent talent; he'd worked hard for years to become a polished, consistent writer. His fears were about intangibles. Was he special enough? Every writer he encountered seemed to have some distinctive attribute, while David felt forgettable even to himself. Not just in writing, but in life. Was he destined to just be missing that elusive X factor?

This condo, with its ghastly stairs, was just another reminder that he was unable to contribute to their finances the way Bonnie deserved, though she was too hopeful and superstitious to ever acknowledge that.

"A two-year lease is required . . ." the realtor was saying. David was planning their sprint out the door. Trapped here for two years! That would take them into the summer of 2010, which seemed like an eternity. They should hang around a few more minutes to be polite, he decided. Then they could tell Sharon they had to discuss it, or that it didn't quite seem to fit their needs, and get the hell out. Maybe grab lunch and laugh about how they'd dodged a bullet.

David took in the view from a window overlooking the yard.

"Think of it like this, David," Bonnie said, resting a hand on his lower back. "If it wasn't for the stairs, they would have sold this a long time ago, and it would never be available for rent. Remember some of the dismal places we've looked at? This one could be meant to be, even though the rent is a stretch. Otherwise we'll end up in a treehouse."

"Bonnie," he started to reply, but he was tongue-tied. Maybe he was a writer in part because when he was writing, he could revise until he sounded sure of himself. He should just cut Bonnie loose, he thought. Let her be free to be with someone on his way to being somebody, someone fulfilling his potential.

They'd met at a birthday party they'd each been dragged to, in an apartment where they felt out of place. Talking about their mutual discomfort had made them feel comfortable and confident, and they'd struck an easy rapport. Now he just felt selfish. Selfish for wanting Bonnie, and immature for wanting to prove his worth to her instead of proving it to himself. "I just wish . . . I want to be able to do more to contribute—"

"Writer," the realtor broke in, looking down at her notes.

"What?" David asked, pulled out of his fugue.

"The neighbor downstairs. He's a writer, and his wife is . . . a guidance counselor at a high school."

"Writer?" David asked.

"Silas Hale," the realtor said, reading from the printout. "You know Cambridge. You throw a rock and hit a writer of one kind or another. In fact, my own neighbor across the hall . . ."

David stopped listening.

Silas *Hale*!

Silas Hale!

With a dozen complex novels written for sophisticated readers, with an arsenal of national and international awards, Hale was the writer David sought to be one day. Silas Hale, as his downstairs neighbor, sharing the same roof? Silas Hale, "a writer." That was an oblivious understatement. Silas Hale *the* writer, and *New Yorker* fiction editor at large, one of the few in the magazine's history. Pulitzer for fiction. David's heart fluttered. He knew, at that moment, that this was all meant to be, as Bonnie would say. Hale was meant to become David's neighbor, to introduce him to elite culturati, to put him on the fast track to literary achievement and to becoming the respected partner Bonnie wanted. To unlatch and swing open the gates to his future. David could never have dreamed this. This would be his X factor. This was the best day of David Trent's life.

He tried to keep his poise, and to appear detached in the eyes of Bonnie and the realtor, even though, if he were completely honest with himself, he might have burned the world to the ground for this chance.

"We'll take it," he said.

"Really?" Bonnie threw her hands around him. "With a two-year lease?"

"The longer the better, as long as you're happy."

As the young couple celebrated, each with different reasons in mind, the realtor sighed. It was a sigh of surprise and relief. Sharon did not like those stairs any more than David did, and she was glad she would not have to climb up and down them in heels. But neither she nor her clients noticed the scribbled note on the packet of documents prepared by the last realtor in her office to have handled the property. In the margin, where the downstairs residents were listed, it advised realtors to "warn" potential tenants that the resident was Silas Hale. Not inform; warn. Still not spotting the unusual gloss, Sharon slid the documents into her bag. There was no need to look at them again.

She began to toggle light switches off. "Let's go get you to write out some checks!"

2

SIGNING THE NEW LEASE SUPERCHARGED David's writing. His motivation to finish his novel had never been stronger. Now his creative drive wasn't merely aspirational, as it had felt many times in the past; it was a rush of adrenaline. With three weeks before their lease would begin, David was determined to have a full draft by the time they moved into the top floor of Silas Hale's bright-orange house on Observatory Hill Drive. His newfound goal in sight, he glowed with purpose and clarity as he tackled his growing to-do list, a mix of creative work and practical chores.

While on one errand, he stopped at a popular sandwich place that required the right level of patience to squeeze into a long line in an insufficient space. They made a favorite sandwich of Bonnie's, a baguette stuffed with turkey and smothered in Russian dressing, which he planned to drop off to her when she was done with work. As David approached, a young woman was struggling to push her stroller inside.

"Let me," David said.

As he held the door and she angled the stroller inside, another customer came charging by, sidestepping David and the woman to bump the door open and then closed again, knocking it hard into the stroller while muttering what sounded like "Move!"

"Excuse me?" David called out accusingly, but the man had weaved through the crowd. David had a burning compulsion to chase him, but instead he continued to hold the door for the stroller and woman. She seemed a bit rattled, but otherwise showed no particular emotion. While the woman and David were both stuck in place on line, he kept scanning the shop for the marauder, but the man must have picked up an advance order and slipped out the exit door on the other side. All David had spotted was a plaid-checked baseball cap and chunky shoes that might as well have been boots. Why did David seem so much more indignant than the woman with the stroller? Mother or nanny, he couldn't tell—he could make the case for either. She'd apparently let the incident slide, and nobody else who witnessed it seemed to care, at least not compared to their sandwich orders, which he tried to interpret as a reminder not to be distracted from his priorities.

He had tried many times before to stick to self-imposed deadlines. Finish the novel by the time Bonnie gets her public policy degree; finish it before leaving to attend his cousin's wedding in Honolulu. But whatever he tried, deadlines floated by. He had never fully convinced himself that they would matter. In his low moments of self-confidence he would ask himself, Who is waiting for my novel? What difference will it make to finish it today, tomorrow, a year from now? Better to try to make it great, he would think, momentarily ignoring the fact that writing projects did not necessarily improve given more time, they just got wordier. "I am, I really am thrilled to have this time to write," he would say to Bonnie when she asked why he couldn't just feel satisfied by doing what he said he wanted to do. These conversations tested Bonnie's natural cheerfulness, which U-turned into outrage more easily than with someone not as cheerful. He was nervous to tell her his fuller thoughts, which, if he was completely transparent, would have run something like, "I just want to be on the other side of it. I want to have already shown that I can do it. If I could skip my terror that I won't be able to do it, I know I could."

People never understood that writers did not really want to write; they wanted to have written—a sentiment misattributed to a dozen famous authors throughout history, none of whom actually wrote that, but no doubt felt it.

When David was growing up in suburban Michigan, his father had urged him to follow his path into engineering. Then David expressed interest in writing. After that, his father lavished praise on David's classmates' slightest mundane achievements, but he never said a word, positive or negative, about the stories David was working on, so he stopped sharing what he wrote. His father wasn't home much, anyway, and his mother's priority was to make sure she was agreeing with his father. In general, David never felt either of them directed much in the way of emotion toward him or toward each other—it seemed to be the secret to their long relationship. On the rare occasion that his father commented on David's creative pursuits, he expressed general mystification: "I don't know where something like writing came from. It might be better to do something concrete. Statistically, nobody makes it in a creative field." He had a way of making David feel he could never defy the odds. "So few," he'd say, "are meant to be writers."

Those words were a curse, hovering over him whenever there would have been a chance at advancement. The darkest valley in his career came when he was twenty-three. Having begun his novel in a surge of optimism and excitement, he decided to apply to graduate programs in creative writing. He was working as a copyeditor at the time for a marketing start-up with a logo featuring the John Hancock Tower and the Prudential Center rising above the Boston skyline, even though the office was located in an industrial complex in a nondescript suburb. It was a miserable slog, most of the time, though there was a comfort in the fact that he never felt the work was bigger than him. Preparing his MFA applications, he needed two recommendations for his top-choice grad schools, and had the option of submitting three. Two were supplied promptly by writing instructors who taught him as an undergraduate.

For a third recommendation, he decided to ask the novelist Melody Bradshaw. He had met her at a writing conference, where she and other established writers were paid by organizers to mentor writers' short stories and chapter drafts. Melody was a tornado, filling a room with a big voice and energy, and was in demand throughout the duration of the conference. The conference organizers had matched David with her, which meant she'd critique his work. Over the course of three one-on-one meetings, she volunteered enthusiastic praise about his writing that he'd never have believed he would hear from someone of her stature. After the conference, he sent her occasional updates on his writing, and when it came time for his MFA application, he emailed Melody, asking if she'd consider providing a recommendation. **With pleasure!** she wrote back. He was thrilled. His college instructors were generous and earnest and had each published short stories in respected literary journals, but Melody was different. Another species. She was what was known as a literary darling.

He thanked her profusely, providing her with a date by which the recommendation had to be sent to the university. Knowing how busy she was, he provided a date before the actual due date in order to build in a buffer. But this time she didn't reply to the email. He sent a warm, self-effacing reminder a few days before the date he had given her, but that date came and went. He tried one last, excruciating time. Sending that email was like yanking his own fingernail off. She never replied.

He didn't need that third recommendation, and he knew he should put it out of his mind. Her name recognition would not matter as much to an admissions committee as it did to him. Besides, recommendations played a small part in the decisions. Yet he had so specifically envisioned his application with Melody Bradshaw's endorsement, the whole thing seemed tainted. Besides, how unjust it was! She'd promised. Maybe she thought he was pitiful for asking. Maybe she'd only agreed in the first place as a kind of extended performance of her obligations from the conference where she mentored him. Maybe she had figured out he'd given her a too-early due date, and was insulted that he assumed she wasn't responsible enough to get a recommendation in on time. He tried to wipe all of it from his mind—the embarrassment, the disappointment, the confusion, the conviction that it was a bad omen, that it signaled the difference between having a flourishing career waiting for him and having none.

But he couldn't stop thinking about it. He decided to do something. He wrote the recommendation himself in her name.

During the brief but meaningful time of our mentorship and ongoing correspondence, David Trent showed a dedication to the process of improving his craft. Emboldened by his open-minded attitude toward writing, I have been left impressed with his ability to convey passion through vital prose. His voice sparkles with erudite storytelling.

He especially liked the touch of "vital," a catchall compliment often applied by critics to books that they didn't understand or only skimmed, as they did with some other words including "unflinching" and "fulsome." Next, he composed some filler language. But he still needed to add a wrinkle, a mild critique that would make the recommendation sound unbiased. He fiddled around with this, ending up with:

If a weakness recurs in David's approach to writing, it would be a tendency toward dogmatic ideas around literary style.

He wasn't exactly sure what that meant, but it sounded harmless enough as flaws went, and in fact he had very few dogmatic ideas about writing, so it could be argued that he had already overcome the fabricated criticism. He sent the recommendation from an email address he had created for the occasion, also under Melody's name. After he submitted it, he put the episode out of his mind until he was admitted to one of the MFA programs. He knew, deep down, that the falsified recommendation probably had nothing to do with his acceptance. He also knew that he had breached academic and professional ethics. Even so, it still felt—strange as it sounded—like the right thing to do. He had achieved a measure of justice not only for himself but for everyone who had ever been denied a chance by someone who could have helped but decided not to on a whim, amused by watching a less fortunate person wriggle in discomfort, a lifeguard sitting on a throne hovering over the beach while a swimmer sank to the ocean floor. Besides, he had composed the recommendation with phrases Melody had spoken directly to him, or emailed him, or at least implied to him, about his writing. Wasn't that authentic in its way? He deserved that record of her support.

He saw Melody again a year into his program, when she visited his campus to give a talk to students. For weeks beforehand he walked around petrified. But he reminded himself that she had no reason to know about the application at all. There were seventy or eighty students attending the event in the departmental library, none of whom probably remembered their own applications particularly clearly, much less wondered about someone else's. Why would his admission application be more likely to come up than his classmates'? He could easily have avoided Melody altogether amid the adoring crowd, but he lingered, then went right up to her after the talk. That was either the least suspicious or the most suspicious course of action—he couldn't decide which. After the agonizing few seconds it took for her to recognize him, they exchanged greetings. She told him how happy she was that he was pursuing fiction, and recalled how much she'd enjoyed their meetings. He was gratified, and vindicated in his decision to write the recommendation. She wanted him to be there.

Still, even that congenial exchange was fleeting. The genuine mentorship once sought from Melody now could come from Silas Hale. He saw it so clearly. Saw Hale himself greeting him on the sidewalk in front of their house—*their* house, his and Silas Hale's! An echo of Henry David Thoreau living in Ralph Waldo Emerson's backyard! He saw himself talking to Hale—no, Silas; surely he'd say "Call me Silas, David, I insist"—about his soon-to-be completed manuscript, and casually mentioning the literary agents outdoing each other to represent him, soliciting Silas's opinion on whom he should select. (Silas would know them all personally from dinner parties and literary award banquets.) He envisioned the details, again and again, as he charted out what was left to finish pulling together his novel draft. He used unlined notecards to jot down brief scene descriptions, sometimes just a few words each, and rearranged the cards to identify the best order and keep track of what came before and after. By this point these notecards, stacked together, were as thick as three decks of playing cards.

He had never been very productive inside his apartment, where he would feel distracted by a single unwashed dish or a piece of unopened mail, and where sometimes he'd realize he hadn't slept well and put his head down on his crowded desk, inert. As he geared up for his Observatory Hill deadline, he chose a better routine. He would go to his favorite coffee shops comfortably before the lunch rush to snag his favorite table.

Writers evaluated coffee shops differently than anyone else. There was an eccentric mental checklist of rules that could be processed at a quick glance to lay the groundwork for productivity.

Rule one: tables needed to be small enough not to attract unwanted requests to share, yet large enough to fit a laptop, drink, and plate of food. Tables should not wobble—that was the second rule—a subtle but maddening distraction from writing. (When necessary, David and other veteran coffee shop writers swiftly propped up wobblers with sweetener packets.) Rule three: there had to be enough capacity and turnover that nobody would be hovering to wait for your table or, the almost worst scenario, *asking* you directly how much longer you'd be sitting there, or, the actual worst scenario, asking a manager to ask you how much longer you'd be sitting there. Then there were the baristas. It was fine for them to be aloof, and most in Cambridge were as aloof as they were effortlessly stylish. But, rule four, you didn't want to get stuck sitting in their line of sight, where they might decide that you hadn't ordered enough over the course of several hours and eyeball you. They were unlikely to do much more, but their stares would put a hex on your writing. Finally, electrical outlets were a must-have to keep laptops charged. One coffee shop had become so overrun with writers that the owner deactivated the outlets, leading a cadre of local novelists and poets to show up with fully charged laptops and portable chargers to spite the place before grudges lost steam and writers drifted to friendlier (or at least more apathetic) environs. Other coffee shops saw a play for money, offering an option to pay for wireless internet, while the rare larger spots in Cambridge, usually on the periphery, had begun providing free Wi-Fi over the last few years.

To combat isolation, some writers formed small writing groups. The truth was, those groups tended to become cliques invested in keeping people out rather than nurturing those inside their cocoon. David never tried to insinuate himself into one of these. But sometimes he would arrange to meet another writer at a café to share a workspace. He liked low-key meetups, particularly with friends who were working on nonfiction, so there was no competitiveness. Jace Chaikivsky, for instance, was a ghostwriter putting together memoirs for business executives and athletes. His mouth would twitch into a nervous frown most of the time he was working at his laptop, but he would grin when David seemed stressed by some creative choice in his novel.

"I don't get why you'd be sweating it," he'd say. "What are you sweating? You write fiction, all you do is make things up—lie. What I wouldn't give. What I wouldn't—really! You just have to lie, lie, and lie, and your book's problems are solved." David laughed, explaining that invention was different from lying, though he couldn't articulate how. Jace's big complaint in life was that other writers did not respect ghostwriting. "They think I'm not a real writer. But writing is writing, a paycheck is a paycheck. It's a business just like anything else, don't you think? But they judge me. You're the only one who doesn't, David."

David actually did judge Jace, but silently. Jace always had a curved wireless earpiece blinking over his ear, which David thought better left to stock traders and financial advisers who spoke loudly at airports, especially since Jace rarely received calls, as far as David could tell. It also bothered David that Jace's ghostwriting propped up people who didn't have the skills to write but had enough name recognition to profit from someone else's work. That ultimately undermined everyone else who wrote. Still, David couldn't blame Jace, and he enjoyed how Jace dismissed David's creative complaints. It made him feel less worried. Jace also had an ear for all questions of syntax and grammar, every rule of which he had internalized. He would even correct grammatical violations during conversation and, oddly, sometimes correct mistakes David had not even made, as though anticipating future errors.

During the pre-move-in weeks, David met with Jace a couple of times, but otherwise gave his book his full concentration. Today, he was on his own. Among the scenes he was still returning to again and again was the end of the draft, closing lines that tormented him. His desire to encapsulate the entire essence of the book into those few lines alternated with an urge to have those lines subtly clue the reader in to the fact that the draft fell short of what he wanted it to be. He typed, deleted, and retyped the last sentences over and over, changing them slightly each time.

I tried not to think of him at all anymore, to close and lock a vault around the memories.

Not right. The imagery of a vault felt generic. He wanted something simpler, but potent, an immediate surrender to emotion.

I tried not to think of him how I saw him last. It was too great a loss.

Too bleak; he didn't want readers tumbling into grimness at the end of the book. From the beginning of time, after all, writers had written to share what was possible in life, not what was irreparable. Nobody ever needed to memorialize the coldness of life to know it. Whenever he got to those lines, he'd tinker until the words on screen blurred.

He caught sight of Brandi, a playwright, out of the corner of his eye. Her hair was cut short, with purple highlights, and she had a silver stud on one side of her nose. Writers were domesticated dogs, easily suspicious just at the sight of each other for no particular reason. Brandi annoyed David, always finding a way to crow about having her plays performed, no matter how briefly and how small the theaters.

Three tables away, Brandi was pecking at her MacBook keyboard with such speed that David imagined enviable productivity on her part. He knew she had seen him, but she ignored him until she got up to order an espresso, then chose a path back to her table that took her past his.

After obligatory small talk, Brandi asked, "Working on your . . . novel?" She made a purring sound whenever she finished speaking.

The pause and her purr managed to vaguely question his novel's existence. He knew some of his writer acquaintances saw him as in over his head, leaning on Bonnie's reliable life as he was spinning in a wheel of unrealistic dreams.

"Plugging away," he said, a neutral answer to end the line of conversation.

"I don't know how you do it. Working on one project for so long. So, so long. God, hasn't it been years? I'm jealous you can do that, and I would hate it, but I would do it, just for the sake of being able to do it. My last play took six months to draft before we started casting, and I was burned out."

It was a one-act play and it's a few pages long and your parents pay your rent, he wanted to say.

She brought up another writer in their circles whose novel in progress had dragged on, then ended up getting rejected by publishers. "Did you hear what happened to him?"

"Is he okay?"

"He got a nine-to-fiver. I was so surprised, I can't picture him in an office!" Her purr this time emitted artificial sympathy. Only among writers did having a job qualify as gossip.

"I'm actually almost finished with the novel," David said.

"Really? I'm so jealous. Congrats!"

"I guess I've been on a streak, now that I have a mentor." He hadn't planned on saying that. He had practiced the line in his mind for a hoped-for future, and now it slipped out. Maybe she hadn't noticed.

But her eyes brightened with curiosity. "Oh? A mentor?"

He nodded. "Silas Hale."

Her jaw locked at a severe angle. She looked like she had to pull her heart out from her stomach before she could speak again. "What is he like?"

"Great. Really great guy, very generous with his experiences and insights. Just how you'd imagine him."

"Wow, David. Really, I'm impressed."

Luckily, she didn't ask him anything else about Silas Hale, whom he still hadn't met, but excused herself and went back to her table. David smiled to himself, watching the utter misery on her face while she stewed on his turn of luck, a Cambridge writer's most coveted commodity.

3

EARLY ON THE BIG DAY, the movers picked up stacks of boxes and furniture from David's apartment and then from Bonnie's place, which had more in it; it had always felt more like a real home than David's, which resembled a storage unit with a bed. Bonnie then drove David to their new address in her car, beating the truck there. Since moving to Cambridge, David had never had a car, an expensive luxury inconvenient to maintain in the harsh winters. Observatory Hill, like most of Cambridge and the surrounding cities, also had many fewer parking spots than vehicles.

But Bonnie remained undaunted by those challenges. She had submitted a permit request to the city to block off spots for the moving truck, a space the enormous vehicle now occupied. Newbies to the area usually didn't know to apply for this permit, or only found out about it a few days prior to move-in, rather than the required seven calendar days in advance. They had to hope the moving truck would get lucky and fit along the side of the street. This rarely went well. Best-case scenario, the truck would stick out past the curb cut of a neighbors' driveway. Even if the transgression amounted to an inch or two of the moving truck's bumper, Cantabrigians relished the chance to leave a nasty handwritten note, call the moving company office, and phone the police (the nonemergency number, usually, but sometimes 911). These steps were not necessarily taken in that order. An angry Cantabrigian might call the police as soon as the shadow of a vehicle fell near the curb cut of their driveway, and then compose their incensed note at a leisurely pace while waiting on their front porch, coffee in hand, for the cops to show up.

Sharon, the realtor, had originally told Bonnie she could pick up their keys at the Coldwell Banker office the morning of move-in, but then she left a message that she had to meet them in front of the house. She showed up soon after they did. Gone was the chipper demeanor. Her hair and clothes were in disarray, as though a commentary on the chore. Now she stomped instead of walked. Still, she had the key, and that's what mattered to David. The nickel-brass shone and shimmered, hinting at infinite promise as Sharon passed it to Bonnie.

"I can hang on to it, Bon," David said, hiding the extent of his eagerness. The metal chilled his palm as he squeezed a greedy fist over it.

That key would open the door into the crooked stairs that went up to the third-floor unit at the back of the house. Sharon also dug out a second key, attached to her oversize Coldwell Banker keychain—the key to the Hales' front door.

"They aren't home?" David asked the realtor. In his imagination, Silas and Rebecca Hale would appear side by side to welcome their new neighbors. Maybe they'd have a fruit and cheese basket, probably with exotic jams.

"Who isn't home?" Sharon asked.

He paused before answering tentatively, "The Hales?" as though he had to make an effort to recall their name.

"I believe they're in the Vineyard through the end of summer." Martha's Vineyard was three hours plus a ferry ride south. "That was the holdup"—she sighed with annoyance—"getting ahold of this key so the movers could carry your furniture up through the Hales' part of the house."

David nodded with an air of indifference to their new downstairs neighbors. As the realtor swung the doors open, the stale air of the Hales' closed-up rooms greeted them, slightly musty, with hints of mahogany and leather.

"The Hales asked that you accompany the movers at all times while they are inside their floors of the house," Sharon said with the air of a strict schoolteacher. "And that everyone take off their shoes."

David slipped off his canvas runners. The chance to walk through Silas Hale's house at his own pace almost made up for the writer's absence. He turned to Bonnie, handing her their new key. "Bonnie, I can go in through the downstairs and walk up with the movers through the Hales' place. Do you want to go around to the apartment and meet at the trapdoor?"

The two movers might have been a bit heftier, considering how much they charged. David presumably was supposed to ensure that they didn't scratch, bash, break, or steal anything on the Hales' two floors while transporting David and Bonnie's furniture. Instead, he split off from them. Could he be expected to resist this opportunity? These were the rooms that Silas Hale used each day, where his brilliance rekindled on a regular basis, where he prepped his creative muscles to prepare for long hours of quiet creation. These passages were hallowed.

On the walls, family photos captured the Hales in moments spanning decades, the majority of those moments being centered around Silas at events where he was honored or otherwise a focal point. There were dramatically fewer photos of the Hales' two children, who were, going by the more recent photos, adults in their twenties, rambling around the world. There were some pictures of family trips to Europe, where they were all together. David was glad there were none of them aboard cruises, not wanting to envision Silas Hale watching faux-Vegas magic acts trapped in a ship auditorium. Through his eyes, the Hale family photos were French Impressionist paintings, glimpses of a world filled only with picturesque lakes, sophisticated gardens, and infinite sunlight.

Silas Hale's study beckoned him. He stopped at the threshold, knowing that he should be hurrying to the stairs to monitor the movers. But, really, weren't they professionals? They didn't need him hovering! He stepped inside. The mantelpiece and shelves were filled with antiques from a wide variety of periods and places, a reflection of a voracious mind. There was a framed *New York Times Book Review* cover featuring Hale's most famous novel, *Sevenfold*. Paintings hung across the wall, depicting strong men engaged in laborious tasks in austere settings such as Cape Cod or Scandinavia. Men using ropes to haul a ship run ashore in the aftermath of what seemed to be a hurricane; a frontiersman felling a tree while children looked on in awe. An antique pickax, like the kind photographed for books about the gold rush, held up by brackets, was given a prominent position. Moving to the side of the desk where Hale would sit, David opened a few drawers as quietly as possible, finding packages of Post-it notes. He picked up the small wastepaper basket, which was piled with scribbled-on Post-its that had been discarded, a glimpse of Hale's creative process—not too dissimilar, he dared to think, from the way David used notecards. There was also an empty pill bottle for Zestril, which David knew from his father's medicine cabinet was for hypertension.

David could hear one of the movers saying something elsewhere in the house. Maybe trying to ask him something? He carefully replaced the wastepaper bin and closed the drawers, then rushed from the study and looked around as though lost. He found the men on the second floor.

"What's that?" he said.

"I said, 'What a way to have to go up!'" the mover complained, genuinely grumpy about it, unaware that David had ever split off from them. The two men had opened the trapdoor in the ceiling above the Hales' wide central stairway, giving way to the cryptlike crawl space above that David had stood over during their tour of the upstairs unit.

David echoed the realtor's turn of phrase. "Cambridge, right?"

"What?" one of them asked.

"Oh, just that Cambridge . . ." David knew it wasn't worth finishing the thought.

The movers hoisted the sofa up more stairs.

"Please be careful not to scratch the banister," David said, belatedly embracing his responsibility.

Above the crawl space, the trapdoor leading to David and Bonnie's floor was rattling.

"I think your wife might need help up there to open this from your unit," one of the movers commented, glancing at him with disapproval.

David thought for a moment to correct the use of "wife." But instead he hustled down through the Hales' rooms and out of the house, sad to cut short his jaunt into Silas Hale's life. Back out front, where he'd started, he rounded the side of the house to the exterior door that led to his new stairwell. Now rushing up the narrow treads—the steep, sharp, creaking turns were becoming second nature—he found Bonnie in the apartment, pulling one of two handles that receded into the cutout on the floor and was raised by turning it clockwise.

"Needs two people?" he asked.

"That's what I'm starting to realize!" Bonnie answered with a smile, even as she struggled. "Perfect timing." Together they were able to raise the two sides of the trapdoor, each lifting one handle. A burst of trapped warm air thrashed up to them.

With the trapdoor opened, the movers pushed the sofa all the way up from the Hales' portion of the house, through the crawl space, and onto the top floor. The process repeated with the rest of the bigger furniture. Hoping to chip away at the number of hours they'd pay for the movers, David carried a half dozen boxes he could manage on his own, wobbling up their treacherous side staircase. Technically, the lease only gave permission to bring large furniture through the Hales' home, not boxes or smaller items. For the Hales, David felt obliged to honor that to the letter.

After what seemed an eternity, the movers left. David threw himself down on a mattress. His own physical exertions had been modest, but the whirlwind of moving, combined with the gravity of what it could mean to live in this house of literary greatness, had wiped him out, body and soul.

Bonnie, stopping only to drink enough water to meet daily hydration goals, immediately started unpacking boxes and pushing around furniture.

The first phase of settling in began. Sunday morning, after sleeping in, David walked the length of each room of their apartment, filled with anticipation, some of which was identifiable and some impossible to describe, even to himself, except that he registered this as momentous. He stopped at a southeast-facing window that overlooked the manicured part of the yard, with its cypress tables and chairs. He studied the shared space. Here he and Silas Hale might get to know each other after a productive writing day, watching the sun glide down through the leaves and branches of century-old trees.

"This is really exciting," David heard himself say out loud.

Bonnie jumped up and took both his hands. "It is!" With her electric-blue eyes, she seemed to be reading his mind, watching the images that he saw, looking out the window, come to life, though of course the images she was seeing did not involve Silas Hale.

Then a string of other thoughts intruded into David's mind, slamming together into a single, alarmed realization: *The rolltop!* He rushed off.

His thoughts retreated to the year before, around the time of the couple's two-year anniversary, when conversation over a dinner at a Tibetan restaurant toggled between the spices in the dumplings and their future. On that occasion, Bonnie made it clear that she was ready for real commitment. Commitment was something she excelled at. David could not say aloud what he really thought, which was that however happy Bonnie made him, however charmed he was by her passion for movie theater popcorn and her terror of a fly getting into the kitchen, however much he loved her, the same thing got in his way that got in the way of everything else: writing. "If you think too much about your own writing," his friend Jace had once said to him during one of their coffee shop sessions, "it will drive you insane." In his heart, he knew Jace was right, but also that nothing else could be on solid ground until his writing was, or he would always be distracted by the fear that he would never make it, as his father believed. He wanted not to worry about his place in the writing world—more tangibly, not to fret about the fate of his first novel—before planning a wedding, much less a life together.

To verbalize that, he knew, would insult Bonnie, and unintentionally minimize her importance to him. Instead, through the course of several conversations, the plan had evolved that once they moved in together, they would get engaged. Neither David nor Bonnie had been eager to give up their respective apartments, which had bought David some time to feel better about his writing. The thought of proposing to Bonnie ended up exciting David more than he expected, maybe because the future he imagined with Bonnie included a very clear image of being satisfied with himself, finally achieving the dreams that everyone seemed to wait for him to reach (or fail to reach). He browsed jewelry stores, mostly in Harvard Square and some in downtown Boston, and found a vintage ring. He bought it on the spot, hiding it in one of the small drawers of an antique roll-top desk that his aunt and uncle had given him at the time when he moved into his first apartment.

Once the end of their leases was on the horizon, he and Bonnie had begun attending open houses and arranging appointments to see places, but they accepted the fact that apartment-hunting in the Boston area could take six months or more. In the interval, David had forgotten to move the ring. It could have fallen out in his old apartment, or on the moving truck, or anywhere in between . . .

Hurrying into his new office, he rifled through the rolltop's drawers and found the ring. He exhaled a loud sigh of relief.

Bonnie had followed him, concerned, after he launched himself at the desk. "What is it, David?"

"What?"

"You were saying you're excited, but then suddenly you disappeared."

How ridiculous it all must have looked to her, he thought. Him standing dreamily at the window while announcing his excitement before running off. Now his fingers curled over the ring case in his hand, which she may or may not have spotted. He couldn't explain that his excitement had been ignited by thinking of how his proximity to Silas Hale would transform his life. She wouldn't be angry, not at first. It would be worse. She would be disappointed, would scold him for driving himself crazy worrying, and ask that crushing question: Is writing worth it? He didn't have the emotional stamina to pull himself out of that rabbit hole, because he didn't have the answer to that question. He didn't want the doubts to be revived. Those were in the past! It was time for a confident new phase, as a writer and in their relationship.

He dropped down on one knee. They had both laughed about that idea before, including once when it happened two tables away while they were eating at a hotel restaurant in Providence, Rhode Island.

"Let's get married," David said.

"Yes!" Bonnie cried out, and they spent the next hours calling family and friends to tell them the news.

"A new apartment, and now being engaged," she was saying to her sister. "I just can't believe it. The ring? The ring . . . is . . . breathtaking. We're so happy. Oh, we haven't even talked about—no, we can't wait to plan it." She turned toward David as she listened to her sister. "I love you," Bonnie whispered to him.

"I love you, too," he whispered back.

4

THERE WAS NO GARAGE AT the house at 6 Observatory Hill Road, maybe because architects and builders of old Cambridge disdained garages, or the construction of the houses themselves predated cars. Instead, a short driveway ended in a cramped cul-de-sac, with room for three cars to park at odd angles that, if calculated with the precision of MIT engineers, would avoid blocking each other in or scratching each other. One morning in the third week of September, a gleaming black BMW appeared parked next to Bonnie's Saab. A red Jeep was added the next day.

Two days later, David saw a woman he recognized as Rebecca Hale from the photos he had seen inside the house on move-in day: mid-sixties, shorter than average, slender, with streaks of silver in her brown hair. She was retrieving a package from the Hales' front porch while David was crossing the yard. She waved, and he offered back an eager, friendly, possibly frenzied wave that he hoped covered up his previous staring. But then he realized he wasn't sure if she had even been looking in his direction. Maybe she hadn't waved at all, but instead was swatting hair away from her face.

After moving in, David had managed to put the finishing touches on his novel. He had even worked out the final lines of the book.

I tried not to think of him how I saw him last. It was so great a loss. Instead, I thought of him as I had found him at the station, standing in place with his hand outstretched, surrounded by strangers who still had somewhere they needed to go.

He did not think *That is it!* in triumph, but rather *That is it*, with a vague conviction of contentment. It had seemed so improbable for so many years, but the time had come. The finished draft represented to Bonnie another occasion for celebration; she took charge by reserving dinner at a hard-to-book restaurant, having established a warm rapport with a hostess in the course of a two-minute phone call. Meanwhile David began to submit queries to literary agents. Smooth sailing ahead.

While rolling the garbage bin to the street the next day, David heard a voice say "Trent." Having rarely played sports, he was always taken by surprise whenever referred to only by his last name, and the next string of words was drowned out by the racket of the bin's wheels up to the word "rats."

David paused, turned, and saw Silas Hale taking long strides toward him.

Silas, in his sixties, carried himself with a ramrod posture that made him look taller than his actual height, which was a sliver above average. He wore a very expensive, form-fitting T-shirt, short sleeves symmetrically rolled up over his biceps.

He was pointing. "You're David Trent, the upstairs tenant."

It wasn't a question but an announcement, maybe a pronouncement, about David's very identity. "Tenant" seemed an odd choice of word over "neighbor," since Silas was not their landlord, as the realtor had pointed out. "Yes, so nice to meet you. I'm David. My fiancée and I moved in last—"

"The garbage bin," Silas said, shifting his pointing finger at it, his enunciation slowing, then crawling. "You need to get a new one for the house. This one has cracks. Look for yourself, and you'll see. It doesn't close firmly. Securely. It will attract rats." He pantomimed closing it tightly, but never touched the bin. "Go to the hardware store around the corner and get a new one, the kind where the cover flips open, flips closed." With undisguised impatience, he demonstrated the two possible positions with his arm. "You know when rat-breeding season is?"

Was David meant to answer? "Rat-breeding season? No, I—"

"There is none. They always breed. It's a hellscape of rats here. They hide in the shadows, waiting. You know where the hardware store is?"

David was still learning his way around the neighborhood, and had not seen a hardware store. "Sure."

"Good. I planned things out when I was your age, and now you can learn to plan. A new garbage bin. Soon as possible." He ran his tongue across his lips, then turned and walked off. David waited to see if he would turn back to say anything else, but he did not.

"Great to meet . . ." David started to say, then petered out. The interaction, the brevity and the tone, was so disconnected from anything David had expected and imagined, that he could not accept that he had met Silas Hale. He felt numb, too disoriented to reflect on what happened.

"Did you see them?" Bonnie asked when he got upstairs. Stretched out on the floor in a yoga pose, she passed her hand in front of her face, admiring her ring. The diamond looked so small to David now that it was not set in the suede box, but Bonnie never stopped raving and smiling at it.

"Who?" David asked.

"Our neighbors. The Hales."

"You met them?"

"I haven't," she said. "But I think I saw Mrs. Hale from a distance when I was out for a jog. She was getting something from her car. Seems super nice. So funny that he's a writer that you've actually read, right? You'll be comparing notes before long."

"Maybe. He wants me to get a new garbage bin."

"Then you did meet him!" She narrowed her eyes. "Garbage bin?"

David nodded. "The rats . . ." he started, trailing off.

"If the house needs new bins, that would be the condo association's responsibility, not ours. I can tell them, if you want."

David imagined defying Silas Hale after his very first encounter—worse yet, sending Bonnie to defy him because he was too cowardly. "It's fine."

"Those big bins can be sixty or seventy dollars each, and we're renters."

David felt a fresh sense of surprise, as he always did whenever it became obvious how much tougher Bonnie was than him. "I'm sure you're right. But I want to start off on the right foot instead of making it a big deal. You know, show we're neighborly, go above and beyond, just this time?"

Bonnie weighed this.

David could tell she was wavering. He put on a cheerful smile. "It's an investment in getting along."

She shrugged, unconvinced. "Just this once, though, right? You don't want them to see us that way."

David didn't want to get the garbage bin so quickly that Bonnie found his eagerness suspicious, but he also didn't want to take so long that Silas would become annoyed. He decided that two days was the perfect amount of time to wait before buying a garbage bin.

He was getting to know the neighborhood better, starting to recognize the dogs that were walked on his street, and to know which ones were happy to be petted. He began to take notice of details about the surrounding houses, including a narrow, light-gray clapboard house across from theirs, in one window of which there always seemed to be a different number of candles burning. He had formed the habit of counting the candles, as though their number might signify something. At one point, he slowed down to look while on his way home.

"At least wait for me to be inside to peep at me," said a woman shuffling toward him on the sidewalk at a slow pace, pushing a narrow wire cart. She hardly came to his shoulder.

"So sorry, I didn't mean—" he said, stepping out of the way.

"Don't be. It's a pleasure to meet a neighbor."

"How did you know?"

"I saw you across the street when your moving truck came." He knew she would be one of those neighbors who called the police on a truck with no parking permit. "I'm Antoinette. Repeat after me—Antoinette."

It took him a moment to realize that she was asking him to say her name aloud. "Oh . . ."

Then she seemed to forget, cutting him off. "You might as well know me, because everyone around here knows me. Come in and have a cup of tea with us. I want to know all about you and your lovely better half. I don't want to listen to excuses about putting me out—you'll be helping an old woman carry in her groceries."

The sharp contrast with his encounter with Silas—being acknowledged as a neighbor, being welcomed in—was so refreshing that David put up no argument, scooping up grocery bags as Antoinette handed him her key and instructed him to head inside while she folded her cart. She had orange hair with the texture and shape of yarn, and wore a bright floral tent dress. He wondered who "us" referred to, and what the rest of that household would think of a stranger barging in, perhaps, for all anyone knew, after knocking Antoinette down the front steps and grabbing her keys.

The front hall led directly into a large room lined with wine-colored linen wallpaper, a kind of living Lautrec painting that contrasted with the understated exterior, filled with large watercolors and ornate pieces of Victorian furniture, plus an array of candles in elaborate candlesticks, some shaped like animals. He complimented these, a roundabout apology for looking into her window.

"For centuries, it was almost exclusively by candlelight that genius was born," mused Antoinette.

Beyond the living room was a cramped kitchen, where David was instructed to deposit the bags. In it was a woman in her late thirties with long, dark hair, blanched with white streaks. David introduced himself to her and she nodded, not showing any visible interest in why he was there beyond a slight quiver in one thick eyebrow. She began carefully putting away the groceries, which beside a few staples appeared to be high-priced éclairs, tarts, and other bakery novelties. Antoinette called for him to take a seat on an oversize armchair. He now noticed multiple coffee-table books with photos and paintings of operas, and several opera glasses, as well as a baby grand piano. As they spoke, it occurred to him that Antoinette had the aura of a fortune teller, though judging by the various pretensions to high culture, she would have been insulted if David had shared his observation.

"Now, David Trent," Antoinette said, clasping her hands on her lap, from a sofa across from him, "I sense you are an artist."

"Really?"

"You're no investment banker or corporate consultant, obviously."

They both laughed, but there was no explanation as to why he was not corporate material. "I'm a writer, actually." His explanation of what he did often came out that way, not just "I'm a writer" but variations of "a writer, actually," or "a writer, believe it or not," vaguely apologetic, and an unconscious response to an anticipated reaction that would doubt him.

She leaned forward, her eyes, formerly resting in a judgmental squint, widening. "Then indeed you are an artist. I do not write myself, but I am what you might label an appreciator, and that is a calling in itself, and a form of art, which is how I know one when I see one. Writers deserve every bit of adulation and reverence we can spare. I can tell you with certainty, you live in the right place. I have known every important writer in Cambridge, in particular this neighborhood, for the last forty years. Judith, sweetheart, the tea? David is a writer, and is to be pampered."

The other woman hurried from the kitchen with a highly adorned teapot and matching cups, and a selection of teas. Antoinette still had not introduced Judith, and Judith did not say a word, all of which embarrassed David. He first assumed Judith must be Antoinette's daughter, but over the course of their conversation Antoinette's tone toward Judith dispelled this. After a while it came out that Antoinette was a vocal coach, and Judith was one of her pupils.

"Poor girl," Antoinette said in a whisper when Judith had gone to a different room. "She used to be married—awful man, awful man."

She stared in silence, making David feel he had to respond in some way. He also whispered. "I'm so sorry to hear that. Was he . . . ?" He winced at the thought of what Judith's ex might have done.

"Abusive? No! Harmless as a bowl of jelly, but an awful bore, an accountant of some kind, so I took her under my wing when she started training with me, until we could secure her divorce. She's rather frail emotionally and intellectually, poor creature, and I make sure that nobody takes advantage of it. She hasn't a life of her own, true, but only because the one I supervise for her is safer and more enjoyable."

Antoinette, between comments that seemed very intimate to someone she had just met, would foster long stretches of silence in which she seemed to be analyzing David. Staring at him. He had to try several times to excuse himself to get home before she finally allowed it two hours and three éclairs later, turning it into her idea to bring the meeting to a close.

"Well, my dear, we are very fortunate to have you in the neighborhood, quite an improvement over the owners of your unit, who lived there before you—very ordinary people, not befitting a life above Mr. Hale."

"You know Silas Hale?"

"Do I! What did I tell you about knowing every important writer in Cambridge? For many years I have known and encouraged Mr. Hale. I consider myself a kind of muse to him—not in a salacious way, you understand. I see my home as a latter-day literary salon of sorts, David, and a refuge whenever creators like Mr. Hale or yourself need it. You'll remember that from now on."

THE NEXT MORNING DAVID GRABBED his backpack and made his way to a café tucked inside a bookstore to sit for a while with his laptop, submitting email queries to agents. But with too many people idly flipping through books (graphic novels, mostly, David noticed, dejected to think of his illustration-free manuscript) without ordering food or coffee, there wasn't a free seat, or even a stool. Writers who did their work in coffee shops always armed themselves with a plan B, and without losing too much more time waiting for a seat to open, David headed to a bigger café, a remodeled former factory, where he had previously run across Brandi. But his timing was off—it was close enough to lunch that there had already been a stampede for tables by the nonwriters. Brandi was there again, too, this time at a long rectangular table used as shared space.

"David!"

Brandi pulled over a chair and squeezed it in next to hers. More grateful than he expected he could be to see her, David dropped his bag onto the metal seat.

"Thanks, Brandi, this is a lifesaver. Really. This is my second—"

"Oh, do you know Barnaby?"

On the other side of Brandi, a man around David's age stood up. David had spotted him before at literary events. He knew only his name and that he carried himself with an assertive air. David didn't think Barnaby had published a book yet, since everyone chattered when that happened. He was tall and stringy, with large, powerful hands. He wore an expensive cardigan with giant, glossy buttons, and his glasses were stylish enough they might be worn just for show. He was the sort of aspiring writer who seemed to be completely sure of his destiny in the literary world, a trait that mystified David.

"I don't think so," said David.

Brandi perked up with importance. "Barnaby Masters, David Trent. David, this is the incredible Barnaby Masters. You might have seen his short story in the *Oxford Review* last spring—it got a fair amount of attention. Which one was that, Barnaby?"

"You mean 'Whispers of the Astral Loom.'"

David, noticing that Brandi had not attached an adjective to his own name, as she had to Barnaby's, reached out his hand. Barnaby looked like he might be the type to crush a hand when shaking it, but instead he lightly slid his fingers onto David's, then withdrew quickly, as though feeling something objectionable. Seat-hunters eyed them as they stood to see if they were about to leave, so they sank back down into their respective chairs.

During some small talk as David set up his computer, he noticed that Barnaby had the habit of asking if someone knew something they could not realistically know, framing the question as a statement so that the other person had no choice but to announce they didn't, which came out like a confession. For example: "David, you're familiar with Phillippa Yaa de Villiers, the South African performance artist."

"No, I'm not."

"That's—oh, what a shame, brother!" he'd respond, then pause for everyone to revel in disappointment. Then he'd extend the opportunity to the next person. "Brandi, you must know the work of Yaa de Villiers," before proceeding to expound on it at length.

"Look at us," Brandi said at one point, "three writers writing. I'm chuffed at this. That's what I love about living here. Nowhere like it. The creativity that's just buzzing no matter where you turn."

"I'm actually stuck taking care of emails today, sadly," David said.

"Emails?" Barnaby repeated, cocking his head, as though David had invented the term. Throughout the conversation, David noticed that Barnaby wore that same expression whenever someone talked, so that you'd begin to feel everything you said, no matter how routine, was offensive, incorrect, and maybe mispronounced.

"Just a backlog," David said, not wanting to get into detail about his outreach to literary agents.

"Torture," Barnaby said. "Level-three, dark-dungeon torture. I empathize, brother. If my fingers aren't writing, my brain is screaming, raging at me. When I have to schedule a call with Jackie, it zaps me. I still won't get a mobile phone."

"Jackie is his agent," Brandi interjected, and David knew it had to be Jackie Pryce Offelman, one of the top literary agents in New York. Nobody got the chance to sign with Jackie Pryce Offelman!

Barnaby continued. "When I wake up in the morning, I think of all the obstacles trying to stop me from writing, building up in front of me." He picked up a handful of raw sugar packs and, glancing at David, started to rip them open, pouring three or four on the table. David bristled. Barnaby then pointed out the pile symbolizing the obstacles to them. "Then I challenge myself: 'What do I have to get rid of from my life so I can break down the wall keeping me away from my writing?' It's not genius that we need, though we do need it—it's the time to unfurl the genius."

"Well, I happen to think you're very lucky, David," Brandi said, adding her purring sound. "Doing emails sounds so much more relaxing than writing just about now. I'm staring at a blank screen for a project I just resurrected in order to enter into a competition for original two-act plays. Two-act plays should be outlawed, and here I am again, trying to be brilliant, but instead going in circles, circles, circles. Like I'm wrestling with my creative writing thesis in college all over again."

Brandi paused and wagged her finger at Barnaby. "Didn't you go here for undergraduate?" By "here" she meant Cambridge, and by Cambridge she meant Harvard.

Barnaby's upper lip twitched, and he made a show of self-restraint. "A cross to bear, Brandi." He gave a scratchy laugh. "You're a Harvard man, David?"

"Me? No."

"Sorry! I misunderstood," Barnaby said. He bowed his head and blew the sugar pile off the table, watching the particles float and drop through the air.

In that moment, the sugar powder forming into two distinct clouds, David knew everything there was to know about Barnaby. He came from wealth, with a trust fund grown generations earlier, which had converted into a sparkle in his eye. Only someone who grew up rich would waste those sugar packets and leave a mess for someone else to clean up without a thought. He probably came from a household of professors and creatives, empowered by their inheritances, who perceived themselves as deeply in touch with average people's experiences while priding themselves on being above them. His access to his money was capped for years to come, probably, but would increase at certain benchmarks with time, which let him talk as though he had financial concerns. From the time he was old enough to think about it, Barnaby had never battled the fear of not being smart enough to be a writer, nor worried that anyone else would dare think that about him.

David, in contrast, had never met a professional writer until he was in his twenties, and for him to even imagine he could become one had felt presumptuous for such a long time. He remembered meeting an astronaut when he was twelve, during a visit to the Kennedy Space Center with his parents. At that time, going to space would have seemed much more realistic to him than publishing a book. On his Space Center visit, David solved a puzzle, part of an interactive exhibit in which you competed against kids on the other side of the exhibit. "Very good," was all his father said. That trip came long before David even thought about writing. But he thought, recalling it later, that his father might as well have said, "See, David, you can put things back together, figure them out just a little faster than the person next to you. That's what you can excel at—you're an above-average fixer, like me, not a creator. You can stay a step ahead of them, and you must be content with that. You could even thrive through that. But that's where your abilities end."

"David went to college in . . . was it, Maine, David?" Brandi said. "Oh, but you know what, you two know someone in common. Barnaby, I remember you mentioning you took a class once with Silas Hale, right?"

David held his breath.

Barnaby nodded. "One of my favorite humans. Silas was a visiting professor in creative writing at the time at Harvard, and just to get a spot in the seminar I had to slice out my pound of flesh and throw it on the table, raw, oozing. No, Brandi, I'll tell you something right now, that was no class. That wasn't *just* a class. That seminar is why I am who I am. That seminar is why I write, why I breathe. That seminar was my air."

"How fun!" Brandi nearly squealed as she gestured at David. "I'm so jealous of you two. Barnaby: Silas Hale is David's mentor!"

"Is that right?" Barnaby said.

David fidgeted, pretending he didn't hear, hoping the conversation would move on. It didn't. He emitted an ambiguous hum.

Brandi turned back to David. She purred briefly, then slapped David on the shoulder as though to wake him up. "It was last time I saw you here. Last time I saw you, weren't you saying that Silas Hale—"

"I probably mentioned he's one of the models for my writing."

"As he should be," Barnaby said.

"You told me he's been mentoring you," Brandi persisted.

"You know I—I remember. I might have mentioned that I've been talking to him." Parts of David's exchange with Silas Hale, about the rats and the garbage bins, replayed in his mind. "Hellscape of rats" was the phrase that stuck with him. But at least he had spoken with Hale. He could run with that fact. "His mind is so inspiring, so in that way, inspiration counts as mentorship . . ." David didn't finish the sentence. At least he had muddied the conversation.

"Remarkable man, right?" Barnaby proclaimed. He must have tired of Brandi's attempt to parse David's word choice, all the more because it had stripped the focus from Barnaby. His oversize hands arranged themselves in emphatic, almost violent gestures as he spoke. "Going into that seminar under his watch, I was like the ancient exiled Christians walking across the threshold of their first church. Silas Hale is a miracle. Once you believe, there's no turning back."

5

DAVID RANG THE BELL AT the Hales' front door. Rebecca Hale answered with a frown.

"Yes?"

"David Trent," he introduced himself. "My fiancée, Bonnie, and I live upstairs. We haven't had the chance to—"

"Of course. I'm Rebecca Hale. Forgive me. I work at the high school, so there's too many names and young faces in my life to ever keep them straight. Once in a blue moon, one of the more troubled students will show up at our door. How are you enjoying the world upstairs?"

David was pleased by her friendly if not warm tone, approximating a dental hygienist asking about a patient's day.

"We're doing great, thank you. I hope the movers didn't leave any scratches when they brought our furniture through here."

Her expression hardened. "I should do a closer inspection."

David regretted introducing the topic, and covered it with a laugh. "I wanted to stop by to let you know the good news about the garbage bin. Mission accomplished."

She was confused. "What?"

"Si—Mr. Hale asked me to get a new bin."

"Did he?"

"He mentioned the old one had cracks, and could attract rats."

"The rats!" That seemed to open her up, and to send her thoughts wandering. "They get worse when it's cold out, because they're hungrier. They have less and less food, so their bodies store their fat and they become bigger. Pest control comes to put peanut butter traps out a couple times a month, especially in the shed, where the garbage bins are. There are more extensive techniques, like bombing the area with dry ice—you can do that when it gets really bad. We've seen some rats grow to the size of small cats. They have nowhere to go, so they spend day and night gnawing at anything they can to get indoors. For rats, it ends up being a choice between finding a way inside or dying."

David tried to appear as though he was finding meaning in these horrible images.

"Sometimes he asks people to do things who shouldn't be doing them," she continued, reflecting for a moment. "Silas, I mean. You shouldn't be buying garbage bins. You're just a tenant!"

Neighbor, he thought, but didn't say. "I didn't mind, really. Happy to help. I can show the new bin to you, or Mr. Hale if he's home, to make sure I got the right kind?"

"He shouldn't have asked you," she said again, shaking her head with annoyance, an annoyance somehow directed at David. "I'm really very sorry to hear this happened. He gets worked up, and it's bad for his hypertension."

Blood pressure seemed an odd reason not to demand that a neighbor buy a garbage bin. But David reiterated what a pleasure it was, which sounded absurd even to him. In fact, rolling the bin from the hardware store had been tortuous, weaving between strollers and wagons pushed or pulled by nannies who didn't want to be near a garbage bin, on the one hand, while on the other two men, loud and intoxicated, laughed at him, fascinated by his ordeal, while cars hit their brakes inches away from him, offended not to be able to run him over, as he tried to get through crosswalks, or honked in a kind of condemnation of his rolling a garbage bin around in the middle of the day. Maybe Rebecca Hale's disapproval of the whole matter would benefit him. She would want to reimburse him and invite him in for coffee, where Silas would join them.

"Something wrong?" Rebecca said, looking over her shoulder.

David realized his gaze had been fixed on the rooms behind her, thinking how content he would be to be inside, not talking about rats.

"No," he said, "of course not."

The conversation ended with Rebecca having to go answer her phone, and David had no chance to show off the garbage bin.

At times David's day-to-day routine when he was leaving or returning home was redirected by Antoinette, who would show up from across the street and insist he come inside for tea, which continued to feature long stretches of awkward—though somehow comforting—silence. Antoinette's singing pupil, Judith, was present on all but one of the visits, and spoke a little bit more than on his first encounter. David realized that she was significantly younger than he had originally thought. He speculated that Antoinette had, for reasons only fathomable to Antoinette, convinced Judith to dye her hair with white streaks, which made her appear older at first glance.

Two weeks after his conversation with Rebecca Hale, David heard back from a literary agent who was intrigued by his query. She was well respected, though not a power broker in the book publishing world. This response was followed in rapid succession by boilerplate messages from four other agents who declined to consider his manuscript. David found himself simultaneously grateful and irrationally resentful toward the well-respected agent, as if somehow her lukewarm interest had prevented others from showing any interest at all.

Silas never acknowledged the garbage bin. In fact, he never seemed to go near the shed behind the house where the bins were stored, leaving to David and Bonnie the task of pulling out the garbage and recycling to the sidewalk on trash day before facing an irreversible pileup. (What had the Hales done, David had to wonder, before he and Bonnie moved in?) He spotted Silas multiple times, though always at a distance, from the yard or sidewalk. He sometimes saw him with neighbors, chatting warmly. At one point David happened to look down from the upstairs window and noticed a young man walking his dog toward Silas, who was bringing home takeout in a white plastic bag. The young man paused and appeared to find some pretense to introduce himself. David cringed. He recognized the younger man as a frequent attendee at local book signings—maybe a college or graduate student in writing, or a recent literature PhD. Then, as David continued to watch, the young writer seemed to have just remembered something, and took one of Silas's novels out of his backpack, which Hale signed. It boiled David's blood, thinking how this dog-walking hack must have contrived the encounter, probably having spotted Silas near the house before, maybe even memorizing his routine like a common thief, while David could only watch from above as Silas laughed and bantered.

Would David have been better off if he'd never lived at 6 Observatory Hill Road, so he could be a stranger stopping Silas to chat? Would Silas have embraced him as a promising writer, rather than lecturing him about waste disposal and rats?

David talked a little about Silas to Jace during their café meetups, but he refused to reveal the extent of his disappointment in his interactions with the Hales. Somehow it meant something to David that Jace was impressed with his proximity to Silas. Jace, like Antoinette, took for granted that David was special, something that David felt the need to preserve. Jace's insecurities, he supposed, lessened his own. Even Jace's last name caused him consternation, since nobody ever spelled or said Chaikivsky right—David wasn't quite sure he pronounced it right, after years of knowing Jace. Jace talked about how he had contemplated changing his name, but then would be offended at his own thought, at which point David would reassure him. Still, David silently admitted to himself that he was glad his own name was short, as though it made his vision of a novel with his name on the cover more likely to come true.

One night David had a strange nightmare in which he had recommended a novel to a stranger, who then told him that she hated the book, before morphing into the writer Melody Bradshaw. He woke in a panic. It was 5:00 a.m., and he never got back to sleep. Instead, he watched Bonnie sleep, appreciating the fact that nothing buried in her thoughts was prodding her awake. Later that morning, while glancing out his third-floor window at Observatory Hill, David noticed Silas picking up a package from his porch, while Antoinette trundled over from across the street as fast as she could move, which was extremely slow. She was wearing a light-brown full-length fur coat that David guessed had been passed down in the family from the 1930s or 1940s. She spoke at such a pitch that David could hear her through his closed windows. "Mr. Hale! I have my Judith over with tea and cake . . ."

Today's Silas was not the chatty version that David had seen with the dog walker, though, and he brushed Antoinette off, leaving her panting for air. David felt relief that someone else was the subject of Silas's disinterest, and an embarrassed awareness of the implausibility of Antoinette's claims of a close friendship with the man.

WINTER BROUGHT DARK AFTERNOONS AND the soft beauty of intermittent snowfall before the slushy rain and harsh ice storms set in. With temperatures sliding, David gradually wrestled the heavy old wood-framed windows into their locked positions and adjusted the old-fashioned radiators. Pipes thumped in the walls, but it was hard to tell whether the radiators were kicking in, and David and Bonnie searched the walls for a working thermostat without success.

"It's definitely turning on now!" David would say after a session crawling around by the pipes, twisting and tightening valves. A few more minutes would pass, and then they would doubt themselves.

"I just don't know," Bonnie said. "I don't think it feels warmer."

"Maybe there's a main valve that is turned off, or something's blocked?"

Walking over the trapdoor in their hall felt like passing over a portal to the arctic; the crawl space below must have been even worse. They moved a rug from the living room over it, though it was too wide and the edges curled up against the wall, becoming a tripping hazard until they moved it back. Bonnie began calling and leaving messages for their landlords, the Rosfelds, who had provided a six-page printed packet of tips for the unit but nothing related to the radiators, an almost conspicuous omission, they now realized, as their breath turned into mist clouds.

One afternoon David came back to the house to find Bonnie wearing her puffy winter coat, pacing with uncharacteristic restlessness.

"You're home." Her tone was never so grim. Something was very wrong.

"What's going on?"

Bonnie explained that she finally got a call back from the Rosfelds, who now resided in Winchester, a leafy suburb a half hour's drive from Cambridge. Bonnie spoke to Carrie Rosfeld, who was chasing a toddler during the call. Bonnie asked for help getting the radiators running.

"First off," Bonnie reported to David, "we were right. The radiators have not been going on."

"It could have saved us a lot of trouble to know that. Did she say how to turn them on?"

Bonnie gave an ironic laugh.

"She wouldn't tell you?"

"There's nothing to turn on, David. Not up here."

It turned out that there was only one thermostat in the entire house. It was on the second floor—belonging to the Hales. That thermostat controlled all the radiators from the first through the third floor.

"How can there be one thermostat for a house that's divided into two units? What if the Hales went away for a month without turning the heat on? Could that be legal?"

"It's Cambridge," Bonnie said, unintentionally harking back to the realtor's justifications of all shortcomings. "These houses are so old, that even if there are requirements, quirks end up getting exempted somewhere along the way."

"What did Carrie say to do?"

"She said the Hales are under no obligation to adjust the heat for our benefit because they're not our landlords. Carrie's solution was that we get heavy blankets and drink hot chocolate."

They laughed in disbelief. After more discussion, they realized it might just be a brief inconvenience. As the Hales felt colder, they would have no choice but to start turning on the heat.

But the Hales didn't, not from what David and Bonnie could tell. Their apartment became so uncomfortable that Bonnie bought a thermometer, which showed air temperatures on their floor hovering around sixty to sixty-two degrees, dipping further during the night. She began to document the temperatures, creating a log complete with photos of the thermometer. They tried hot water bottles, thermoses of hot tea and coffee, and electric space heaters, which popped the electric breakers when more than one was used. When Bonnie started to feel sick, her toughness solidified. "I'm going downstairs to talk to them right now."

"No, you've been so busy at work. Let me," David said. "You don't need extra stress. I'll explain what's going on."

"You sure?"

It could be a blessing, was what David did not say. It was another chance to connect with Silas, assuming he was home. At least talking about heat was less demoralizing than talking about garbage. A fresh start.

That evening, David knocked on the Hales' front door. *Don't even knock, just come in,* he had envisioned Silas saying once they'd bonded. *You and Bonnie are welcome here, always.* Silas came to the door wearing a sky-blue wool cardigan. He looked like a man ready to sit by a crackling fire and share worldviews, with big leather-bound volumes all around them. His heavy eyebrows slipped down, demonstrating how he had to concentrate to remember David.

"David Trent," David reminded him, pointing upward toward the top floor.

"Yes?"

"Sorry to bother you. Our heat doesn't seem to be going on. After talking to the Rosfelds, we realized there's only one thermostat in the house . . ."

Silas's mouth stretched in a big smile. "You came to the right place. Come in." He quickly retreated from the door, then called back to David, who was struggling to take off his shoes to add to the rows of them belonging to the Hales in the inside corner of the front hall: "Come!"

David hurried behind Silas into the kitchen, sliding along in his socks.

"Don't be shy, step lively, come along. Rebecca, we have a little visitor."

"Someone here?" Rebecca, reading the latest issue of the *New Yorker* at the kitchen table, looked up. Even as she made direct eye contact with David, there was only vague recognition.

"Monsieur Trent, from upstairs," Silas said.

She returned to the magazine after nodding at David.

A few items stood out to David that he hadn't noticed during his solo exploration of the Hales' rooms during move-in day. In a frame was a Best of Boston award, given by a local magazine to a writer each year. There were also some book covers and best-seller lists hanging up, mixed in with photos from literary galas over the years, artifacts of achievement that David dreamed about, symbols of what he might become one day.

"Now, over here, Signor Trent. Come, you can do it."

He led David by the arm to the far end of the kitchen and into an adjoining hallway, where a large water pipe was coming out of the floor and continuing into the ceiling.

"Heat travels, David. It travels upward. So there will always be enough heat traveling to your floor. You never have to worry about that."

"Well, that's . . ." David cleared his throat to cover up his conflicting trains of thought. "But it seems like the thermostat hasn't actually been turned on. So the heat can't rise . . . if it's not on?"

"Beautifully spoken, David! There's that thermostat you heard about. Go ahead, let's turn it on and test it out. Do the honors."

"You're sure?"

"I want you to feel the heat in its full glory."

With Silas's encouragement, David hesitantly tapped the thermostat on, then up a couple degrees.

"Be a man, Trent! Give it a real kick!"

A few more taps caused muted rumbling in the walls to come from every direction in the house as the radiators activated. David broke into an embarrassingly big smile. Silas led him back to the large pipe.

"Go ahead," Silas said, gesturing.

David put his hand near the pipe.

"Grab it, Trent, like a lopped-off enemy head!"

David closed his fingers around the pipe, nearly scalding himself. He had to hold in a scream.

"Already hot?" Silas said.

"Very," he muttered.

"Happy?"

"Beyond. Thanks so much, Silas. I'm relieved we could solve this."

Cradling his throbbing hand, David imagined Bonnie basking in the welcome geyser of warmth upstairs, as if stepping out of an airplane at a tropical destination into the first sweep of air through the jetway.

"Excellent. Now let me show you something else while you're here, David."

Silas retrieved a glass jar filled with a cloudy green liquid, for a moment giving the impression of a mad scientist in his lab.

David sensed that Silas was waiting for him to identify the object. "Pickles?"

"Exactly. I make them myself. You have to internalize the choices that go into the transformation of the cucumbers, exactly how fresh they must be without being overly so. The salt I use is imported from the Dead Sea, David. From the rich soul of history. There are men who home-brew beer. There are even some among them who feel they're accomplishing something as they create drinks meant for hooligans to guzzle before vomiting it out later. But the real craft is in pickles. I always make my own pickles and my own champagne, and never accept either if storebought."

He put a strong hand on David's shoulder and shifted him toward a wall of shelves filled with glass bottles organized into flavors. There was a tap and a tank. David was nodding, attempting to hide his bewilderment. Though he couldn't muster interest in the pickles or champagne, he felt a rising exhilaration that Silas was sharing his hobbies, initiating him into his personal life.

"The French insist that the only champagne comes from Champagne, France, but I defy them. I engage a vineyard that signed an agreement with French authorities in World War I to preserve the right to make authentic champagne grapes, and among home winemakers that now extends only to me."

David sensed the chance for a segue.

"It seems like a great break from writing, Silas. I'm not sure if we've talked about it, but I also write."

"Fiction?"

For a moment, David could not speak. Then he stumbled through a smattering of details about where he had received his MFA degree and about his novel. Somehow, this ended up with him reciting from memory the opening to Silas's classic novel about a disgraced friar, *Sevenfold*:

He called it the mark of Cain, that last dot of orange extruding from the ash, then he crossed himself sinuously and ironically. At the monastery in Chartreuse someone had explained to him the distinction between blasphemy and sacrilege, but he had since forgotten.

Silas's gaze turned to glass. "How strange—don't you think?—that so many claim to be writers, when in truth almost nobody is. It also occurs to me, hearing those lines, how few understand that 'he had since forgotten,' which at one point was printed on T-shirts on more sophisticated college campuses, is an axiom for mankind. Look closely at the masses around us, and you will realize that they have all 'since forgotten.'" He clapped his hands together. "One other thing before you go . . ."

Silas's tongue traced the edge of his upper lip. He returned to the thermostat and theatrically switched it back to OFF, turning to David with a grin that flatlined. The rumbling in the walls and floors quieted, the warm air receding.

"Look around, Trent. Rebecca and I spent quite the small fortune on new windows a few years back, hermetically sealing this whole place from the elements! Thankfully, I received a generous book prize shortly afterward, which paid for it all. Sometimes what comes into your life and what goes out of it balances perfectly, David."

David was stunned. "Oh," was what he mustered in response.

"Since we put in those windows, whenever we turn the heat on, it gets too warm for us. Right now, for example, I'm starting to perspire in the few minutes since you hounded me to turn it on." He wiped his forehead with his fingers and showed drops of moisture to David. "We—Mrs. Hale and I—tend to like a neutral temperature. In fact, the radiators get so hot that we'd have to open windows if they're left on. If it's cool upstairs, you could certainly invest in new windows, too."

"New windows? How much would that be?"

"For the entire third floor? I couldn't say exactly. Maybe six, seven thousand. And then there's the crawl space above us, below you. That has virtually no insulation to the outside, so that stockpiles the cold air. We have no interest in changing that, but that would be another thousand or so to fix—so where does that leave you, at eight thousand total?"

David could tell Silas was dead serious, and also that he wanted to be finished with the conversation.

"We're just renting. We can't do that. And the Rosfelds don't have any plans to replace windows that we know about. We can't force them to. It's not realistic. We just need the heat on, Silas. It's freezing up there. We won't be able to stay there otherwise."

"That's too bad. It really is! Come." He led David to the front door.

"Hold on. There must be something we can do."

"There is one thing. Or at least there's one more thing I can explain, which is the following, and I sincerely hope it helps. David Trent: we're not your landlords. I'm deeply sorry if I wasn't clearer earlier. If I was opaque, let me try to articulate myself better while trying not to raise my blood pressure and having Mrs. Hale get on my case. Here it goes: We have no responsibility to you at all. Never speak to us about this again. In fact, to make it easier, do not speak to us. You have ten seconds to leave my property. Because, make no mistake, you may live above us, you may walk upon our ceiling like so many pigeons, but you may not step inside our property without permission."

"Silas . . ."

He held up one finger, then a second. "And do not make eye contact with us again when you walk by us." Five. Six. "We want nothing to do with you or your life, or your so-called writing, or your girlfriend's life. You have nothing to do with us." Eight. Nine. "Have a good night!"

He slammed the door into David's face as David was trying to put on his shoes. David realized he was trembling, his head spinning, trying to make sense of it and face the fact that there was nothing to be done, and that Silas Hale hated him. Absolutely hated him.

Reaching his stairway back to the top, David lumbered slowly, the creak of each tread taunting him as he stalled telling Bonnie what had just happened.

"David?" she called from above.

She was waiting for him. He hadn't noticed before how the acoustics in the narrow stairs were tunnel-like, making the sound at one end seem to be closer to the other end. He did not reply. He felt so small.

"David?" she called again.

As he reached the vestibule, Bonnie ran to him and threw her arms around him. "You did it!"

"What?"

"I felt the heat kick in! What a difference. It was heavenly. Now I feel silly for worrying. We should have just talked to the Hales all along."

"It's not on, Bon," David said, bracing himself.

"What do you mean?" She walked over to the radiator. "You're right, the heat went off again. It was hot when I felt it before, I swear. What happened?"

"You're not going to believe this . . ." David started, then paused. "Some kind of faulty auto shutoff is being triggered. Probably old wiring in the thermostat, Silas thinks. They're going to get it looked at as soon as possible. Tomorrow, maybe?"

6

DAVID HADN'T INTENDED TO LIE to Bonnie. He had tried to solve their problem as he would have with a typical neighbor. That had been a mistake, but he could not tell Bonnie that. She would hardly empathize with the idea that a person who was a writer should be treated differently than someone who wasn't. Still, in the process of David's faux pas, Silas had given him clues on how to successfully enter his rarefied sphere. What Silas valued was a person's unique interests, like pickling and champagne-making. David just had to buy the time to strengthen connections with him, to win his allegiance.

Besides, maybe there was a way to resolve the heating issue without involving the Hales. Regardless of Silas's bedside manner, it was true that he and Rebecca were not their landlords and were not responsible for the top floor. That was the harsh reality. While Bonnie was at work, David called the city hall offices. Without giving a name or address, he was able to find out that in this scenario, landlords were not required to install a separate thermostat for each floor, which could cost thousands of dollars, because another heating zone would have to be created inside the walls. Regulations did exist, however, for minimum temperature in a rental, and the Rosfelds could be fined on a weekly basis if David and Bonnie reported temperatures below those levels. If this happened, the Rosfelds would in turn invoice the two-unit condo association—which would only serve to infuriate the Hales, who would then be on the hook for half.

The next day, Bonnie texted him from work.

Thermostat getting repaired today?

David, sliding the keyboard panel that sat hidden behind his phone screen, pecked out on the tiny keys: **Checking!**

When she got home, she looked at him expectantly. He didn't hesitate. Apparently—this he reported with a disappointed shake of the head—the repair was going to take longer than expected to schedule. There were backlogs with the equipment they needed, and the whole procedure would have to be expensed through the condo association for tax purposes.

"You shouldn't even worry about this, Bon. I have the free time to deal with it. I'm waiting to sort things out with the literary agents who are interested in my novel. Look, I have an idea. I know you've mentioned trying to stay with your sister to help her out for a while, and the commute from their place is basically the same as ours to your office. You would get time with your nephew, and she would get a break. It's perfect timing. Camp out there, and in the meantime I'll figure all this out. I promise."

Bonnie's sister, who lived nearby in Allston, had a six-month-old son, and David knew Bonnie had been feeling guilty that she wasn't able to be there much, even though her sister had never lifted a finger to help Bonnie or anyone else. Bonnie had a tendency to feel responsible for everyone, and he urged her to fight that feeling. But in this case, her guilt, and her sister's eagerness for help, proved convenient.

She hesitated. "That would be nice if I could pitch in for her more. But are you sure you'd be okay here?"

He showed off a new set of portable space heaters he'd bought that day at the hardware store, which used less voltage and so would be less likely to overload the—circuits? breakers? David wasn't positive about the terminology, but it had the intended effect of putting Bonnie at ease, and setting their plan in motion.

The electric heaters did make a difference, though being lower voltage, they were less powerful. On the truly frigid nights, the little black boxes seemed to shrink and vibrate, as though shivering themselves, while attempting to emit enough heat to stay relevant. He would wear long sleeves, a hoodie sweatshirt, and a coat to bed, piling up four thick blankets over himself and three rubber hot water bottles. Still he'd tremble. Those nights, he'd be thankful Bonnie was comfortable and warm elsewhere. Privately, he'd think of himself as one of the old arctic explorers of the nineteenth century he had enjoyed reading about in oversize books with glossy old black-and-white photos in his high school library, on a journey that others would think unhinged but that deep down he knew he had to complete, and if he did, his life would be forever changed.

The Siberian temperatures sent him out of the house even more than usual to cafés, sometimes meeting Jace and sometimes on his own, savoring hot drinks and toasty rooms. This helped foster an early start to his writing days. On one of these outings he overheard a snippet of conversation from a nearby table. The older of two men turned out to be a professor of poetry at Boston College, whom David had once seen speak on a panel. To his surprise, David heard them talking about plans to attend "Hale's party again" at "Hale's place." He strained but couldn't hear much else, the pair's exchange being drowned out by a young man on the other side of him, pontificating on the need for wider bicycle lanes in Cambridge. Still, he was able to piece together that Silas had an annual end-of-the-year party at the house, a kind of soiree for the local literary scene. The fact that David had never heard a word about this event in the past suggested its exclusivity.

By the time Bonnie returned from her first stay with her sister, he had mastered the new space heaters' placement and timing. Life's usual distractions accumulated, with busy schedules at her office and the early stages of their wedding planning. Bonnie had settled into a routine of staying for a few days at a time with her sister, and when she came back David lucked out with a mild stretch of weather, so that heating their unit receded as a topic.

When the subject did come up, he glossed over the reasons for the delays. She did not seem entirely convinced, but he could sense she didn't want to distract him from his process of submitting his novel. On that front, he had lied to her—again, without exactly planning on it—by indicating that multiple literary agents were interested in representing his manuscript, and he had to decide between them. In fact, still only one agent had expressed any interest, and her enthusiasm remained limp; she was essentially asking David to convince her. He was disappointed but did not want Bonnie to know, as he knew she would urge him not to take this personally, which was impossible.

Amid bouts of colder weather and snow, he seldom spotted Silas outside, and when they crossed paths, Silas didn't acknowledge him. No wave. Not a glance. Not only as if he did not exist, but as if everything in his general direction vanished from the face of the earth. Garbage duties—rolling the bins from the driveway to the curb and back again through mud and slush and ice—had by this point fallen to David alone, since Bonnie was away so much. He imagined the Hales brought down their trash bags to the storage shed in the middle of the night, as he never saw them do it, but the bins would all at once quickly fill up with four or five of their oversize trash bags.

The same went for shoveling snow. When Bonnie was staying at the house, there were several nights when the driveway was snowed in, and nobody seemed to do anything about it. David or Bonnie would call the Rosfelds, who would swear that 6 Observatory Hill was on a waiting list for a snow removal company to come by, but that the companies had priority houses that had been clients for forty or fifty years, which had to be cleared first. Bonnie had to get out of the driveway to go to her office in the morning, so David inevitably ended up shoveling, with a Kafkaesque routine involving the city's snowplows periodically speeding by, pushing dirty, brick-heavy ice and snow blocks right back onto the driveway. The snow shovel, he noticed, was always positioned outside the storage shed, leaning against it, as though placed there for him to find.

He hadn't heard the date of the Hales' holiday party during the eavesdropped conversation at the café. But one evening, when Bonnie was at their place with him, at around four thirty—in December, Cambridge would fall into bone-chilling darkness by that point in the afternoon—a large number of cars squeezed into the driveway as well as into the nearby on-street parking. He realized the day of the party had come. *I'm not going to spy, it's not my business*, he told himself, though his dedication to that principle could be debated. He sidled to the window to peer down between the blinds.

"What's up?" Bonnie asked. "Aren't we watching a movie?"

"Let's do it," he said, turning from the window.

The party emerged as a series of muffled sounds that night, drifting upward to the third floor while he willed himself to ignore them. The unfairness flooded him.

In another month, with Bonnie still back and forth from her sister's, the worst winter weather had long passed, with the end of the season very mild. After a few rounds of revisions, David's lukewarm literary agent worked up some positivity and started sending out his manuscript to publishers. He could barely function that week, missing meals and hearing phantom rings from his phone. Several big publishers slowly circled, considering the book, but his agent explained that the editor who came closest to making an offer had been overruled by colleagues in the marketing and publicity departments, who did not feel there was enough unique about David to promote him as a first-time author. At the end of the process, an offer was made, during a second round of submissions, by Parable, a smaller but very respectable boutique imprint; the offer itself was financially modest, but the publisher had a track record of landing reviews for their books in the *New York Times Book Review* and could point to several of their books that had won awards over the years. The latter was a tiny percentage of their output, but it represented tangible hope. The other publishers he had once envisioned fell out of his mind with surprising speed. David was ecstatic to be on his way to being a Parable author.

Like many writers before him, he soon experienced the paradox of working on a novel with an editor, which was that she did not edit much. This was particularly true at Parable, which had limited resources, permitting only a single round of notes between him and his overworked editor before the manuscript was copyedited for grammar and continuity, by which point nothing substantive could be changed, on the threat of charging him money if he tried to edit any more. David was not given much choice about the cover design, either, though as a courtesy his editor emailed the image to him, while politely making it clear that input would be dismissed. The cover was a cornfield at sunset, on which was superimposed the image of a man's face falling apart like a jigsaw puzzle, with the letters of the title, *The Crises*, also on puzzle pieces. He tried to imagine being a reader wandering through a bookstore and feeling compelled to pick up, over any other book, a book with this cover. He could not quite conclude he would have. Still, he felt grateful for the cover, because it was his cover. Soon enough he loved it.

The thrill of the publication with Parable gradually succumbed to the fear of bad luck. What if reviewers were assigned whose taste in fiction happened to differ entirely from his own? What if they used the opportunity to amplify their voices at his expense, depriving him of his one chance at a debut?

Summer came, and with it the publication of *The Crises*. Bonnie celebrated with enthusiasm, writing a countdown on a mini chalkboard at home and arranging a small get-together with their friends in the private room of a nice hotel restaurant on publication day. She ordered a cake decorated with a fondant facsimile of the hayfield cover of his book, and he couldn't stop thinking about how the dinner and cake might cost more than he expected to make from the book.

"To our published author!" She raised a champagne glass in a toast. "My published author, David!"

"You were born for this!" Jace called out in complete earnestness, which elicited a few cheers.

As weeks passed, David occasionally heard from his editor, then didn't hear from her at all, until the point came when it seemed the book might never have existed. Reviewers did not write negatively about his book to put themselves in the spotlight, as it turned out; instead, few wrote anything about it at all. He couldn't blame his publisher for focusing on other books, nor could he fault Bonnie and the rest of the world for moving on to their day-to-day lives. One day all he could think about was his book, and, it seemed, the next day there was nothing to think about. The whole experience hit him hard. It was cruel and cold confirmation that he would not achieve his dream, that he would not manage to be special, and that he would forever be on the outside looking in on the future successes of other writers, the ones whom Silas Hale would embrace, people like Barnaby Masters. The trust fund baby, blustery and pretentious, handed a place at an Ivy League school that gave him an undeserved sheen, being mentored by Silas Hale! Maybe people like Barnaby deserved it more than him, maybe less, but the moral assessments did not matter; they somehow got it, and he hadn't.

Fall brought with it a crisp chill. One morning Bonnie was stuffing laundry into the machine when she called out, "David, did we confirm the heat situation is fixed?"

The washer and dryer were located at the top of the stairs, in the vestibule, which had no insulation. This had made her think about the upcoming winter.

David was sitting on the sofa in the living room. "What?"

"It was such a hot summer," she said, "and then with your book coming out, I kept forgetting to ask."

"Don't worry. I still have all the space heaters."

Bonnie fell silent. She walked over to the couch and sat down next to him, a slow, careful movement intended as a precursor to a discussion he could not wriggle out of.

"It was supposed to be fixed last winter, David. And, as you're aware, another winter is coming up."

That counted as sarcasm for Bonnie, which did not bode well. "Whenever it gets cold, there's a backlog for these companies. There are people without any heat at all."

Bonnie squinted. "You mean like us?"

David laughed, but she didn't.

"I'll call the Hales and ask what is taking so long with the repair."

"You can't."

"Why?" she asked.

"Silas Hale."

They both fell silent. Revelation hung in the air.

"I'm confused," said Bonnie.

How to explain?

"They're not going to repair it. Silas isn't going to repair it. Ever. Because there's nothing wrong with it. They don't want to turn on the heat. He says they get too warm. I didn't want to upset you, so I tried to stall in order to solve it myself."

"What?" Bonnie's eyes fired with purpose. "Then we're getting out of here before it's cold again. Let's pack up. Come on. I'm sending a certified letter to the Rosfelds, too. We're not paying another dime in rent until this is taken care of."

"Bonnie, let's think this through."

She was in action mode, grabbing luggage from the closet and marching toward the bedroom. "What the hell is there to think about it—" She stopped walking, processing the information in a different way, her anger rearranging itself until it aimed at him. "You lied to me, David. You didn't want to upset me? That's what you said. So you knew this, you lied to me, and you thought that wouldn't upset me? You told me there was something wrong with the wiring that needed to be fixed."

"I know. There was so much going on. I can explain all of it."

"Why did you lie? Really."

"That night, when I went downstairs to talk to them, Silas Hale was very angry at the whole exchange. The writing community is a small world, especially in Cambridge. It fits on the head of a pin, Bonnie. Everybody doesn't know everybody, but everybody knows somebody who knows anybody you can think of. And Silas Hale knows them all. Norman Mailer used to hang out in our yard."

"Who cares? You're published now. You don't need Silas Hale."

"It doesn't work like . . . Bonnie, if we make this a big thing with the Hales, Silas will despise me. That feeling will trickle down right to the chairs of committees who consider writers for adjunct teaching positions, to the organizers who put together writing conferences and fellowships, even to publishers. I'll be blackballed."

"Silas Hale doesn't care about you. He despises us already for being an inconvenience to him, all while you shovel out his car and drag his garbage to the street. If you dropped dead he'd step right over you. And if he dropped dead, you should step right over him." More than ever, Bonnie struck him as a woman who would quietly survive an apocalypse. "Our health, our relationship, our wedding—those should all be more important than anything Silas Hale thinks or does. Why would you think of letting this continue for another minute?"

David could not say why, could not explain what he wanted, what he believed—that he still had some chance, however slim, of turning Silas's feelings around. That once he left Observatory Hill behind, he wouldn't, he'd be surrendering that forever, and maybe with it his career—now teetering on an unnoticed book—that maybe, just maybe, Silas could save.

"I don't believe this," Bonnie said, left to interpret his silence. "You're really not going to leave?"

"I can't. I can't leave yet."

"You're staying here?"

"You make it sound simple. You always make everything sound simple—that there's one right thing to do—and there's not."

"Is that what you think of me?"

"It's not just me. You think in black and white about everything—your sister, your work, me. Sometimes it's not simply about doing what's right, it's about doing what needs to be done to make things right. Don't you ever consider that?"

"Apparently not, David." Pain reverberated through her voice.

"Bonnie, let's both calm down and talk."

"I'm done talking, and I'm done with this. This isn't you. It's not the version of you I love. You want to stay here and lose sight of what matters, then stay here. But it will be without me."

Gathering up essentials, she was out the door within minutes, ignoring his pleas to talk more. Over the next hours, she didn't return his texts. Over the next weeks they only communicated a few times, once over the phone, a couple of times over text, and in a long email exchange filled with venting by Bonnie, who concluded by urging him to consider their many blessings and put Observatory Hill Road behind them. **The engagement is off, though I'm not giving up on you,** she wrote. **But you need to be able to decide your priorities, and that starts with walking away from that house. It's not just about the heat, I hope you see that.** She went a step further, too: in her email, she pointed out that if fiction writing had led him to a miserable place, maybe it was time to leave the writing to miserable people. Was it better to be happy or to be a writer? He was so bright, he could do anything, even if it meant going back to school. Maybe you're trying to be this, I mean be a writer, because you think it would make you a more valuable person in other people's eyes, not because you love it. Words he had always feared hearing from someone, especially the person who knew him best.

David stared at the words: *The engagement is off.*

The worst part of it all was that he had no plan, no solution to counter anything or justify his decision. Silas still wouldn't look in his direction. There was nothing he could do to change that except to hope for some miracle to transform their dynamic, perhaps involving Silas taking notice of his writing. David's novel had been reviewed in a small number of newspapers and websites, but those came in the doldrums of August while the Hales were away in the Vineyard, and he imagined Silas probably not paying any attention to fairly brief reviews of new fiction. If people weren't forced to notice a book, they usually didn't.

Far more concrete, he knew, would be a plan for patching things up with Bonnie. That was the key to his happiness and his future. He began to mull over how to prove to her that he was as reliable and committed as he really was. He was going to arrange a dinner at the restaurant where they had their first date, but it had closed down, so he tracked down a restaurant with the same owners, which was trendy enough to be booked up for weeks. He snagged the first reservation he could, and hoped she would agree to meet him there. It would be a chance to reset their emotions and the conversation. He picked up brochures from two area law schools. He would bring them to dinner, not a firm commitment to applying, perhaps, but a step to show his open-mindedness.

A week and a half before Thanksgiving, David received a letter in the mail, lodged between utility bills. It was from the Boston Literary Society, and he assumed it was a solicitation to join for a fee. He couldn't believe what it said.

> . . . Our committee is pleased to inform you that your novel, *The Crises,* has been submitted by your publisher and has been awarded the Boston Literary Prize for Best First Novel. Arrangements will be made in the coming days for you to meet the other prizewinners with representatives of the committee. The prize includes a $15,250 award and a two-year membership in the Boston Literary Society. Past winners of the Boston Literary Prize for Best First Novel include Tom Perrotta, Jennifer Haigh, Silas Hale . . .

He stopped reading the list of past winners at the sight of Silas's name. His heart raced. He was receiving the same award that Silas had won early in his career. There was no way for Silas to avoid hearing about this.

He called Bonnie. He had found his miracle, but he couldn't say that to her, and couldn't get his words out in a way that made sense.

"What? Start over, David."

"I did it." He corrected himself. "We did it." He was breathless, and when his words came out, he unexpectedly choked up. "We did it, Bonnie!"

7

DAVID WALKED ON AIR. HE threw the law school brochures in the recycling bin. At first, he loved thinking that no one else would know the news for a few days until the awards were posted online and published in the society's newsletter. To delay telling anyone would make their reactions later even more pleasurable. Reactions to good news never lived up to what they should be, so why not savor the perfection that came in the anticipation of those responses? But in the end, he managed to restrain himself for only a few hours before beginning to send excited emails and texts, which he started firing off one after another while still on his jubilant, disjointed call with Bonnie.

"I am so happy for you," Bonnie said on that call. She was almost hyperventilating after he finally managed to explain the news. "I can't believe it, David!"

He fought his impulse to overanalyze her word choice. Was she admitting that up until this point she had suspected, just as he did, that his work would never really be noticed?

"Thank you, Bon. I can hardly believe it either. I hope the team at Parable will be energized, too. You know I don't like to let myself be excited, but I have to say, I'm excited!"

"It's such a great feeling to know that your writing means so much to people reading it. Give yourself permission to enjoy that."

"We should get together and celebrate."

"David, I'm not . . . I don't think that's where we are right now."

David knew he had to find a way to finally explain why he had lied to her about the heat. But as his mind spun in circles to catch up with years of unfulfilled feelings and ambitions, he was distracted. After a few choppy comments about repairing their relationship, he ended up reading her the letter from the prize committee twice, and their conversation ended without any noticeable path toward healing.

After they hung up, he rationalized that pushing off bigger conversations was a good thing. He owed it to her, he told himself, to give her some space for a bit longer. The truth was, he rationalized with greater enthusiasm, that he needed to concentrate on the award for Bonnie's sake as much as for his own—for their future together. He had to properly build upon the honor of the award to blaze his path, not just for the present but for the rest of his career for years to come. He nearly convinced himself.

"David Trent," Jace said, as though anointing him. "Best First Novel. How amazing is that? How amazing?"

David could barely contain himself when a local library called asking about his availability for a speaking event. Libraries affiliated with the literary society received the lists of award winners early. The library proposed that David, Silas Hale, and two others do a joint appearance, putting together the current winner of the Best First Novel Award with past ones. David tried to remain blasé while agreeing to any date, anytime they wanted him.

He had reached out to share the news of the prize with about two dozen people by the time the society announced the winners widely. There were so many awards—for poetry, nonfiction, biography, and a slew of other categories—that he wondered if his own name might be overlooked, but he felt like Best First Novel had a ring to it that other categories lacked. In fact, he was startled by how many people had heard about it. He received messages and shout-outs of congratulations from people he had known as far back as grade school, with more from his MFA classmates. They had never seemed to him to recognize his potential, and it shocked him how casually they could now say they were happy for him without acknowledging, or maybe even apologizing for, previous attitudes.

Closer to home, Antoinette intercepted him on the sidewalk, waving her short arms wildly. She had also somehow heard about the award and was saying how "we" had much to discuss about the award, by which she might have meant her and Judith, or maybe her and David, but he had more emails and phone calls to return than he could get through, so he put Antoinette off.

A courier buzzed at his door with a bouquet. It was from Parable. David choked back tears as he put the flower arrangement in a vase. Though the combination of lilies and hydrangeas was nothing extraordinary, he admired them to the point of obsession. Those flowers, however modest, more than anything else, made it feel real.

The Harvard Bookstore, an institution in Cambridge, emailed asking that he stop by and sign copies of his book when he could. He expected the owner or manager to welcome him as he walked in. Instead, there was hardly anyone in sight. The one cashier he tracked down had to look up his name and found six copies of *The Crises* stored behind the desk with a sticky note, on which was scribbled "to be signed by," the scribbler presumably having been interrupted before continuing to write "author," and then forgetting.

The cashier found the closest pen at hand, a plastic ballpoint not suitable for book signings, and then paused. "Do you have an ID?"

"What?" It took a moment to process the question before David took out his driver's license.

"Huh. The photo on the book jacket makes you look older. That's a compliment, by the way. Here you go." Her tone struck David as odd, as though the store was doing him a favor, despite the fact that the email to him had the subject heading **A favor for Harvard Book-**

store and had noted how meaningful it would be for their customers to have signed copies.

As he was signing the books, he noticed Silas Hale at the other end of the store, chatting with the manager and a few staff. David knew Silas's publisher had recently reissued a set of some of his novels, with new covers and forewords by the author, in which he described his creative process in detail, providing insights that included how his novels were essentially murder mysteries without the murders and without the mysteries. Silas had stopped by to sign these special editions. The manager must have dashed off a cluster of emails around the same time to local authors with new books out.

David stalled. "I'm really excited about this. The Boston Literary Society prize, I mean."

The cashier looked around to check if he was speaking to her. "What?"

David shook his head. Having signed the copies as slowly as humanly possible, he pushed the sad pile toward the cashier and turned to walk away, glancing only for a moment at the huddle around Silas that he wished surrounded him instead.

"Herr Trent!" Silas called out. "Hold on there a minute."

David stood at attention, then started moving toward Silas, but Silas held up his hand, palm facing out. The gesture said: *I am going to talk to you, but not yet.* David stood there in the middle of the store, his shoulders and arms alternating in poses of awkwardness. The cashier now squinted in his direction with much more curiosity about him than she had shown during their exchange. Silas finished holding court with the manager and staff, then turned to a young woman in an oversize sweater who had been waiting to one side for a chance to talk to him.

She presented a well-worn hardcover of *Sevenfold*, one of his early novels.

"Mr. Hale, I wonder if you could sign this to me. Cleo, C-L-E-O.

This novel really changed how I look at life. I think it's fair to say it changed me in—" She had more to say before Silas interrupted with a gasp.

"Is this a first edition, Cleo?"

"Yes!" she said proudly.

Silas offered a grave nod, as though a serious thought weighed him down. "Of course I'll sign it for you with great pleasure, dear. But I'm not going to write your name on this."

"Oh . . ."

"You see, my first editions are worth significant money, particularly signed ones, but as soon as we add your name to it, it will decrease sharply in value. With my signature only but without your name to blemish it, if there comes a time when you run low on money, you can sell this. You will thank me later."

He signed and returned the book to her, and then approached David.

"You should have told me you were a writer, Trent."

"I did."

"I must have been distracted! Sometimes, when you're starting off, you have to just shake a giant by the shoulders to be heard over the din and the nuisances of Lilliput. That award that is being bestowed on you was critical to my career trajectory, and shall be to yours as well, I don't doubt."

"Speaking of that, actually, a library reached out about organizing a reading with both of us together."

"I look forward to hearing about it. And in the meantime you have to come to our end-of-the-year party."

"That sounds great, Silas, thank you."

"You'll find it's filled with writers as well as writers' enemies."

David laughed. "Enemies?"

"People whose role in life is to deeply appreciate writers. You think they are your friends, but they are not. You'll realize they're impossible to please. Of course, don't think any of this changes your duties at my house!"

David laughed, but he was quite serious in confirming his continued servitude.

"We all do our part, don't we?" Silas said. "I paid my dues to be where I am, you can count on that. Now that I see you again, I begin to see it in your eyes."

"See what?" David asked.

"A writer's soul, my young friend."

How many times David had looked longingly through the display window of this same bookstore, other people's success staring out at him from the covers of books that projected talent and drive he hoped he could match. Now Silas Hale had invited him inside his world, wholeheartedly, a deceptively big leap from living just a floor above him. He wished Bonnie could have been there with him in the bookstore to witness the exchange; it would explain everything to her in a way he was not sure he ever could.

The event organizer at the library left a message that the reading would be David and two of the other three invited writers. She commented that Silas Hale declined to participate, then quickly apologized, realizing she had given him more information than she should have. David was dejected at learning of Silas's refusal, but busy enough not to dwell on it. A few days later he received an email from Lee Van Knox, the head of the prize committee at the Boston Literary Society, to meet him for coffee at Darwin's on an out-of-the-way stretch of Mount Auburn Street. The original letter about the award (which by now David could have written out verbatim from memory, backward if needed, and had decided to frame) had specified that he and the other winners would soon meet with *representatives*, plural, which made him relish with satisfaction that he was asked to meet one-on-one. The society likely wanted to arrange a special event or ceremony for the Best First

Novel prize without the honorees from less exciting categories. (Facts were facts, after all, in terms of comparative public interest in, say, "Best Nonfiction Anthology.") This was reinforced by Van Knox inviting him to meet as soon as the next morning, if it suited David's schedule.

David knew Van Knox was not a writer himself; a writer looking for a meetup spot would have picked some other location. Darwin's layout made finding and keeping seats difficult. It was also loud, and the tables were too close together to expect any privacy, though none of this could bother David today. Nothing could.

Van Knox waved at him. He had come early to secure a table, while scanning the customers for him, which made David feel a few inches taller as he made his way over.

"David, so nice to meet you," Van Knox said, exuding a deference that David was not used to. "Please sit. I must say, I'm really looking forward to reading your book."

During their small talk about the crowds and the coffee, Van Knox showed himself as firmly in the category of "people whose role is to appreciate writers," as Silas named it. Van Knox may have read prodigiously, but lazily, and did not suffer from any compulsion to create. He was slender from endless running and cycling the Charles River on a daily schedule, something that would be too disruptive to the typical writer's routine. When he removed his jacket, he revealed reflective gear on his clothes, as though he might be on the move again at any second. His helmet hung on the top of his chair by a strap. The strange comment about not having yet read the book lingered. Surely, even if his role in the Boston Literary Society prize committee was largely administrative, Van Knox should make the time to read the award winners' work!

"Well, let's get down to the business at hand, shall we?" Van Knox said.

"Yes, let's."

"I don't want to use up more of your time than needed."

"Honestly, I've been crazed," David said, "but in a good way, so it's nice just to catch my breath."

Van Knox held a tight-lipped grin for too long. "I wish we could meet under different circumstances."

It was another out-of-place comment, or maybe a misguided joke.

"Diving right in, David, here's the situation. I'm in charge of the award committee for the Boston Literary Society. The voting is all done by secret ballot by our judges, and then we have software that tabulates everything. It's essentially automated, thankfully. Still, there can be human error."

"I don't understand."

"When I was reviewing the files for myself, I discovered that another first novel had been submitted with an almost identical title to yours. It's called *Crisis*, and it's by an author and professor of writing named Valentina Maldenado. Quite delightful work. She actually won the highest number of votes, but when the list was compiled, one of our interns accidentally copied out the information for your title, *The Crises*, which had been submitted by your publisher. Imagine that! An understandable mistake, of course—he never even knew he did it, and he's now in Paris for a semester abroad. In any case, there are so many books that titles are destined to collide and resemble each other. I remember when I worked for an independent press in New Hampshire, that was my first job related to publishing as a matter of fact . . ."

David couldn't listen to the anecdote. He was running his hand back and forth through his hair as he tried to catch himself on the table to prevent himself from collapsing.

"We do have good news," Van Knox said, which snapped David back to attention.

"Good news?"

"We'd still like to extend you the complimentary two-year membership to the Boston Literary Society. It's very prestigious to be a member."

"I told my parents, my fiancée. About the award! I told everybody."

"I am so sorry. I can imagine . . ." He gave up the sentence, which suggested he could not actually imagine what David felt.

"What am I supposed to do? How do I possibly undo that?"

To his plea for help, Van Knox sighed with sympathetic frustration and shook his head, as though he had just learned David was given the wrong coffee order. After they sat for a while in their awkward tableau, Van Knox's expression softened, projecting genuine compassion.

"We are really apologetic, David. Really. Look, this is just between us at the moment, and I'll make sure it stays that way for now. Please take some time to inform those closest to you about our mistake the way you'd prefer to tell them."

"Thank you. I appreciate that. So the other writer . . ."

"Ms. Maldenado doesn't know yet. We want to make this as easy on you as possible, David. Blame it all on us, since it really is all our fault!" Van Knox surveyed their surroundings, maybe trying to think of something to add. He shook his head back and forth, upset with himself and his helplessness. "Let me buy you another, David. Macchiato?"

He had an uncharacteristic urge to stand up and punch Van Knox's face, something he had no reason to think he could do. In his youth in Michigan, he had earned a schoolyard reputation as a peacemaker, helping to break up more than one physical altercation that broke out between other kids. Even then, high on self-righteousness, he'd wonder what it would have felt like to have thrown one of the punches, to channel all your force, your pent-up frustration, into a physical act that proved the strength everyone doubted you could possess, and that flouted the rules he was terrified of breaking, in the name of retribution.

"Thank you, no," David said, numbed. "I'm fine. I'll be fine."

How would Bonnie take this? This train of thought was interrupted by considering Silas Hale. Silas! What was he going to think of him now? David knew the answer to that. "There are so few real writers," Silas might say, "and I knew from one glance that you were never one."

Van Knox settled on giving David a week to tell people. David could console himself that some people who had heard about his award would never come across the correction. Retracting a piece of news was harder than spreading it. He knew what Jace might say, the pragmatic ghostwriter in him coming out. "It's all a business, David," he would comment with a wry air, his businesslike approach reinforced by the blinking light from his wireless earpiece, "and at the end of the day writing should be left at the office, even if you don't have an office. It doesn't change your worth." Van Knox had spoken about it so casually. If only he and the literary society knew what it had meant to him, and the number of people he had told! Ripping his heart out now appeared hardly more than an inconvenience to them.

In the meantime, the second winter living on Observatory Hill Road was rapidly proving colder than the first. David's meticulous arrangement of space heaters was no match for the New England climate. As temperatures plummeted below zero, the space heaters might as well have been props from a dollhouse, their warmth barely perceptible in the freezing air. The two coldest spots were above the crawl space under the trapdoor, and the similarly uninsulated vestibule at the top of the stairs, housing the laundry machines. David wore a ski hat and gloves when he did laundry. He had no intention of begging the Hales to turn the heat on; in fact, the thought of ever seeing Silas Hale again, knowing what he was about to find out about David's award, made him nauseous.

No matter how much he rehearsed to himself how to explain the award mishap to people, how to slyly convert it all into a lighthearted joke that showed how little it meant, he still couldn't do it. The week passed without him telling another soul, not even Bonnie.

When David first received the letter about receiving the award, he had felt he was on the precipice of being ready to win Bonnie back. But he couldn't face telling her yet that his exhilaration was all mistaken. The longer he avoided her, the more her frustration with him was renewed. As far as she was concerned, he was slamming the door on their relationship that they had worked hard to pry back open little by little since she had left Observatory Hill. She rented an apartment in Brookline and insisted that she take her furniture, in part as a warning that she was serious about moving on from Observatory Hill Road—and from David. Most of the furniture they had brought to the orange Victorian house had been Bonnie's anyway, and once the truck came to collect it all—pointedly without Bonnie showing up to supervise, all arranged through the realtor and the Hales' housekeeper—the top-floor apartment turned even bleaker, colder, harsher. Bonnie rarely spoke directly about being upset or angry, but she made her feelings loud and clear.

David told Van Knox he was having trouble reaching one of his family members, to whom it was vital he had a chance to personally explain the award committee's mistake, insinuating, without saying it, that this beloved relative might have a heart attack or some other major medical setback from the shock, and the society would be responsible. In his correspondence with Van Knox, David tried to subtly remind him at every turn of the fact that it was the committee's error, not David's, that had led to this. Mostly he stayed in bed, staring at the ceiling, trying to will away what had happened. Several times, he could hear a woman's beautiful, searing voice singing arias from outside. He assumed it was Judith, Antoinette's pupil, now providing an accompaniment to his despair from the vocal coach's plush, pastry-filled Lautrec painting of a living room. His life crumbled beneath his feet, and all he could do was try to hide, hide from the crumbling, hide from the ear-piercing crescendos, hide from the expressions on the faces of people who would now know once and for all that he would never make it.

8

AFTER LEE VAN KNOX GRANTED several informal, guilt-induced extensions over email, David ignored his messages. A strange, illogical feeling gathered inside him, a determination that he could change the outcome of the situation if only he could think it through with absolute clarity. He began to draft a letter to the director of the Boston Literary Society, who had authority over Lee Van Knox, proposing a tie between the two books. The more he worked out the argument of why both writers deserved the award, the more he convinced himself that it was a practical idea. He failed to address how the society would explain, on top of the unprecedented idea of a tie, that the co-winners being announced were coincidentally called *The Crises* and *Crisis*. But after all, coincidences happened every day! David had often thought how fiction writers were the only group of people banned from acknowledging the existence of coincidences, merely in order to avoid readers thinking, *That's coincidental!* More importantly, a tie, he reasoned to his hypothetical future correspondent, would show the society's fairness after causing so much confusion thanks to the incompetent, negligent, reflective-clothing-wearing Van Knox (or at least thanks to a former intern).

He felt giddy about his proposed solution, so much so that he had newfound energy to work on his other problems, leaving a message for Bonnie, suggesting a get-together to have a serious conversation upon her return. She was out of town. Her family had organized a winter cruise to the Caribbean to celebrate her grandmother's ninetieth birthday, which at one point he had planned to join.

While he was drafting the letter to the society, a document that was turning into something of a cultural manifesto, David remained covered in blankets in the frigid bedroom whenever possible, his dreams occupied by the salvaged award, with recurring characters Silas, Van Knox, David's father, Bonnie, and Valentina Maldenado. He didn't know anything about Maldenado, but she appeared in his dreams as a female version of Van Knox, tall, gaunt, pale. The longer he avoided contact with Van Knox, the more David seemed to gain an illusory control of the situation.

He was transfixed by watching the next morning's snowfall, which continued without break into the evening. If he didn't shovel the driveway and sidewalk, he risked Silas tracking him down. And he wanted to keep avoiding Silas, who, considering all the preternatural acumen David attributed to him, might look at his face, read his mind, and declare: "Trent! Is it the award? You somehow lost it already, didn't you?" He waited until after dark to go outside, where the fresh freezing air stabbed at his face. He shoveled under the glowing streetlamps and the floodlights on the side of the house. Since his meetup with Van Knox, and his countless hours remaining sedentary inside the house, David had felt himself become physically weaker, creaky in his bones, the shovel dragging more after every time he tossed away snow.

As he labored, he noticed lights flick on inside the second floor; the Hales' bedroom upstairs, then the first floor, in Silas's study. David's lips felt dry and tight from the cold, and slowly running his tongue over his upper lip only made it more uncomfortable. A thought emerged and then stuck. Could Silas have already heard rumblings about problems with his award from the Boston Literary Society? Could he know what had happened? Was he waiting to pounce with glee at the first sight of David?

Fearing he'd be noticed from the Hales' windows, he picked up the pace of his shoveling, but he couldn't compete with the night air, which transformed the snow into something there was no good word for—*slush* was too insubstantial—something impossibly heavy and hard, a material akin to defeat. He had to stomp on the blade with all his weight to force the shovel under the frozen blocks. Lights glowed from the end of the street from a vehicle David couldn't yet see, but knew from its mechanical roar to be the snowplow. All he could do was stand there, waiting for the steel and metal abomination to push a brick wall of snow in front of the driveways to the right. He was taken with the maddening thought that if the house had simply been built on the left side of the one-way street, instead of the right, the plow wouldn't block him in, but now it would make a joke of his labor. He had seen people shout and curse at the plow, but he just stood and waited, the urban dweller's version of watching an avalanche fall over him.

More lights glowed from the Hales' house, including an outdoor porch lamp. David surrendered, spearing his shovel into the snow and hurrying toward his door, but he was too late.

"Trent!" Silas said, stepping out onto his porch in a too-thin kimono and a red-checkered hunting hat with flaps over his ears. David stopped his flight and turned toward him. Silas held his gaze. "I believe there's something you've failed to tell me, Trent."

The plow drowned out the conversation. David couldn't bring himself to look at the street, but Silas watched it go with delight.

"There's a beauty about those," Silas said, as though ruminating on buffalo running through a valley, or another scene out of the paintings in his writing study. "There is poetry in their ugliness, blasting through whatever stands in its way, a capacity for brutality we've lost in our residential interments."

Silas was shivering. He turned to go back inside.

"Wait," David said, the inside of his mouth now as dry as his lips. "What were you going to say? About me not telling you—"

Silas paused. He nodded, remembering. "Our end-of-the-year party on Saturday. You have not sent in an RSVP, my friend. Don't give it another thought, I am doing it for you now. You RSVP yes. We will see you there."

So Silas didn't know anything, it seemed, but David's fate for Saturday was sealed. He would have to show his face at the party to prevent Silas from asking questions.

When Saturday came, he decided to go early to the Hales', before most guests arrived. The more important people in Boston literary circles considered themselves, the later they tended to show up to events. A National Book Award nominee would come twenty minutes late, while a Booker Prize winner with a visiting professorship might come in the second hour, or even text an apology later about how something had come up. It was an expression of power.

David calculated that arriving fifteen minutes before the start time seemed reasonable, considering he lived right above. That's what he would do. His premature appearance would be inconvenient for the Hales, and he would make sure to have so little to say, to render himself so dull, that the hosts would hardly notice a quick departure; in fact his exit would be so insignificant to the party, coming amid a crush of arrivals, that a goodbye would be unnecessary, and David could disappear to continue plotting how to sway Van Knox to do the right thing.

9

"THE MAN OF THE HOUR! Ser Trent! Right on time," Silas said. It was a dispiriting declaration in light of David's hope that he would be ostracized for showing up so early.

He followed Silas through the house into a warm kitchen with swirling cross-smells of food that could only combine harmoniously at social gatherings.

Rebecca Hale was chopping vegetables, alongside another woman in her late thirties who did not look up from her preparations, the demeanor of hired help that David did not grow up with, but had learned to recognize on trips to friends' homes during college, often in households around Boston and Manhattan where he didn't expect them, in rooms where loquacious dinner guests mused on inequality. In early instances of these encounters, David would introduce himself to these employees, but the surprised reactions of the residents made it clear they were meant to be left aside and alone, to be invisible—which made David relate to them all the more. He had seen this woman before, hurrying into and out of the house, sometimes with buckets and cleaning supplies. There was also another, younger woman, petite with jet-black hair and bright eyes, who seemed less sure about her presence in the kitchen, carefully pouring Silas's homemade champagnes into decanters.

"Rebecca," Silas called to his wife, "you remember David. Turns out he's a writer of apparent fine talents—enough to win an award. My award, in fact."

Blocking the bleak reality from his mind, David prepared to respond in a tone balancing modesty and pride in the Best First Novel Award, but Rebecca did not seem interested in talking about his award or Silas's. After a moment of deadpan confusion, she seemed to marginally register David's identity, nodding and smiling at him, an unusual level of warmth for her that she must have reserved for the times she hosted parties. She was giving directions to Paula (the woman, whose name he now learned, who worked for the Hales) while Silas was instructing Leni (which was how Silas addressed the younger woman who seemed unsure) regarding the house-made champagne. David marveled at how the Hales—how anyone, come to think of it—could muster, at will, a tone of superiority and authority over another human.

As they walked, Silas curtly introduced David to his son, Markus. He was broad-shouldered, with red cheeks and ears, and quick to flash his big, sloppy smile.

"My son is taking some time after college to decide on his next steps," Silas said in a tightly coiled voice.

"Nice to meet you, Dave," Markus said. David smelled alcohol on the younger Hale's breath, and guessed he had been sampling the holiday punches and eggnogs throughout the day. "Dad, my friends are going to come over for a while."

"There's free booze. They can smell it from Essex County. Bring in those buckets for ice, Markus," Silas said, giving the impression he wanted him out of sight. "We're going to put you to work, too, Trent, don't you worry." David was assigned to arrange Silas's homemade pickles onto silver platters engraved with illustrated moments from ancient legends: the Trojan Horse being pulled by ropes, Achilles dragging Hector's body behind his chariot, Achilles, again, this time hiding in women's clothes at the court of King Lycomedes. Silas brought tongs that David was to use to spread out the pickles on three different platters—garlic, half sour, and dill—each to be presented with two tongs so that guests could serve themselves, and set down with the other food spread out along the long dining table.

The ambience was strained, with the only voices to be heard mostly Silas and Rebecca, giving orders, while David and the growing number of helpers, some of whom he only glimpsed as they hurried around with dishes and glasses, stayed quiet, or perhaps cowed.

"It's like getting ready for a really big, competitive Thanksgiving," someone said.

David turned and saw that the comment was made by Leni, the young woman with the dark hair, who was arranging decanters behind him. Her voice had a sardonic tone that surprised David, clashing with her demeanor. The voice seemed to harbor grievances.

"Except instead of being the one writer having to explain to your uncles what a writer does," she continued, "there will be a hundred writers, all trying to sniff out what the other ones are working on. You ever notice how writers congratulate each other on things nobody else would congratulate them for, like starting a chapter, or *almost* being finished writing a book?"

"You're a writer, too," he said reflexively. "Sorry, stupid question. I'm David."

"No, it's fine. Leni. Actually, I have a corporate job, a small cog in the big wheel. I did toy with writing, to be honest, but I lost my confidence along the way. I found that creative failure is a hole that only gets bigger once it cracks open."

"Hey, corporate cogs get a steady paycheck and perks," David said, "which is more than I can ever say." He tried not to think more on the topic. Since Bonnie had called off the engagement and moved her things out of Observatory Road, he had been struggling to keep up with the rent and everyday expenses. "Publishing isn't exactly reliable."

"People who don't know writers are always interested in them because they imagine something genteel. Writers, more than other people, are sociopaths. They turn ruthless on a dime. Especially the good ones. Charles Dickens emotionally abused his children and abandoned his family to run off with a teenage actress. Charles Dickens! What hope does anyone else have?"

David smiled and nodded. "How did you end up on kitchen patrol? You're friends with the Hales?"

"Actually, I only met Silas just now, and the wife has only grumbled at me thus far. I somehow got invited by a friend of theirs, but I didn't expect to be indentured. Crowds give me hives, so I show up early to things so I can leave early."

David laughed. "Great minds."

She softened her voice to a whisper. "Honestly, I've read a couple of Silas's books, like everyone else who has taken creative writing, but they didn't stick with me. How did that one start about the apocalyptic friar that is supposed to represent modern man? 'He crossed himself sinuously and ironically.'"

"Well, if I remember, those lines from *Sevenfold* were chosen as one of the fifteen most memorable openings of a novel in the *Paris Review*."

"They're manipulative, right? It's not a man he presents us, it's *man*. It projects a power and control in the guise of a character that even the ancients rebelled against. How he writes is manipulative, and maybe that's the whole point. People want to be manipulated."

"Let's get this over with, now!" Silas announced, coming over to them expectantly. "Seventeen!"

Leni glanced at David with a confidential air about their exchange, turning into confusion over Silas's exclamation.

"Seventeen each," elaborated Silas.

"Seventeen?" David asked.

"Dollars."

Leni laughed uncomfortably, but David could tell Silas wasn't joking, and he shook his head at her to warn her.

"I've calculated what the average person at the party will consume in food and drink," Silas continued. "There's a certain amount of money and energy that goes into hosting this in our home, and I only ask my guests to respect that to a minimal degree. I do the same every year. You should both learn that all our roles in life are like that of electric currents. People are either conductors or insulators. As a conductor, I throw my energy into the world, and you, tonight, are insulators, taking all of that energy in, benefiting from it."

David, too distracted to try to scrutinize Silas's line of thinking, dug out a twenty-dollar bill from his wallet. "I don't have exact change."

"I'll take it," Silas said. "Next time, bring smaller bills."

Leni added, "I'll have to get my wallet from my coat."

"You'll know where to find me, madame," Silas said.

"Will do!" she said.

As he walked away, she mouthed *never* to David. They broke up into more laughter. After feeling isolated for longer than he realized, he appreciated Leni's conspiratorial wavelength. At downturns in their forced labor, he opened up to her quicker than he usually would with someone he just met, talking about his hometown and about how he met Bonnie, neglecting to mention how their future was in limbo.

Having run low on ice, Rebecca had ordered more to be delivered from a nearby convenience store, and when Silas could not find Markus, he sent David outside to carry it in.

To his surprise, Antoinette was standing in front of the house, unsure what to do with herself.

"David!" she said. She clapped both of her hands on her cheeks as though the sight of him might bring her to tears. "My boy, my dear boy. Thank goodness."

She was in one of her dresses shaped like a tent, but this one was sequined, sparkling in the streetlights reflected from the snow as she waited.

"Antoinette, what are you doing? It's too cold to be standing out here. You'll get sick."

"I'm ready!"

"Ready for what?"

"For the soiree!"

David thought back to seeing her chase Silas, who had ducked her. The last thing David needed was to bring attention to himself by letting someone inside whom Silas had not invited, someone he viewed as a pest. That would hamper his goal of slipping away unnoticed.

"Antoinette, this isn't my party."

"Yes, yes, I know. Mr. Hale hosts this soiree every year, of course. Like clockwork."

"Did Silas tell you to—"

He stopped mid-question when he saw her expression quiver. She recovered her haughtiness. "I told Judith to come with me, but you know how reserved she can be. It borders on rudeness, I hate to admit that, the poor girl."

"I'm just not," he stalled, ". . . I'm only helping the Hales for a few minutes." The two bags of ice, which he had heaved up against his body, were starting to sting his cheeks and chest. He backpedaled toward the Hales' kitchen door. "I have to get these inside."

"David! Wait for me, David!" She was struggling in the snow to get closer. "I've welcomed you in, David, to the neighborhood, to my home!"

"Antoinette, it's not my place to . . . to . . ." he stammered. "I'm really not staying." She could find some other way in, one that didn't involve him. But she was not going to stop. He envisioned her dragging him with her to Silas, narrating how close they were, gripping his arm and holding him in place. Then, even if he managed to shake loose, Silas would no doubt berate him for allowing the intrusion. "Antoinette," he heard himself snap, "really! If you weren't invited, you can't go in!"

Her face fell. She appeared disoriented, groping for a way around her embarrassment. "I'll stop by your place later, my dear, and we'll catch up over tea. What about that? Is it a plan?"

"We'll talk soon," he said, his voice cracking with regret at having gone further than he'd intended. She went on again about having tea, her words fading away as he worked his way inside the Hales' kitchen.

The atmosphere of the house had changed as guests arrived in bigger waves, half-sliding around in socks. While the house had a large square footage for Cambridge, it was an artifact of the late nineteenth century, tweaked by sporadic renovations over the years, leaving long, narrow spaces alternating with half-size rooms, cramped hallways, and arbitrary alcoves. Even after the arrival of the first dozen people the party had felt overcrowded, and all of a sudden a few minutes later it was claustrophobia-inducing, more so as alcohol was consumed and voices became louder and closer. On the plus side, it would be easier than David would have hoped to slip out unnoticed. At ten after eight, he had exchanged polite, anonymous greetings with enough guests not to be accused of being unsocial. Perfect time to bolt. He was at the far end of the house from the Hales' front door, so he started to pick his way through people at an intentionally slow pace to pull off his inconspicuous exit. He noticed several of the *New Yorker*'s local contributors—scholars of philosophy, medicine, history—and two fiction writers who had their big breaks when Silas, in his role as an editor, placed their short stories in the magazine. David couldn't help but notice that Silas seemed to ignore the latter altogether, as though to say to them, "Don't forget your place—you are nothing, I owe you nothing, you owe your futures to me."

David would have made it right out the front door if not for two developments. The first was the appearance of Melody Bradshaw. The rare times he had seen her over the last years, David never felt confident she would remember him. To his surprise, she locked in on him upon entering and waved excitedly.

"David! It's been so long!"

She wrapped her arms around him, pressing him into her lavender aroma. "I heard what happened. The award! Wonderful!"

She kept talking. His aspiration from years earlier of her mentoring him flooded back with her bubbling enthusiasm and the perfume cloud of her presence, and with her throwaway mentions of her own children, in whom she seemed—at that moment, at least—so much less interested than she was in David's life and his award. She didn't mention anything about his long-ago request for an MFA recommendation, and he was certain she hadn't the slightest memory of it.

"It means so much to me, Melody," David said. "The award, I mean, and seeing you again."

"Come, let's sit. Tell me everything, David, don't dare leave anything out, and we can't let this much time pass again before catching up. What are you working on now?"

David practically levitated as Melody showed him a successful novelist's ultimate sign of respect, complaining by name about editors and critics. Even when she was finally coaxed away to another part of the room by other acquaintances, he was flattered that she had to be coaxed away from *him*. Broken out of the spell Melody had put him under, he realized how packed the Hales' house had become, filled with familiar faces from writing festivals, conferences, workshops, and bookstore talks. His goal of getting out early had imploded.

"There he goes." The words came from Leni, who was being jostled behind him by the increasingly sloppy crowd. She held steady when bumped and bumped people right back, her face overtaken with anxiety as her eyes darted around the room.

"Who?"

"The worst of them all. Him. I met him once at a friend's dinner party. He showed a rare talent for making me feel stupid in seconds flat."

David followed her gaze to the other side of the room, in front of the Hales' massive bookshelves, where the second development materialized to undermine his retreat. It was Barnaby Masters, chattering and laughing with three or four women around him. Barnaby was tall enough to look down upon his listeners, and he did so with great satisfaction. He was born to have conversations while standing around at a party.

"Still going to make your great escape?" David asked Leni.

"You bet. I put in my time. See you later."

She found an opening in the crowd.

"Trent! David Trent!" Silas called, sending a shiver of excitement and stress through him that made him forget he was on his way to exit. Silas was pulling him by the arm into the denser parts of the room. "You two must meet. David Trent, this is Barnaby Masters, my mentee."

David was forced into Barnaby's circle of admirers.

Silas continued. "Barnaby was born to write short fiction—short pieces express everything and nothing. And David, here—well, David has just been awarded the Best First Novel from the Boston Literary Society."

Barnaby grew rigid for a fleeting moment, then relaxed as he looked David up and down. "Wait. You got your MFA at Iowa?"

"No. I did do an MFA program, but not—"

Barnaby broke into a sympathetic laugh, as if David had meant to tell a joke but inadvertently humiliated himself. "If we didn't do it at Iowa, then we didn't do it. I thought I remembered meeting you when I was at Iowa. But I know I've seen you before."

"We sat together at—"

Barnaby loudly snapped his long fingers. "That's it! I knew I was right. I met you at the café with Brandi!" Barnaby shook his hand. "Congrats on the award, brother, that's fantastic to hear, really fantastic." He cracked a smile, which seemed to light up the room. "They have you doing events for it?"

"Pretty soon, I think." He felt the need to prove himself, even though nobody was questioning it, sort of like Jace reciting a grammar rule that nobody had violated. "I'll do some readings and—"

"If it were me, I would refuse. Their events, I mean. I couldn't be a trained monkey for hacks. You'll do incredible."

By this point, Silas had his back to them, talking to other guests before drifting away into another part of the room. With Silas distracted, Barnaby immediately became less interested in David, inching closer to one of the nearby women, whom David overheard was a ballet instructor who also helped at the dance program at the school where Rebecca Hale served as guidance counselor. It was a moment of luck for David that would finally allow him to leave without further obligations. But he couldn't quite pull himself away. The fact that Barnaby had the satisfaction of boasting Silas as mentor and now felt justified in ignoring David nagged at him. It was David, not Barnaby, who had just won an award! (At least as far as Barnaby was concerned.) He wanted to somehow make the point before leaving. He thought of calling Barnaby "Barney" before he exited, which he imagined would eat at him for a few hours. To slink away, to surrender to this lucky barbarian, seemed fundamentally wrong and unjust.

"What are you at work on these days?" he asked Barnaby, prodding him with the fact that David had not run across any of his writing. "Fiction?"

"That's my heart and soul."

"Working on a novel?"

The question got Barnaby's attention. "No, no. Oh God, no. I hope I never become so desperate. I'm writing a series of linked short stories. I admit I do some magazine work for the glossies, too, to keep the lights on. But novels, no, brother. Novels have long been a dying art form, fated for doom since Henry James was dictating to his typist, now bequeathed to a fading generation of bored housewives. There are a few titans who can overcome it. Silas, of course. Melody Bradshaw, who's here. She cuts your heart out every few words."

"I know her well."

"Fantastic. She can write the way a woman shouldn't be able to."

David felt Barnaby was trying to avoid revealing anything about his work, which came across as an insult. "I would love to hear what your short stories are about, Barnaby."

"A writer should never be able to say what his writing is about, don't you think, David? If a writer knows what his writing is about, he's lost."

"When you win an award, I'm learning that your writing gets summarized far and wide, to encourage people to read it. Summary is a form of art in itself, I guess."

Barnaby stiffened. "If forced, I'd have to say my stories are about the nature of good and evil, seen through the lens of artificial intelligence, intertwined with the close third-person narrative of a graduate student archivist. There's one—'Lamentations of the Oracle's Last Breath'—that is my thematic cornerstone."

"One of the stories?"

Barnaby grimaced. "Right—although, you know what? Now that I've said it out loud, I'll throw that title out. That ever happen to you, David?"

David was looking past Barnaby. At the end of the room connecting to the front hallway, Lee Van Knox was shrugging off his jacket and shoes. David's stomach clenched. How could he be such a fool? Of course Silas knew everyone who was part of the Boston Literary Society. If Van Knox cornered him here, David wouldn't be able to stall him any longer, and everything about the award would erupt without giving him one last chance—however remote it was—to stop it.

"You feeling unwell?" Barnaby asked.

"What? No—"

"You went a little pale."

"I just didn't realize how late it was getting. Have to get going."

His obvious discomfort elicited a long, inquisitive stare by Barnaby, engrossing him enough to ignore a question from the ballet instructor. David rushed through the crowd. He might have barreled through one of the back doors despite the deep snow of the backyard, but it would have caused a scene in the middle of the party, particularly without recovering his shoes at the front of the house. Instead, his path was a slow, carefully choreographed dance until he finally found a clear way to the front. There was now a mountain of shoes and boots, with his somewhere at the bottom. He couldn't do what he desperately wanted to: grab handfuls of shoes and toss them aside until he found his. Instead, casually as possible, he had to pick through one shoe after another, dividing many from their counterparts without a second thought, until he spotted his, threw himself out the door, and slipped them half on only once he was on the front steps. More snow had fallen, blanketing the paved paths he had cleared.

Markus Hale and his tipsy friends were outside, roughhousing and launching snowballs at each other. David took a deep breath, trying to remain calm as he continued to his door around the side of the house.

"David! David, wait!"

At the sound of the voice, David unlocked his door as quickly as he could, but he was not fast enough.

"There you are." It was Van Knox, hurrying toward him, holding a flute filled with Silas's home-brewed champagne. He hadn't stopped to put on his jacket and was now hugging himself with one arm for warmth, but he had somehow recovered his boots quickly enough to catch David.

"Lee. Great to see you here."

"Where are you—"

"Oh, just going home." David indicated his door, then pointed up, managing to communicate what he meant.

"What amazing luck! You live right—well, I didn't realize you lived in Silas Hale's house. Talk about a literary bastion."

"Not really part of his house," he said. "It's a separate unit, the top floor."

The point was lost on Van Knox. "A literary bastion," he repeated, pleased with the phrase. "What a great neighborhood to be in, David—terrific restaurants, some of the best. This is perfect, because we need to talk."

The din of the party and the brutish shouts of Silas's son and friends combined, hanging in the air.

"Listen, Lee, I'm just a bit tired."

"Regardless, we do need to talk, David. The situation—"

David hesitated. When he saw that Van Knox was going to say more right there, where they might be overheard, he spoke over him. "Of course we should catch up. Let's go inside."

"Yes, out of this cold, please."

David opened the door and gestured Van Knox in.

"It's a narrow stairway up," David said.

He paused to collect himself as he watched Van Knox climb up, taking each tread with a surprising lack of grace for an accomplished cyclist. When they reached the top floor and David's unit, Van Knox developed a look of consternation. "It's freezing up here, David!"

"I can offer you some coffee or tea."

"Why is it so freezing?"

He didn't feel like turning on the space heaters, which struggled at these temperatures, anyway. Let Lee Van Knox freeze.

"No use driving up the gas bill." The last thing he needed was to explain the heating situation and risk Van Knox talking to Silas about it as some misguided favor to make up for ruining David's life. In a rush of thoughts, he grasped for some way to put off what they really had to talk about. "How has the cycling been going lately? Harder in the snow, I'd guess. You put on special tires?"

"David, I'm sorry. I'd like to chat, but we have to—well, this is serious. You haven't been getting back to me, and I cannot wait any longer to tell the rest of the committee and the rightful winner."

"Then you haven't told them?"

"I promised to give you time," Van Knox said with a noble air, "and I have done that. It's been just between you and me. But I can't draw this out longer. You understand. I know you do. You must understand!"

"I appreciate your discretion. But I told you, Lee, there are people I still haven't been able to reach—"

"Let me stop you there. Think of it from my side. For chrissakes, David, I invited Leni here, thinking the correction would already have been announced before this, and I could introduce her as the winner before everyone goes away for the holidays. Instead, that poor young woman doesn't know, and she thinks I dragged her here for no reason!"

"Leni? Leni from the party is Valentina Maldenado?"

"Yes. Well, she was at the party. But she left."

"Professor Maldenado?"

"Such a hard worker. Teaches writing, when she has time, on top of full-time office work, treasures that chance to encourage young writers, and—never mind that. Listen, David, I sympathize with your position, I do."

"Do you?" David asked, reacting with a quickness that he hadn't intended.

"What do you mean?"

"I don't think you really know. You certainly don't know me well enough to care how it affects me. And I don't think you even know what it means to have a dream, Lee, much less to live for that dream. And to miss it, sometimes by a hair's breadth, every time you get close to it. To watch other people get those same dreams handed to them gift-wrapped. I don't think you do know, Lee. I don't think you can possibly understand that the only thing worse than missing your dream at every turn is to be told that for once in your life you got there, that you were the one, you were chosen, it was finally your time, and then have that ripped away." David realized that his voice and his hands were both shaky, which upset him more. The blind urge to punch Van Knox's face returned—to take him by the neck, to wipe away his shallow, mechanical, calculated expressions.

Van Knox stood up. "It really is too cold to be in here, David. You're going to get sick. Really. I think you can acknowledge by now that I've apologized amply, again and again, for the unfortunate mistake. Let's be blunt: It's not the end of the world! You're a young man, with so much ahead of you. And at this point, you are being self-centered. I know you can be happy for Leni, though, for her to get what she deserves, too. I find writers can be a bit inward looking, which leads to selfishness if you're not careful. It's my humble suggestion that it's worth fighting that tendency."

David snapped back to a rational frame of mind. He modulated his tone to one of frank negotiation. "I had an idea, if you can just hear me out. I think you'll agree it could make everyone happy. A tie, if you will, that could split the award up . . ."

Van Knox was speechless at first. "Not going to happen. There's never going to be any tie. I'm sorry, David. There was a mistake, and that's that. It happens. You'll be fine. I'm going to see if I can reach

Leni on her cell and tell her to come back to the party, explain to her that she won, and let the society know your name was announced in error."

"Can't you at least give me the respect of listening to my proposal before you say no? Can't you do that? Just give me two minutes."

"Proposal! You can't be serious, David."

Van Knox was walking away. The man whose task was to maintain patience with one of the world's most maddening categories of people—writers—had reached the end of his rope. "This isn't your time, David, you have to accept that! There will be other books and other awards. I have always had confidence that in life, things ultimately work out how they should."

"Wait!" David rushed after him. "Please stop, just listen!"

Van Knox was rubbing his temple with one hand. "I'm so sorry, David."

As Van Knox started down the stairs, David grabbed his arm. There was a jolt in time in which David pulled in one direction, Van Knox the other, and in the next moment they seemed to reverse themselves in a blur, with Van Knox pushing David away and David grabbing him. Then Van Knox tumbled, crashing against the sharp turn in the stairs before launching farther into the stairway's next angle with a sickening crack.

David remained stock-still at the top of the stairs, where he could see part of Van Knox's akimbo legs below. "Lee?"

There was no response. No movement. David couldn't hear anything but the thumping of his own heart. He backpedaled into his apartment, starting to take heavy breaths, then retraced those steps, as though the passage of a few seconds would change what he saw below. He tried to call Van Knox's name out again, but this time couldn't find his voice. He crept down the stairs one tread at a time, moving closer, and still detected no motion. All he could think was: Help. Help. He needed help, anyone's help, because his mind was blank. He rushed down the stairs, stepping over Van Knox, not wanting to look closely to confirm what he suspected, and then almost falling as he stumbled to the front door. As he opened the front door wide, forming a cry for help in his head and at the base of his throat, all that came out when his mouth opened was a gasp. He could hear the snowball fighters from the other side of the yard. He swallowed hard, and this time felt strength returning to him as he prepared to shout.

He stopped. Fear at what was about to happen overcame his desperation for help. Hadn't he been holding or at least touching, maybe pulling, maybe pushing, Van Knox when he fell? They had been arguing—no, nobody knew that! Or could someone outside, partygoers from the floors below, have heard? Either way, there were Van Knox's calls and emails to him. Those might easily be overlooked, might blend in with the records of dozens or hundreds or thousands of other calls and emails, but not if Van Knox was found inside his apartment. No. With the body in David's stairwell, police would obviously zero in on their connection, and it wouldn't be long before they tracked down the mistake with the award, Van Knox's numerous requests to speak to David, David's avoidance, and now Van Knox, presumably, confronting him, preparing to destroy his life, leaving him no choice but to . . .

He could very clearly imagine Silas Hale marching up to a crime scene from behind police tape, with David surrounded by police officers and detectives. The chaos would part for Silas, who would stand over David, crouched on the floor. "What happened here, Trent? What have you done in my house?"

David stepped back into his stairwell. As quietly as possible he pulled the front door closed, then with a flick of his wrist softly locked the deadbolt. He forced himself to move back toward Van Knox. Maybe the man was just knocked unconscious! But his eyes were wide open, his jaw loose, his neck twisted into an unnatural position. David tried to remember what he had read or seen in movies about how to check whether someone was still alive. He reached out his trembling fingers and pressed them on Van Knox's wrist, which felt like putty and turned white under his touch, then did the same with his neck.

Suddenly there was a pounding at the door. David ducked down. Had Antoinette shown up for tea, even after he had embarrassed her? Would she ever pound her fist like that?

"Come out and play! Dave! We met inside my dad's place, remember? Come on, Dave!"

It was Markus Hale and his drunk friends. He must have seen David leave the party.

"We need a fifth to make a snowball team! We know you're in there. Open up or we'll—"

Markus and at least one of his pals pounded a few more times on the door before they moved on. Then David's phone rang from upstairs, which freshly terrified him. After what seemed to be an eternity, it stopped.

He found himself curled up on two steps, his legs stretched out on one tread and his head down on the other. He closed his eyes, feeling as though he had just fallen asleep and been woken up, or had just woken up and fallen back asleep, disoriented and uncertain where he was or what time or day it was. The most unexpected and sorrowful feeling distracted him—how happy and content he remembered having been minutes ago, and how miserable he would be from now on.

When he lifted his head once more, he felt tears burning his eyes. He could not look away from Van Knox's body without feeling panic, as if keeping his eyes on it meant he had something under control. He had no choice about what to do next, not really. He had not meant to hurt Lee Van Knox. Sure, fleeting thoughts might have ricocheted through his mind about punching him, pops of aimless anger, natural under the circumstances. And he hadn't punched him, had he? All he'd done was touch his arm! If there had been a push at all, hadn't it been Van Knox who pushed against *him*, then lost his balance? If David opened that front door again and called for help, exactly who would it help? Not a dead man, obviously. David would only be tearing down his own future, without accomplishing anything else. And all the problems with what happened between him and Van Knox would—

No, he couldn't think about his writing, couldn't think about his career, not now.

What he did next seemed so obviously the right thing that he felt his body move in an automatic way, like someone performing long-practiced CPR in an emergency. He took Van Knox by the arms and began to pull his body up the stairs. Everything else flowed from there. Once he'd put his hands on the body and moved it, he convinced himself, there was no turning back. Even if he wanted to change his mind, they would know right away he had moved the body. How would he explain that?

Van Knox's head and hands fell in a series of grotesque poses as David dragged and manipulated his body to fit through the angles of the stairs like an oddly shaped piece of furniture. David half closed his eyes to avoid seeing the body, at several points almost slipping down the stairs onto Van Knox.

You'll think more later. Figure out a plan later. Get him out of sight, just get him out of sight, and you can make it right later. Everything can be fixed later.

Once David was up the stairs, on level ground, the body moved with relative ease. Stopping to regain his breath, he went to the trapdoor in the floor of the hall. He pulled up one leaf but couldn't grasp the other. He remembered opening it with Bonnie on move-in day, how it was designed for two people to open, with one person pulling up each side, and for some sadistic reason—or probably as a very reasonable safety measure—built in such a way that both had to pull at the same time, not one after the other. He tried over and over again, but couldn't find a place to stand that didn't block one leaf of the trapdoor. He couldn't help thinking of the anecdotes of mothers miraculously lifting cars to free their children, feats attributed to adrenaline. Were those urban legends? Could he access that strength for the sake not of children but of his own future? This time he stood away from the trapdoor, leaning forward and extending both arms at an almost impossible angle, finally throwing open the doors with a shout of exertion.

The air that blasted up from the darkness in the crawl space was at least ten degrees colder than the third floor, and the sounds of the unsuspecting partygoers below wafted in from the other trapdoor below that connected to the Hales' central stairs. The noises, he thought, were just enough to cover up the sounds he made as he lowered himself into the crawl space and pulled the body behind him. Van Knox crashed down, partially falling on top of him and making a racket. He braced himself for the noise below to change in some way, maybe to give way to silence as people tried to locate and identify the sound of a falling corpse over their heads—but there was no obvious alteration. As he waited, immobilized, the din became happier and drunker. He was so close to the people below that he could hear bits and pieces of conversation.

"That time will come," someone was saying. "No, I'm telling you . . . No. That time will come."

David was hastening to climb back up toward his apartment when panic overtook him. Wallet. Van Knox had to have a wallet. As he contorted his own body to look down, he slipped, landing hard, and again was relieved and surprised not to detect any change in the sound below. He found Van Knox's pockets positively stuffed—a wallet, earphones, multiple sets of keys, though no cell phone. For such a tidy man, his pockets were a mess. David slipped everything out of Van Knox's pockets into his own and resumed his ascent.

He closed the trapdoor and spread Bonnie's blue area rug over it. The worst was behind him. More than an hour later he was still breathing heavily to the point of wheezing. Suddenly a stray thought calmed him and his breathing. The award. Once he allowed himself to think about it again, it was all he could think about. A balm that made everything better. The award!

The award. Van Knox had said he hadn't told anybody else about the mistake yet—not the committee, not Leni Maldenado. The idea that it was an error had been erased from existence. It was as if it had never happened, just some passing nightmare extinguished by the light of dawn. The award would be David's now, really, truly his. All his.

10

DAVID WOKE THE NEXT MORNING drenched in sweat, even though the house was colder than ever. He had fallen asleep without turning on the space heaters, then thrashed around all night, his mind whirling even as he slept, images of Lee Van Knox alive, dead, alive, dead again, Van Knox delivering moralistic lectures to him, a kaleidoscope of horrors running through his dreams.

He spent the next day and a half pacing the apartment in a long-sleeved shirt, a sweater, and his winter coat, slowing down whenever he came to the throw rug over the trapdoor. He was half stalking, half guarding the tomb, awaiting the arrival of, well, anyone, everyone—a party guest who'd heard and seen everything and come back to confront him, the police, ambulances, firefighters, the Hales, SWAT teams, Van Knox's family, if he had any. Bonnie had been texting him. She, as it turned out, was the person who'd called him when he was in the stairwell with the body.

After imagining the variety of people who might show up to inquire about Lee Van Knox, he brought himself to research the man's life in news databases online, finding occasional references to him related to literary events in the Boston area or to debates over adding or improving bike lanes in Cambridge, a cause for which Van Knox regularly advocated. He was spearheading an idea—considered far-fetched, David gathered—to replace on-street parking with dedicated bike lanes. He also volunteered at a soup kitchen, once a month helping to dish out food to the needy at the back of a church. As far as David could tell, Van Knox lived alone in an apartment in Mid-Cambridge and went on interstate bicycle tours several times a year. He had posted on a cycling forum about his plans for taking part in two winter bike tours spanning thirty-three days and seven states.

Bike! Bicycling was a religion for Van Knox. He cycled everywhere. David could see in his mind's eye a bike, somewhere outside in the yard, gradually buried in snow, and then dramatically revealed once it began to melt. No chance of it being a secondhand bike that could have been anyone's; it would be a high-end bicycle that could be traced to the nicest bicycle shop in Cambridge with carefully maintained records of all their sales, where Van Knox would surely have lovingly selected and purchased his ride. David's heart sank as he realized how much he hadn't thought through. He ran to the vestibule and pulled on his boots, now so stiff from the cold that he could hardly stretch out the tongue and instep enough to get them on. He rushed outside and into the yard, relief flooding him when he found no trace of a bike. Not wanting to be spotted going about this peculiar search, he hurried back to the sanctuary of the third floor.

He thought more. Van Knox was a bicycle obsessive. If he had really cycled to the Hales' party, might he have gone to the trouble of hiding his bike to make sure it wouldn't be stolen? Yes, David thought, he would have.

A knock on the door at the bottom of the stairs interrupted these thoughts, the peculiar acoustics making the sound ricochet. Panic seized him: it had happened, he'd been caught. A few slow steps at a time, he headed down the stairs. The knocking resumed, its cadence impatient yet resigned—not how police knocked, he imagined, if they even knocked at all, rather than just ramming the door. He opened it on Bonnie.

He threw his arms around her. "Thank goodness," he blurted out.

She stiffened and pushed away, casting a quizzical look at him. "You didn't forget, did you? This was the day you said we should get together after the cruise." He had forgotten entirely, forgotten that each passing day signified anything but another set of hours in which to grapple with what had happened on those stairs. "I tried to confirm, but you've been missing my calls, ignoring my texts. I almost didn't come. Why would you . . . What's happened to us? Can't we still sit down and talk to each other, at least?"

She took his hand and started to climb the stairs.

"No!" He pulled away. The sight of Bonnie on these stairs chilled him to the core. She stopped—right where the body had come to rest. "Not up there."

She frowned. "Where do you want to talk?"

He couldn't think of an answer that would make sense. "You're right." He led the way to the third floor.

Almost as soon as they'd stepped inside, she spun around and glared at him. "I can't believe this."

He looked around, struggling for a response.

"Are you serious?"

"What?" he managed.

"It's freezing, David! It must be fifteen degrees colder than it was last time I was here."

He steered her into the living room, which at this point held only an armchair and an ottoman. "I've gotten used to it."

She looked at him as though he had lost his mind. "Don't you have anything to say to me?"

"I know I've been out of touch, Bon, but I just have to sort through some personal things. I promise it's all for us."

"Not talking to me is for us?"

"There are things going on."

"What? Is something wrong? Are you having health problems? You can tell me. Why can't you talk to me? When you found out you were receiving that award, I really thought it might start a new phase, that you could stow away your anxieties and concentrate on the future."

"Exactly, Bonnie, that's exactly what I want! There are some complications."

"How? Why is it complicated?"

David remained at a loss. Bonnie stood up and started pacing, rubbing her hands together for warmth and gazing in judgment at the barren apartment. The sheer bleakness of the place struck him all at once as he imagined seeing it through her eyes. Her expression softened from stern to sad. "This is no way to live—barely any furniture, the sickening cold. Don't you think I can see what's happening?"

"What?"

"Something is wrong, and I know what it is!"

He waited.

"The Hales," she continued. "They're trying to freeze you out in the most literal sense of the expression, David, and for some reason you just can't see it. This is about the award."

He could hardly force himself to get a word out. "Bonnie?"

"You told me Silas was supposed to do an event with you because he'd won the same award. I'm guessing he sabotaged that—maybe badmouthed you to the literary society? Is that what happened? I've had enough. I'm going to talk to him myself. You earned that award, and nobody is going to mess it up for you."

"No!" He jumped up. "That's so thoughtful, Bonnie. But that's not it. The award has been—it's presented some new responsibilities I didn't expect, but I'm handling them."

Her pacing took her into the hallway. She gazed at the floor, noticing the throw rug that he had moved over the trapdoor.

David rushed to block her path. He didn't want her near there. "Not that way."

She looked toward the bedroom door past him. "Is someone else in here?"

"No!" He was shaking his head, smiling unconvincingly.

"Are you— Were you having an affair when we were living here?"

"What?"

"You heard me. That's it, isn't it? If it's not the award, then something else has to explain your moods, your behaviors, especially around this house. Your suggestion that I stay with my sister. How nervous you are now. Are you seeing someone? Someone who has been coming here?"

"Of course not."

"Was it—what was the name, you've mentioned her a couple times, meeting up with her at one of your coffee shops—Brandi, wasn't it?"

"Brandi? No, not at all! Brandi's just . . . ! There's nobody else! It's just a mess in here."

She threw her hands up in frustration. "I really expected more than this when you said you were ready to talk things through, David." She started walking away, then stopped and turned to him again, her voice strained. "I deserved more. And if you make me walk away now, then it's really you walking away. From us."

He wanted to follow her out, wanted to keep her talking, but he knew the longer she was there, the longer she was around him, the more chance there was that her future would end up in as much jeopardy as his. He had no choice but to let her go.

Once she'd left, he hurried outside into the yard and threw open the shed doors. He looked in terror at what awaited him: an expensive bike, as well as Van Knox's helmet, a sleek silver sphere David remembered from their meeting at Darwin's. The helmet began to shake, while at the same time a putrid odor, like rotten meat closed up in a drawer, hit him. A squeal rose up. A giant silver rat, wet from snow and ice, ran out from inside the helmet, then another, bigger one from below the bike. A third rat, larger than the other two, had been crushed at the neck in a big metal trap at the back of the shed. Were the other two guarding the body, hoping it would come back to life, or maybe shielding it from animals that might find and eat it? David stumbled backward, dropping the helmet. After circling a few times, the rats darted out through a crack in a plank that formed part of the back of the shed.

The thought that the helmet had housed a rat just moments before sickened him, but he had no time to be precious. He wiped it with his glove, then struggled to secure it over his head. It was too narrow for him, but finally he managed to cram it on. He was thankful, for once, for the Hales' near-religious determination to stay away from the garbage bins. It meant that they rarely opened the shed, and when they did, they hurried to close it again.

The bicycle's front wheel was clamped to the frame with a U-shaped lock, preventing it from a full rotation. The lock had four dials that spun around to form a code. He tried futilely to guess the code, then attempted to force the whole lock off, before stopping to wonder at the level of obsessiveness that led Van Knox to apply a lock to his bike even after tucking it inside a shed. That suggested Van Knox also would have considered the off chance that a combination mechanism could malfunction, which would have led him to purchase one with a failsafe. Fidgeting with the lock, he found a rubber flap that concealed a keyhole—an override for the combination code. David retrieved the key ring he'd found in Van Knox's pocket. The smallest key fit right into the bicycle lock.

He hurriedly yanked out the bike from the shed and jumped on it, cycling away as fast as he could manage.

At first, he pedaled in a frenzy, trying to get as far from Observatory Hill Road as possible before anyone saw him. The faster he cycled, the harder the frigid air stabbed his face, which felt invigorating and painful at once. In his first year living in Cambridge,

David had purchased a bike and cycled to get around sometimes, until both that bike and another he bought secondhand were stolen from roughly the same area, admittedly without the kinds of security features Van Knox had invested in. He decided the safest way to dispose of Van Knox's clearly expensive bike would be to ensure that it was stolen. He crossed over the abutting city limits, into Somerville, then picked a side street equidistant from the two streets where his own bikes had been swiped, which was also around the corner from a café where on more than one occasion he had seen people arrested outside the front window, one of whom had been pulled by the police off a bicycle when he rode up to the curb. He had wondered at the time if that bicycle, which the police left behind, would end up stolen and ultimately reported to the same police.

Once David abandoned the bicycle, he realized what a long walk through the cold he had in store. Hailing a taxi or calling Jace for a ride would be too risky. He didn't consider what an absolute wreck he would look until he reached his street and saw himself through the eyes of Antoinette, who for some reason was standing in front of her house in the darkness, illuminated by the flickering light of the candles in her window. He wished he hadn't glanced in her direction, but though he had no intention of crossing to her side, he gave a stiff wave. She offered no gesture in return before he ducked onto the footpath to his door.

Disposing of the bike had filled him with an unexpected feeling of accomplishment. Hiding in his apartment was no answer to anything. He had to rise up and solve his own problems. He went back online. He didn't see any news about Van Knox's disappearance. He searched Van Knox's social media, wondering if anyone posted comments to question him about his whereabouts. At one point he almost screamed aloud with surprise. Van Knox's MySpace profile appeared to have been in disuse for a year and a half or so, but his Facebook page had been more regularly updated, and another Facebook user had tagged Van Knox in a photo from a bicycle tour that had begun days after his death—taken in Maryland—amid a group of two dozen cyclists. Zooming in to the tagged cyclist, David could see how the mistake was made, as the rider was mostly hidden by his cycling clothes and helmet and sunglasses, and could have been almost anyone of a similar build to Van Knox.

Walking through the neighborhood, David stopped at the window of the popular sandwich shop where he'd always get Bonnie her favorite lunch. He thought back to holding the door for the young woman with a baby, and the man who slammed the door into the stroller. "Move!" the boor had shouted. In David's hazy memory, that man had a bike helmet tucked between his arm and messenger bag. Could that man, obscured from David's sight, have been Lee Van Knox? He realized it may well have been—in fact, it likely was! Van Knox had told him the neighborhood had great restaurants; he had to have spent time there before he and David met. Maybe Van Knox was not as nice as he had appeared when he thought people were watching.

David's thoughts then turned back to the absence of a phone amid Van Knox's belongings. It was possible that Van Knox, like Barnaby Masters, didn't have a cell phone, or hadn't brought one to the party. But there were fewer mobile phone holdouts with every passing year. In fact, David had run across a handful of people who no longer had landlines. And even if Van Knox had his share of eccentricities, a year-round cyclist would almost certainly have a phone and keep it with him for safety. Plus, shortly before he died, Van Knox had mentioned the possibility of calling Leni Maldanado and asking her to return to the party.

David rang the bell at the Hales'. Silas answered, glancing at him with a smirk, as though he was expecting him.

"Our esteemed neighbor," he said, bellowing each word out with equal emphasis. "More snowfall out there? 'The snow doesn't give a soft white damn whom it touches.' Cummings. I think of that line often in the winter, as should you. It reminds us to stay humble."

David reminded himself to be careful: the more casual he seemed, the better. "Silas, I was wondering if I might have left—"

"Coat, yes? Take your pick."

David was about to correct Silas and say he was looking for a phone, but caught himself. "Right."

"You'd be surprised. We had three or four coats left behind at the party, a pair of socks, two stray gloves. People drink and get rides with friends or stumble into taxis. They'd forget their own heads. Our lost and found is over there."

Silas gestured to a windowsill where the cast-off items were stacked. David knew Van Knox had rushed from the party without any coat on, because he'd complained of the cold in David's apartment. He'd have been more likely to leave his phone in a coat pocket than to put it down elsewhere. David tried to remember first spotting Van Knox at the Hales' door when he was tossing down his coat, and also seeing him shimmy out of his coat at Darwin's, but he couldn't recall anything about the coat itself. Black or brown, dark tan maybe, but that only ruled out one red jacket in Silas's stack. He patted down each one until he felt a large rectangular shape in a zipper pocket.

"I found mine," he called out vaguely.

"Very good," Silas said. "Whatever has come to pass in your time here, my young friend, I think you'll be a stronger man and a stronger writer for it."

Silas's comment didn't strike David as relevant, but he didn't have time to parry with his ego. Before he left the Hale house, as though possessed, he wandered a few steps toward the central stairs, looking up at the trapdoor to the crawl space from the Hales' side. Nothing seemed different or out of place. David stayed too long there, staring, but Silas didn't notice.

Back on his own floor, David threw the coat down. He studied the bulky phone, a BlackBerry a year or two past its prime. He began to imagine with horror that it had been ringing over the last two days, but the battery was dead, and with any luck it already had been low when Van Knox arrived at the party.

Since he found out that his award had been given in error, David had been letting emails pile up. Now he reminded himself to deal with them, to deter anybody from becoming too determined to check up on him. Multiple emails had come in the last weeks from their landlords the Rosfelds, asking if they could treat him and Bonnie to lunch in the suburb where they now lived and discuss updates they wanted to share about the apartment. He finally wrote back, trying to stall. But the Rosfelds were persistent about going over the details in person, and David was hesitant to push against that too much, since other than the realtors, the Rosfelds were the only ones with keys to the apartment, which posed a unique risk.

When the day came for their lunch date, he was surprised to find Carrie and Tim Rosfeld harried and uneasy, incongruous with his mental image of stringent, stoic landlords. Rather than rendezvousing at the generic chain restaurant he'd imagined having to endure, he followed directions to take the commuter rail and a taxi to their house. When Bonnie left Observatory Hill, she had taken her car with her, making it more difficult for David to get to most places that weren't in easy reach of public transit.

The married couple didn't really welcome him as much as wave him in, while Carrie fed a baby in a high chair and Tim shadowed a toddler who was dispersing magnetic tile toys around the house.

"Thank you so much for bearing with us, David," Tim said. "Sorry your fiancée couldn't make it. Please." He gestured at a seat at the

Cheerios-covered kitchen table. Lunch was reheated eggplant lasagna. Both Rosfelds had short dark hair and dark circles under their bespectacled eyes. He wondered if they had always looked so similar, or if marriage and children had blended them.

"David, we just wanted to sit down in person to give you some context," Carrie said, now strapping the baby into a carrier around her chest and bouncing him. "We bought the third floor where you're living from an elderly man who had lived there for decades. Silas Hale had his lawyers draft the condo association papers before we purchased the apartment. We loved Observatory Hill, and we were so excited to own our first place together. We didn't look at the fine print closely, to be honest."

"Yep," chimed in Tim, a fond smile for memories of that time turning into an expression of befuddlement.

"Once we lived there . . ." Carrie paused to gather herself.

Tim put his hand on hers for strength. "It was pretty tough on us. Carrie was pregnant, our heads were spinning, and the Hales had the tendency to . . . to hound us, I guess you might say."

Carrie nodded, quickly wiping her eyes, which startled David. "Their lawyers would add these provisions to the condo papers," she said, "and we'd have no time to look at them, and then Silas would threaten that his lawyers would fine us if we didn't approve them quickly."

It hit David all at once: the Rosfelds hadn't moved to the suburbs just for more space. They'd moved to get away from the Hales. To escape them. They were scared to death of Silas.

"They spent thousands on new windows and insulation for their part of the house, so those two floors were probably fifteen, twenty degrees warmer in the winter than our top floor. But Silas refused to let us add a thermostat to the heating system, saying we would run up the bill for the whole house. We think Rebecca might have let us if it had been up to her alone, but Silas wouldn't hear of it, and she deferred to him—always. It became so cold there that my doctor warned me I had to get out, or I could put myself and my pregnancy at the time at risk."

David took this all in. "I'm confused. Why wouldn't the Hales just buy the top floor themselves when the elderly man's family put it on the market, instead of waiting for you to buy it and then terrorizing you?"

Carrie nodded vigorously. "We never understood that. Silas had received the Nobel Prize a few years before—I think you're given a million dollars for that!" David did not interrupt to say it was the Pulitzer, which was a much smaller sum of money. Carrie went on: "He obviously coveted that floor. But at some point when we were there, we started to think that maybe part of him needed someone up there, someone to lord it over, and that Rebecca knew that Silas needed that, too. Almost like we were sacrifices."

"We want to cut to the bottom line here." Tim looked concerned that they might be saying too much. "Silas Hales has notified us that he wants us to rent our unit to a friend of his daughter's, who needs somewhere to live starting the first of the year. That's why we've been trying to reach you."

"That's in a week," David said.

"Yep, but like I say, we have been trying to reach you for quite a while now."

"Tim, our lease has seven months left in it."

"We know, of course," said Tim apologetically. "Believe me, we know. It's just, well, we spent nearly two full years trying to sell the place, and after a while the realtors told us that the stairwell was a dealbreaker for every single interested party who looked at it. To get over that obstacle, we would have had to drop the price so much, we would have been in the red. When we put it up for rent, Silas inserted language in the condo papers that if the Hales were ever to put in a request for us to rent to someone specific, we would be obliged to fulfill the request or have to pay fines to the condo association—steep fines."

"We can't really afford them, David," Carrie said. "It's not as expensive to live out here as it is in Cambridge, but with two children . . . we're just keeping our heads above water as is."

The baby fussed and then began to wail, and Carrie nursed her. David wondered whether he and Bonnie would have this one day.

"We know you and Bonnie have no obligation to leave the house early, David," Tim said in a quieter, helpless tone. "Please understand, we would help you however we could. You two could even stay here for a while with us, rent free. We have an extra room."

David didn't want to get into his current status with Bonnie, and he couldn't let on a hint of his actual stakes in the situation. "The fact is, Tim, it really is unacceptably short notice."

Tim and Carrie nodded, nervous and desperate.

"But to be totally honest, we were actually planning on doing some traveling, anyway," he continued noncommittally, as though coming around to a compromise. "It's possible, though I'm not sure, if things line up right—we might be able to make it work."

Carrie and Tim could have collapsed with relief, which gave David time to calibrate how to get what he needed from the exchange.

"With conditions, of course."

"Name them, David," Tim said. "Anything."

First David listed a variety of red herrings related to the security deposit and assorted logistics. Then he got to his actual priority, which he could not say directly—that nobody be given a reason to open that trapdoor any time soon, a temporary and wildly imperfect solution, but at least a goal he could manage. "We've actually gradually put most of our stuff in storage in anticipation of traveling. But we don't want to bother with the hassle and expense of dealing with the little we have left in there. If we're going to agree to make this work on such short notice, we'd like to leave the last few bigger items behind. It's not much—a chair, a mattress, one dresser. I can make a list, if you'd like. We were going to donate most of it, but even those pickup services get booked up months in advance. It would be easier just to leave them to be used by the next renters."

Carrie's face brightened. "That's perfect!"

"The Hales hate whenever someone has to use their stairs to move things in and out," Tim added in a confidential tone. "At one point, they found a few scuff marks on the wall of the stairs and swore it was a bureau we brought up a month or so earlier through the trapdoor. We never heard the end of it. So leaving some items there is a win-win. This is excellent, really excellent. It's meant to be, I think!"

The Rosfelds seemed like they could finally breathe, celebrating with more helpings of lasagna all around once the baby was in her crib. They chatted with David about what they missed about living in Cambridge, the playgrounds for the kids where they'd run into all their friends, and what they liked better in their suburb—the grocery stores were a big plus, they said, where more than one shopping cart fit down the aisles at a time, and nobody got into screaming matches over parking spaces. They were far more relaxed and easygoing once they stopped talking about the Hales, but when it came out that David was a writer, they tensed.

"Then maybe you could explain," Carrie said in a lamenting tone.

"Explain?" David repeated.

"What makes him like that."

"Carrie . . ." Tim said, looking nervous again.

She ignored him. "What makes Silas Hale need to break people? Maybe because you're also a writer, you can comprehend it better than we can. We'd see Silas's name mentioned in articles—he was always being honored for this or that, given another award, the key to a city in the Midwest, some humanitarian recognition. Humanitarian! That was the part that we could never get over. I couldn't take it anymore—not just having this bad person treat us like garbage over and over again, a tyrant in an orange Victorian mansion, but having to watch him be feted."

Her train of thought knotted up. David chewed his food slowly, thinking, as he cut his lasagna. He had learned that Carrie worked in health care and Tim in corporate marketing, probably career paths they'd had since the end of college. He knew the Rosfelds, like most people—even Bonnie, deep down—perceived writers as a kind of alien species, with some unfathomable inner life. He wished he could explain that writers' outward behaviors had little relation to their creative identities.

Back at Observatory Hill Road, David jogged up and down from the third floor, packing what remained in the apartment and stuffing everything into Jace Chaikivsky's car. The lower floors of the house seemed quiet, suggesting that the Hales were away. Once David thought he saw Antoinette peering through an opera glass from a second-floor window of her house, but when he didn't see her again, he decided he had imagined it.

Until that day, David had felt safest keeping watch over the apartment, but the closer he came to leaving, the more urgently he wanted to flee. It felt as if every moment he was present was a moment closer to the body being discovered and linked to him. He needed to be somewhere else, anywhere else. Even as he walked to the driveway and back, over and over, he locked the apartment door each time. He seemed to be done after a few hours, but then he'd find more odds and ends in a drawer, and then some clothes in the corner of a closet shelf. Two hours became three, and then three and a half, as he felt his energy draining, forcing him to take more breaks.

The slowdown was excruciating. Every instinct and impulse in David screamed louder for him to get far away, that his life depended on it. Each time he hurried across his central hallway, the trapdoor beneath the throw rug rattled, and David's heart raced with every hollow vibration in the floor. As he gathered up loose papers and the last days' mail, he found an envelope with a check for $15,250—the award money from the Boston Literary Society, signed by the person who must have replaced Lee Van Knox.

While he was folding up the check, he heard noises from downstairs, surprising him so much he assumed he must have imagined them. Then the startling sound of his front door being unlocked, followed by hurried bootfalls up the narrow stairs.

He spun around, trying to think of some other way out before remembering one of his very first conversations about the apartment, when the realtor acknowledged the fire hazard that came with having only one exit.

"Trent."

It was Silas, kicking snow from his boots onto the hardwood floor.

"How did you—"

"Get in?" Silas said. "I have a key. I've always had a key. We need one at all times, of course, in case of an emergency in the house."

"You can't just walk in!" David wasn't sure why he was picking a fight with Silas now, of all times, when he was leaving, when he should have already been out the door. But he was overtaken by pure, profound indignation. "I'm your neighbor, not your tenant. You're not the landlord, Silas. The third floor is not part of your house."

"If it's under my roof, it's mine, Trent. Whether I own it or not!" Silas was studying the apartment with a mixture of pleasure at its emptiness and disgust at its condition. "So, we both find ourselves on our way out, to very different destinations. I'm meeting Rebecca and our kids in Aspen. They ski while I write. They laugh, they drink, they enjoy, and I write. That's the life we chose. I noticed you packing up a car, so I suppose you've made your decision to move out."

"There wasn't much choice, and it wasn't exactly my decision. I think you know that."

"It would have been the Rosfelds who suffered for you staying. You could have said no to them. They're strangers. They're civilians, not artists or writers, not creators. They should mean nothing to you, Trent. Your mistake, Trent, was thinking that the award meant you belonged."

"Is that what made you so happy to force me out? You're resentful that I received the same award as you?" His urgency returning, David gathered his bag. "I have to go, Silas."

"This space will work fine. Fine," Silas said. "As for the furniture—"

David froze, stumbling over his response. "The Rosfelds said . . ."

"Normally I'd insist you take every last piece of junk with you, but Julianne, my daughter's former college roommate, will be living here for a while after spending two years in Japan, and she can use what's here."

"Good for her." David resumed his walk toward the stairs.

"Aren't you forgetting one thing?" Silas added.

David paused and turned back, watching as Silas, standing in the hall, stomped his boot over the trapdoor. He slapped his tongue across his top lip, then ran it in a circle across his bottom lip.

"You think I wouldn't notice? This . . . vile . . . atrocity!"

"Excuse me?"

Silas frowned, kicking the throw rug toward him.

"I don't mind the dresser, the mattress, but take that ugly rag with you."

David kneeled on the floor, rolling up the rug, one section at a time.

Silas stood over him as he struggled with it, looking down on him with a fixed grin. "Trent, I'm sure it feels unfair to you, your time here being cut short. I can imagine how thrilled you'd be, a young writer, to have the opportunity to be under my roof. But becoming a real writer isn't about your writing. Not really, despite what they tell you in a classroom. It's about understanding the reality that you have to take what is yours, at all costs. Because everyone wants to see you choke, and because everything that makes you happy outside your writing will wither and deteriorate. Now I've gifted that realization to you, you'll be better for it."

David heaved the rug over his shoulder. "I won't forget," he mumbled.

As David drove away from the house, a weight was lifted. He knew it wasn't rational, but it really felt like Lee Van Knox would vanish altogether as he pulled into the next intersection, crammed full with cars and bikes and pedestrians dodging each other. The house receded out of sight. Everything bad that had transpired, all that had gone so unaccountably wrong, also faded and dissolved, surrounding David in a New England haze of safety, contentment, solitude, the chill of other centuries.

Neither David nor the Hales would be at the house less than a week later when Paula, the Hales' housekeeper, was cleaning their dining room on the first floor and turned off the vacuum several times because she thought she heard something, a series of faint bumps, from somewhere in the ceiling, where the stairs led to the trapdoor.

11

NEW HAMPSHIRE QUIET WAS ALL-CONSUMING. David would wake up unable to tell the middle of the night from midmorning. The sky stayed gray in the winter; many of the stores in the small town kept short seasonal hours or closed altogether. David had found a rental listing for a bedroom above the garage of the lodge-style house of a retired couple. The house was three miles outside town, and Barbara and Stan Steadman, his landlords, were shocked by the idea that he had not brought a car. After borrowing Jace's car to move his belongings out of Observatory Hill Road and sleeping on Jace's couch for a week, David had rented a car to get to New Hampshire, but if he rented it any longer he'd chip away too quickly at the award money, which was funding his refuge. The Steadmans had a twenty-year-old metallic blue pickup, a spare vehicle for them, that they encouraged him to use whenever he wanted. Barbara regularly left Tupperware containers of salad and soup at the door to his room. After the Hales, the Steadmans' kindness felt shocking, making him suspicious of their very existence.

Stan was a onetime military pilot who later flew small planes for government agencies, which is where he met Barbara, who had been in administrative middle management for the government. They explained to David that their area of the Granite State was filled with ex-government workers, and while they had never been in the intelligence community themselves, it was said that their unassuming small town had more ex-spies per capita than anywhere in the country. David supposed there couldn't be statistics on that, but everyone, spy or not, certainly seemed to keep to themselves there, which suited him.

Before his arrival at the Steadmans', David had been offered a two-month residency at a small liberal arts college in North Carolina, starting in April. It would be an opportunity to live rent-free without much responsibility in return, and with a small stipend—all on the strength of his Best First Novel Award. Spending the rest of the winter away from Massachusetts until it was time to go to North Carolina seemed wise, both because it was cost-effective and because he felt safer. There was spotty cell phone reception in the house in the woods in New Hampshire, so he mostly communicated with people over email, barely staying in touch at all with Bonnie—who hated using email for anything but work—and occasionally trading messages with Jace and a few friends.

Though deep down he knew the body of Lee Van Knox had to be found, with time passing it started to seem as though it might never happen. He was shocked, more than he should have been, when he scrolled through the *Boston Globe* online early in March and saw a brief report.

> **CAMBRIDGE**—Police are waiting for autopsy results for a man whose body was found Sunday at a private residence in North Cambridge.
>
> **Investigators are currently waiting for a report on the cause of death.**

Maddeningly, he couldn't find anything else. Twice, he started dialing the Cambridge Police Department with plans to blather something about being a reporter—a role close enough to being a writer that it was tempting to think he could convincingly claim it—and ask for up-to-date information on the case. He thought better of it.

Then he got a call from a Massachusetts State Police detective, asking that he contact them. The call, like most that came in while he was in the house in the woods, skipped straight to voicemail. David listened to the message again and again for any clues. The detective didn't give any indication what it was about. He thought about waiting a day or two before calling back to demonstrate a lack of interest or knowledge. Could that end up prompting detectives to show up in New Hampshire? He couldn't risk it. Instead, he took the Steadmans' blue pickup truck into town to get better cell reception. It was too cold to have a long call outside, so he went into the Chinese restaurant, the only place in town for non-diner cuisine. The dining room was dimly lit, and they mostly did takeout business, leaving the spacious faux leather booths private.

"Detective Unit," a voice answered his call.

"Hi, this is David Trent."

"Who are you trying to reach?"

He had formed a mental picture of the entire police force gathered together waiting by the phone. Maybe, instead, speaking to him was a formality, an item low on their priority list. "I'm returning a call from Detective Braddox."

He was put on hold for a long time, at one point checking that he hadn't been disconnected. Then the voice came back on to say the call would have to be returned. An excruciating half hour passed, sipping hot tea and a second bowl of egg drop soup to pass the time, before the phone vibrated. When he picked up, a woman's voice came on.

"Thanks for returning the call, Mr. Trent. We're reaching out because we're investigating the death of Lee Van Knox."

There was a silence that David realized he was supposed to fill.

"I've been away for a while. Lee Van Knox, that's terrible. What happened?"

"We can't discuss much publicly yet, Mr. Trent. You knew him, correct?"

"Yes, though not well. I met him a couple times. Twice."

"What was the context of those meetings?"

"I won an award. He worked for the organization that had chosen my book, so he invited me to have a coffee. Do you know Darwin's café, the one on Mount Auburn? That's where we met up. And then I saw him again briefly at a holiday party."

"Where was that party?"

"That was at the Hales' house. Silas and Rebecca Hale."

"The writer Silas Hale."

"That's right."

"Had you seen him since then? Mr. Van Knox, I mean."

Since then? He tried to unpack the question to understand what she expected that he might say.

"No. That was the last time I saw Lee." True! "Actually, I moved up to New Hampshire shortly after that."

"Did you witness any exchanges, any conversations, that Mr. Van Knox might have had that evening? Mr. Trent?"

David had fallen silent again as his mind spun, only barely registering her words.

"Sorry. Reception here—sorry. No, I can't really remember anything specific that he said."

"I understand. Can you confirm when you moved out of the Hales' house, and when you were last there?"

David told her the date that he drove away in Jace's Volvo. He confirmed that he hadn't been back to the house since then. She seemed to be organizing existing notes, or writing more, leaving another uncomfortable gap in the conversation.

"You're certain you didn't return to the house, where you might have seen something else?"

"Yes, I'm certain. Obviously if there's some other way I can be helpful . . ."

He had no intention of finishing the sentence, scared he would say the wrong thing after having felt relatively unscathed so far, but the detective abruptly lost interest. It seemed peculiar. She hadn't asked what seemed to David to be obvious and important questions—about the night of the end-of-the-year party, about David's access to the crawl space and how often he had gone into it, questions that would be almost impossible for him to squirm out of. "Thanks for bearing with me, Mr. Trent. There is one other thing to clarify."

"Sure." No! Too casual. "Please."

"Were you on hand during any arguments, any hostile exchanges, while living in the house?"

"Me? No, not that I can think of."

"You're certain?" He said he was. Typing sounds. "Thank you, Mr. Trent, that's all from our end, then."

Those last moments of the call, talking about arguments, left him trapped in a state of panic. Had someone heard David and Van Knox arguing that night from his apartment? Had Markus Hale seen Van Knox going in while he was running around during the snowball fight with his friends? Had Antoinette still been wandering the yard for a way into the party, eyeing everyone who might assist her, maybe waiting at David's door, debating whether to demand tea?

David obsessively followed developments that were reported in the news, but they were few and far between. He devoured online news about everything and anything in case there was anything relevant, watching clips from the Boston nightly news posted on the network's websites and on Facebook. A steady diet of anchors boasted about sports teams, reported stories about neighbors arguing over saved parking spots, and relayed details of violent crimes. At one point he came across a news segment about a bicycle thief busted in Somerville, which David nearly ignored. A police officer said the perpetrator was running one of the biggest bike theft rings in the area. There was footage of recovered bikes, with information on how to claim them. David swore he spotted Van Knox's bicycle in the footage, amid dozens of others; he paused the clip and zoomed in, over and over. There was no reason to think the police would consider connecting a stolen bike with the Van Knox case, but if they did, who knows what clues that bike would yield.

At the same time, he worried that some important development might not show up online, so he went out to buy Boston-area papers from town whenever possible. The clerk at the combination ice cream and newsstand, which a sign boasted had been around since 1953, began to expect his arrival, which in itself worried him. On the one hand, David didn't like the idea of any local thinking he had a preoccupation with the news, which could pique the interest of the Massachusetts detectives, were they to ask around about him. On the other hand, he could explain that he was buying the newspapers because he was homesick for the city while living in the middle of nowhere. He made sure not to be observed reading the paper until he was somewhere private, in case even a facial expression could provoke interest in what he was looking for.

While he was exiting the newsstand with the latest papers tucked under his arm, he got a call from Jace.

"David, didn't you hear?"

"What?"

"Silas Hale."

David stopped in the middle of the sidewalk. "What about him?"

"Arrested, David! Silas Hale was arrested for murder!"

He told Jace he'd call him back. He planted himself in the Gothic-style town library, dotted with a handful of slow-moving retirees. In front of him, he laid out all the latest newspapers, booted up his laptop, and plugged in his earbuds while listening to all the Boston radio talk shows with online uploads, piecing together what he could.

The coroner determined that Lee Van Knox's death had happened weeks after David had already moved out of the house. Because of the Hales' refusal to heat the house, it seemed, the body had remained so cold in the uninsulated crawl space that it was preserved far longer than normal. By the time the body did finally begin to thaw and decompose, rats had burrowed their way into the house through the walls and into the crawl space, gnawing at the corpse's face, legs, and arms and pulling apart toes and other chunks of flesh, as well as chewing through Van Knox's clothes, leaving little that could reconstruct the circumstances and causes of death, and destroying any fingerprints that might have been left on the body. With the Rosfelds' new tenant (the Hales' daughter's friend) delayed by logistical issues traveling from Japan, the only people present at Observatory Hill Road around the coroner's estimated date of death had been the Hales and their housekeeper. Paula, the housekeeper, had reported hearing noises in the ceiling above, which turned out to be the growing convoy of rats that continued to squeeze into and out of the crawl space, attracted by the body.

Meanwhile, the investigators discovered that Silas had angered and alienated half of the writing community around Boston, though for many years people had been too frightened of his power and influence to speak out publicly. One of these angry individuals happened to be Lee Van Knox himself, who had left behind a years-long paper trail of complaints about Silas's long-standing verbal and psychological abuse of Van Knox and others affiliated with the Boston Literary Society.

One exchange between Silas and Van Knox overheard at the end-of-the-year party, according to various sources, went something like the following:

VAN KNOX: "Silas, I wanted to talk to you about some of the board commitments at the Society that we've noticed you're behind on—"
SILAS: "I answer to you? Don't you dare speak to me like that."
VAN KNOX: "Nothing personal, Silas, really. It's just as a member of our board, you must—"
SILAS: "I must. I must what? I must nothing. Don't speak to me unless spoken to. Don't even make eye contact unless I do, you pathetic snake."

No wonder the detective had asked David if he'd heard arguments. Boston media made much of exposing a dramatic schism, an epic rivalry that had come to a crescendo in a murder, not realizing that Silas could as easily speak like that to someone he'd met minutes before, and then forget he had done so minutes later. Comments from the police and prosecutors also didn't reveal any particular understanding of the nuances of the cutthroat literary community. As for the timeline leading to the body's discovery, once the rat infestation in the crawl space became obvious from the racket they were making, Silas ordered their housekeeper to help him open the trapdoors, when they came upon the semi-frozen body.

David searched every article and blog for his own name, but never found a mention. The official account, after all, placed David not just out of the house but out of state during the proposed time of the murder. Jace, fascinated by the events, was texting and calling him regularly as news came out, curious for David's opinion, as someone who lived above Silas Hale.

"Can you imagine if you hadn't moved out? It's pretty wild. If you had been there a few more weeks, you might have witnessed the murder, or at least heard something while it was happening. Wild, right? Maybe Silas Hale was planning the murder for a while, and engineered your move, that whole business about his daughter's friend, to get you out of the way and give him opportunity."

"Imagine," David said. It was a good point, and a compelling theory about why Silas had forced him to move. "I hadn't thought of that."

"Hale probably wants to tell his story, right?" Jace asked. "But I'm sure he doesn't have the peace of mind to write behind bars."

"What's your point?"

"Look, I don't want to toot my horn, but this is where an expert ghostwriter can help, David! Could even help Silas Hale. Seriously! Could you put in a word for me?"

David received a call from the district attorney's office in Middlesex County, asking him to provide a statement in person. They offered to travel to New Hampshire to speak, but he still feared Barbara and Stan's reactions to such unusual visitors. He felt self-conscious in front of them just bringing home a pizza, which they thought strange, as they only ate food from restaurants on special occasions ("very special occasions," Barbara had specified). Jace's insatiable interest in the case came in handy. He was willing and eager to pick up David and drive him to the suburban courthouse where the district attorney's office was located.

As David got out of the car, Jace watched his every move with an air of expectation. He seemed to want an invitation to the meeting.

Walking in, David wondered if they would ask to examine his cell phone. Could they find anything incriminating on it? He didn't think so, though for a moment he considered tossing it into a planter near the elevator bank. But that seemed far riskier than holding on to it.

David was led to a colorless conference room, with three lawyers present. They asked him to describe Silas Hale's demeanor in the months before David moved out—the months before the murder.

David told himself to sound measured. "Silas could be abrasive, certainly, but everyone can be sometimes, and he wasn't always like that. At times we would talk about writing, and he would give me advice. He was very accomplished, as I'm sure you know."

The lawyers seemed disappointed by his benign depiction. But it would serve no purpose for David to bash Silas. He didn't want to be elevated to any importance in the investigation or a possible trial, and he certainly didn't want the press to be given any reason to notice him. Remaining inconspicuous was his best strategy.

"I used to try to write a little fiction," said one of the lawyers, who was around David's age. "Sometimes I miss it. In fact, I even tried to start a book club around here, but it didn't take."

"If only we had that kind of time," the assistant district attorney, whose name was Christine Horvack, lamented. She had given David her card and seemed to be in charge. She directed a sidelong glance at her colleague and added, "Maybe it would have helped not to choose a six-hundred-page James Joyce novel for our first book club pick."

David, sticking to his plan of not drawing attention, nodded blandly, refraining from any commentary that might imprint him in their minds. The lawyers returned to the point.

"David, the detective's notes indicate that you never saw Lee Van Knox together with Silas Hale?"

Even with Silas already charged, the prosecutors seemed to be groping for a motive. They could show Silas made enemies easily, but that would not be enough to make their murder charge stick.

"Well, they were both at Silas's end-of-the-year party, as I mentioned. But I don't remember seeing them talk to each other. No." This was entirely true, which made it satisfying to say out loud. He would have liked to repeat it if they gave him the chance.

"And you don't remember other visits to the house by Lee Van Knox?" asked Christine.

David shook his head.

"Our evidence suggests that Lee must have cut a trip short, in the week after the party, to come back and see Silas again. A trip he had planned for a long time."

The bicycle tour. They must have found the same erroneous tagging of Van Knox in a Facebook photo that David had come across, which also happened to fit with the coroner's incorrect estimate of the time of death, and would have meant that Van Knox must have returned to Observatory Hill Road after the date of the photo. Those mistakes should also prevent them from looking at bikes stolen weeks earlier.

"Any ideas why Mr. Van Knox would have some reason to come back in those weeks after the party to talk to Silas—maybe to confront him?"

"I can't imagine," David said, after pretending to contemplate the query. "They were both part of the Boston Literary Society."

"The organization that arranges literary events and awards. Right. We saw your name on the list of winners for those awards. That's the award you mentioned in your call with Detective Braddox. Is that right?"

"I'm honored to say yes. It was an award Silas Hale had won early in his career, too." David threw his hands up, as if he shared their frustration about how Silas could have committed a murder. "Silas is a pillar of our literary community. He's idolized."

"Right," Christine replied, checking her notes. "We spoke to a neighbor of the Hales, Antoinette Saville-Burke, who praised Silas Hale as 'a very generous and gracious representative of the Cambridge intelligentsia.' Might have missed a few more words in that phrase in our notes. She can really talk. In fact, Ms. Saville-Burke had some things to say about you."

"Oh?"

"She said she came by the night of the party. She explained that you turned her away rudely, and that you were, to use her word, 'unusually distracted.'"

"Rude? No, at least, I hope I wasn't. I was bringing in some bags of ice to the kitchen to help out the Hales. Honestly, I don't remember my exchange with her very well, but I used to visit with her sometimes, help her bring in groceries, that kind of thing."

He felt certain by the end of the interview that he had managed to make things murkier. He signed an affidavit that contained a summary of the statements he had made in the conversation. They never asked to see his phone. Christine told him he might be called to testify, but she didn't sound confident about it. He believed he had successfully bored the lawyers by failing to add anything colorful, but he'd still subtly reinforced the fact that Silas was ill-tempered. Sure, Silas happened to have had tension with other people as much or more than his tension with Lee Van Knox, but it was Van Knox who'd turned up dead.

Weeks later, David surprised himself by how quickly he settled into Davidson for his residency. He had imagined that once he was in North Carolina, he would keep to himself in a quiet room in perfect anonymity, but in fact his position as writer-in-residence at the college was a fairly social one. The English department held a reception for him on his first evening in a large room with red leather couches and large portraits of the college founders, and even arranged for chamber music from one of the college's string quartets. In advance, students in the department had been assigned to read *The Crises*. They were genuinely excited to meet David, even starstruck. Once someone has read a book, or even just held it in their hands, the author of the book takes on a mystique, even if the reader had never heard of them before and would never hear of them again. In the Boston scene, writers were surrounded by more other writers than readers, but here

David was meeting students who were just excited at the idea that someone had been published. They were curious about things like how he chose his author photo and why he chose (as if he had) the book cover with the cornfield and the jigsaw-puzzle face. David was in shock at how deferential they all were, including the younger faculty, and how invested in getting to know him.

The morning after the English department reception, the tranquility was broken. He was woken up at six by his phone ringing.

A computerized voice announced: "You have a call from the Middlesex Jail and House of Correction."

Stunned, David hung up, and then regretted it. Was someone from law enforcement calling? No, calls with recordings like that were only from prisoners, he surmised. It could only be from Silas Hale, but why? Why call him unless . . .

He had been trying not to imagine too much about what Silas was thinking about everything. Not knowing anything about the death of Van Knox, Silas would have no basis to doubt the medical examiner's scientifically determined timeline about when the death happened, would he? He wouldn't have known about David's interactions with Van Knox.

David continued to be feted by the English department. He gave an afternoon talk and reading from his book and then had dinner with faculty, where he was surprised how many had read his novel carefully enough to come with well-informed questions, including another fiction-writing fellow named Sloane, with whom he had a fascinating conversation about the origins of writing curricula in the United States. Sloane loved everything about being a writer: meeting other writers, reading other writers' work, learning about the history of writing as a profession. Sloane had received an Emerging Writers Fellowship, meant for writers who had published short fiction but not yet completed a book.

David couldn't enjoy the camaraderie the way he wanted to. He checked his phone repeatedly, on edge that another call might come in from the jail. He woke up several times during the night to check, too, but no call came. He began to consider that the initial jail call could have been accidental, possibly a lawyer or some other official transposing numbers from Silas's contact list on his phone.

The next day, he got an email listed as coming from INMATE: HALE, SILAS STUART.

David,
Arrange to visit me at your earliest convenience.
Regards, Silas

Below the message was the address of the jail. Somehow Silas's language made the jail seem to belong to Silas.

After breakfast, David called Christine Horvack, who had left him her card at their meeting, at the district attorney's office.

"I'm sorry to bother you, Christine, but I had a question about the case."

"No bother at all."

"Silas Hale emailed me, asking to visit him in jail."

Christine paused. "I see."

"I didn't know how or whether to respond. I'm in North Carolina now, anyway."

"Oh?"

"I have a residency at a college here."

"Right, I remember you mentioned that was coming up. I hope it's a nice getaway. When do you return?"

David filled her in, finding himself saying a few words about how friendly the college and the town were. Why had it seemed like David was much more interested in the progress of the case than the prosecutors and investigators? "You had said I might be testifying at a hearing or trial. Would it be a conflict to speak with Silas before that?"

"Not necessarily."

David hesitated before continuing. "I guess the evidence is pretty strong against him."

"How so?"

"I'm not a lawyer, obviously, but I thought someone of Silas's stature and connections would normally have been given bail by now."

"Everyone's equal in the eyes of the law." She gave a hardened chuckle. "Actually, between us, you'd usually be right. But Hale flew off the handle at a preliminary hearing and started berating the judge like she was a child finger-painting on the wall. He told her she was a 'submental specimen.' He had to be dragged out, screaming about his Pulitzer."

"I'm sorry to hear that."

"He's onto his second lawyer now, too. The first one quit, citing personality differences. Apparently Mr. Hale forbade him from looking him in the eyes. The new lawyer has thicker skin, but is even more expensive than the first. This is off the record, too, but we're hearing that Rebecca Hale had to borrow money. Not to bore you with behind-the-scenes details, David. Listen, unless you're notified otherwise, it's up to you if you want to communicate with Mr. Hale, in person or otherwise. You're free to do so, or you can just ignore him."

Even after the call with Christine ended, with her reassurances that he could forget about Silas's message, the email nagged at him, demanding action. What if whatever it was Silas wanted to say to David, or ask him, he became impatient at David's lack of response and relayed it to his lawyer or to prosecutors? There was also an element of raw curiosity on David's part. What *did* Silas want to say to him? The email, which he read over and over, and sometimes came close to deleting in his desire to pretend it never existed, was an enigma. Its tone could as easily be read as civil or seething.

Over the next few days, David made a conscious effort not to think of Silas. He largely succeeded in putting it out of his mind thanks to Sloane, whose fellowship, which came with the duty of teaching a short fiction seminar, had started before his. She showed him around to two local bookstores and arranged a lunch at a Thai restaurant with several writers on the faculty and a local poet, a kind of father figure to the literary community. "I read his last collection," she said. "I cried a couple of times, but to be fair I cry a lot. He's a good poet. The tricky thing is, nobody can really tell a good poet from a bad one, especially other poets."

Sloane, who was in her early twenties, had a nervous laugh that burst out of her often. She had oversize glasses shaped like owl eyes, behind which she often dried watery eyes, which she attributed to the woods in Davidson. She had come from Dublin after publishing short fiction in an impressive roll call of academic literary journals. Hanging out with her in Davidson's circle of writers, David heard mild complaints about their overdue or stalled writing projects, but there wasn't the competitiveness that he was used to, the obsession with agents or imprints or getting past the gatekeepers at the *New Yorker* or Random House. These writers' ambitions and goals, and the familiar complaints of falling short of those, revolved around writing itself, which they seemed to genuinely love doing.

It became a running joke that Sloane refused to advise David on the best coffee shop to write in, since she didn't want to compete for a table. There were only three coffee shops, and eventually he ran into her upstairs at her favorite spot. The place had a wider selection of tea than coffee. The truth was, he was far too distracted to get any serious writing done, and embraced procrastination. Writers have special skills to make an afternoon seamlessly pass without accomplishing anything.

"I'm curious, and feel free to ignore me, but what was it that made you a writer?" Sloane asked, sitting over folded knees on an overstuffed chair by a fireplace, which gave a northeastern vibe to the place that both comforted and bothered David.

"Made me a writer?"

"Made you want to be a writer?"

"Well, I don't really remember, to be honest. I mean, I wasn't one of these people who grew up dreaming to be a writer as a kid."

"Who does that?" She laughed. "Actually, me. It's all I ever wanted. I would dress up as Flannery O'Connor for Halloween, and in retrospect I'm not sure people could tell I was dressed up at all."

"That might be a first."

She wrinkled her nose and brow, then blew her nose into a handkerchief.

"I do admire it, though," he said.

"Why?"

"Well, the clarity, I guess. I mean, if you set out to be a writer from before you can remember, then you don't have to second-guess it, you don't have to wonder if you should do something else. Maybe I'm just doing this because it's the only thing I figured out how to do, because I could write well enough to try. But there's always fear, lurking. What if I'm going through the motions?"

She gave her nervous laugh, but then seemed contemplative. "How so?"

"Maybe I'm not a writer because I write, but someone who writes to become a writer, if that makes sense."

"Honestly, David, that makes no sense," she said, then laughed again before pouring them both more tea from the ceramic pot. "But it sounds nice. That's half the battle. You're an award-winning writer. Think of that if you ever get down on yourself! No matter what you do, nothing can take that away, and nothing can take away that you wrote that novel. 'Award-winning author David Trent.' I'd take that every day of the week over 'emerging writer.'"

They both returned to their work, though David just stared at his screen. It was in the silence—broken up periodically by Sloane's allergy attacks—while staring at his laptop that he realized, or articulated to himself what he already knew. He had to go see Silas Hale. He had to know what Silas wanted to say to him, while at the same time realizing he had no idea what he could possibly say in return. How would he greet Silas in jail? "How are you, Silas?" couldn't possibly be right. "Good to see you"?

Weeks passed as he continued to play out the visit in his head. When his residency came to a close, David was relieved to finally be searching for his answers. After flying into Logan Airport, he stayed with his mother's cousin and her family, who lived about a half hour away from Boston, which was closer to the jail, though he did not mention anything about that to his hosts. He had done in-depth research into what the visit would be like—visitors were not allowed to wear headgear, for example, unless it was religious. Visits were also on a first-come, first-serve basis, so it was possible that if there happened to be many visitors that day, you'd leave without seeing your inmate.

When he confirmed with the jail which day Silas's "dorm," as the subdivisions of inmates were called, was eligible for visits, he headed to the jail, timing his drive to get there when it opened. It looked like an austere early twentieth-century New England church out front, complete with a steeple, with the rest of the massive complex comprised of a series of industrial buildings.

By the time he handed in his visiting form, at least ten people were waiting who had known exactly where to park, which halls to turn down, and which offices to enter, and whose forms had already been processed. The seating area was located beyond a security checkpoint. Once in the room, David tried to keep track of how many people were ahead of him, as if waiting for a table at a restaurant, but it was fruitless, since visit times depended on the prisoner's prearranged schedule and their respective dorm assignments. Even given those variables, it started to seem like too many people were going inside for visits before him. He asked the officer at the desk if there was any update on when he would see Silas. The only update, she said, would be when his name got called.

He began to get a feeling that other visitors and the staff were watching him. A thought crept over him. What if his visit had been a trick, choreographed by the prosecutors? They had discovered everything that really happened on the night of the party, but did not have enough evidence to take him from North Carolina, so they arranged the call and then the email to coax him back to Massachusetts of his own volition. He couldn't actually know if it had been Silas calling him, since David had hung up. The email could have come from anyone. The district attorney's office could have been called by the prison staff as soon as he handed over his identification to the clerk. Perhaps he was now waiting there for his own arrest, unwittingly having turned himself in.

David returned to the officer at the desk.

"I'm sorry, I have to get going."

She glared.

"Do I just go out back that way?" he asked.

"You haven't had your visit."

"It's just getting late. I have some appointments I can't cancel."

"You've been processed already. Once you've been processed, you can't just walk back through security. That corridor is one-way."

"So can I go out another way? That way?"

"No, you can only exit that way once you've been called for your visit."

"I have to wait to be called just to leave? Really, I have to—something came up—"

"Sir, it's not a hotel lobby, you can't go in and out. If you really wish to leave before your visit, I'll have to call for a supervisor to input the changes into our system."

"Supervisor" had a ring to it that he didn't like. "Never mind. You're right. I'll wait."

Back at his chair, he fidgeted. He caught a glimpse of the officer at the desk consulting with another officer, gesturing in David's direction.

Roughly twenty minutes later, the door adjacent to the desk opened and "David Trent" was called in a deep voice, attached to someone he couldn't see even once he went through the door and behind the desk. He was met by a fast-walking guard, who was checking some forms. He was told to follow.

"Relation to the inmate?"

"Sorry?"

"What's your relation to the inmate you're visiting?"

His answer spilled out: "Mentor."

"What?"

"He's my mentor."

"He's your—"

"Advises me on my career."

"Um-hm."

Why did they need to know his relationship? Perhaps it triggered different safeguards, for example if someone was aggrieved and might want to hurt the inmate. He thought it odd when he was brought past a set of stalls where other visitors, most of whom he recognized from the waiting area, were seated, either already speaking to inmates who were on the other side of a partition or waiting for an inmate to be brought there. Those stalls were surrounded by guards, and individual cameras on the ceiling were aimed at each seat. But apparently that wasn't where David was going. The guard ushered him down another hallway to a private room. Inside, Silas was seated at a table. He was wearing a crimson jumpsuit and writing in small, rapid strokes on multicolored Post-it notes. The door closed behind David. They were alone.

Silas held a finger in the air for silence as he finished writing. When finally he looked up, his expression was unreadable. Then for a moment he radiated warmth toward David.

"Trent!" Silas crowed. "I've been waiting for you to visit. I need your help with my case. Where have you been?"

"North Carolina. I had a writing residency there."

"Excellent! Now you see it. You finally see how to do it."

"How to do it?"

"Squeeze out every penny any university or grant-giving body will hand out. We feed our soul into our writing, and we're owed all that the world can give us in return. Speaking of writing, I came across your book in the jail library here."

"Really?"

He seemed to become meditative and distant. "Time goes by quickly here, Trent. 'Time is the least thing we have.' Hemingway said that to a journalist, likely because he wanted her to stop asking him questions, but never mind Hemingway, who only hated sentimentality because he was sentimental, deep down. I was able to request this private room for our visit because I explained that you are among a number of people I believe have material facts that can help my case. This way, they treat you essentially as one of my legal representatives—we have the right to speak without the sheep all around us, and the officials are not permitted to observe us at all—no videotaping or recording permitted. It is the one room in this place where the government does not profess to own you."

David had a look around the room and saw that Silas was right: unlike the visiting stalls he had passed, there were no cameras here.

"Silas, I wanted to say how sorry I am—"

Silas waved this off midway through David's sentence. "I don't whine, so you shouldn't. Let's get down to business. They may not be able to record us in here, but they certainly can declare when our time is over. Did you know this twit Lee Van Knox? The one they found dead?"

"I had crossed paths with him."

"He attended my end-of-the-year party. My new lawyer is as abominably moronic as the first one. If I could go back in time and go to law school, I would, even though it turns passably intelligent men into automatons. I haven't that luxury now, but I have no choice but to take this fraud of a case by the throat myself and throttle it, and I want you to be in the courtroom to see me do it."

"Of course, Silas. I'll be there."

Silas shuffled through a rainbow of Post-it notes, which were filled with overlapping, microscopically scrawled writing. "Recently something occurred to me: the coats. That's why I needed you to come talk to me here, Trent!"

David shook his head, feigning confusion. "Coats?"

"You remember!"

"You mean the coats from the party?"

"Keep up. Yes. Think of it. It's certainly expected that some coats get left by drunken fools at a party stumbling into a taxi. But it's also possible that one of those coats was left by someone especially agitated, worked up over some kind of argument with Van Knox, leaving in a huff. That could be a key to a motive—someone might be carrying a grudge against Van Knox, someone who might have been in my house at the party long enough to study it, to find an ingress to return at a later date, to somehow lure that twit Van Knox back there a couple of weeks after the party and kill him!"

"That makes sense."

Silas ran his tongue across his teeth. He was waiting for more, poised to take notes. "So do you remember anything?"

"About the coats?"

"Are we speaking English today, Trent, or shall I translate into the original Dutch? The coats, yes! You looked through the pile of items left behind when you came back for your coat. I threw them out after another day or two. I'm not a lost and found. But we need to work backward here to find the maniac who set in motion this whole plot to destroy me. You could turn this all around for me. Do you remember anything distinctive about any of them? Do you remember seeing the coats on anyone as they walked into the party? Concentrate!"

"Honestly, Silas, I'd have to really think. That was months ago."

"Not long enough ago to forget, unless you are an imbecile."

David wasn't sure whether to nod in agreement.

"You were there early. You had a front-row seat to see people arriving."

David had disposed of Van Knox's coat, along with his phone, which he had disassembled and smashed into its smallest components, in half a dozen public dumpsters around Cambridge, one of which he tossed the coat into. He had remembered reading that the landfills in Cambridge had long ago exceeded capacity, so trash was being incinerated upon collection. As for the other items left at the Hales' house, he would bet that their owners, likely members of the literary community, would prefer losing a coat or pair of socks to getting on the wrong side of Silas Hale by bothering him.

"Have they tried—your lawyers, I mean—have they tried to find out if Van Knox might have been arguing with anyone?"

"I've told you, Trent, the lawyers are brain dead. The culmination of decades of our system of higher education embracing mediocrity and instilling it with verve into our so-called best and brightest. I need *you*."

Despite the circumstances, he couldn't help but feel flattered. In the moment, part of him really did want to help, wanted to solve the riddle for Silas—as though David himself wasn't the solution. "The little I know of Lee Van Knox, he was what you called the enemy, the people whose role in life is only to deeply appreciate writers."

Silas grinned. He loved being quoted back to himself, cited as an authority on human nature. "Correct!"

"They resent what they can't be, right? You said they're impossible to please, and maybe that's the reason. They say that they love books, that they love writers, but deep down they wait for a chance to try to tear them down to their level. They say 'You're special' only in preparation for saying 'You're nobody.'"

David realized he was speaking faster than he was thinking; he found himself winded, as though he had run a sprint. He felt a moment of panic that he had said too much. He ought to remain vague, general, emotionally detached from the facts.

"Back to the coats, Trent. We have been collecting photos taken during the party from everyone we could track down, and some are of people posing as they arrived at the party, still wearing their coats. I'll have my lawyer send all the photos to you, and you can try to remember whether any of the coats match the ones left behind."

"That seems like a start, Silas. I'll go through those and report back to you."

"Let me make sure I have the right mobile phone written down for you. I tried calling before."

"Of course."

"Phone," Silas said, murmuring the one word.

This made David uneasy. "I'll help in any way I can," he said.

Silas looked through some more of his notes, flipping through the Post-its. Then he grew contemplative, furrowing his strong brow as he looked off to one side of the room, then back at David. He noticed David was nervous. David knew he should just stay quiet, or find a pretense to end the meeting. If only a guard would come to announce that time was up. What was the maximum duration for a visit, anyway?

"I've never been inside a jail before," he blurted out.

"Phone," Silas said again.

David waited.

"A phone," Silas said one more time, wobbling his head back and forth as he followed a silent train of thought. Discomfort raced through David's body and became nausea.

"I know you mentioned they would give us a limited window to meet for today. Should I plan to come back once your lawyer sends me photos of the coats?"

"Do you know why your book is available in a jail library, Trent?"

The sharp turn threw him off. "What?"

"It's in the library in this facility," Silas said, "because someone came into possession of it out in the world, read some of it, maybe a few pages, maybe only a paragraph, and abandoned it, maybe the very first word that dulled the mind. I control my readers with ease. There is a phenomenon in writing, in which if you write about the tongue, the reader must imitate the movement you write about. When I describe a character's tongue slapping across the sharp edges of the upper lip, and traveling down the moistened ridges of the lower lip, the reader has no choice but to do the same with their tongue—I have burrowed into their brain cells, at that point, and never leave. That reader is mine, will always be. If you can't control your reader, then you're no writer at all. When you see your book in a Goodwill, at a garage sale, at a jail library, you've failed. You've lost control over your reader, and handed it back to the world."

David's fists curled into balls on the table. "Did you bother reading my book? Let me guess the answer is no. You just jump to judging it."

Silas was grinning through clenched teeth. He wagged a finger at David. "I see you, Trent. I see you now. Your arrogance, thinking you could leap to the top of a mountain that you're not strong enough to scale. A phone! A phone rang from inside that pile of coats that was left behind. On a few separate occasions. I remember it now. I was about to take a hammer to it if it happened again, but it didn't. Battery drained, no doubt? It was a day or two later that you showed up for your coat and looked through that pile. It's one thing for some dolt to leave behind a coat and be too embarrassed about it to knock at my door. How many people with mobiles would leave their phone behind and not turn back for it after a few minutes or an hour, much less twenty-four or forty-eight hours?"

"I don't understand, Silas. Somebody lost track of their phone. Forgot where it was. It happens."

Silas was scribbling on another Post-it. David leaned forward enough to see the word *phone* and an arrow to the words *Van Knox*. Silas flipped to the blank side and wrote "David" over and over again, spaces falling away, so it looked like *DavidDavidDavidDavid*, before adding "ItwasDavid."

"Van Knox," Silas said. "It had to be Van Knox's phone! Had to be. He didn't get killed in January, when they said he did. He was already gone the night of the party. You came back for your coat. But you didn't leave your coat, did you? No. You never needed a coat to come down from upstairs to our floor. You'd only be walking outside for a minute from your door to the front of our house. How foolish I was not to see that before. To not see you, the real you!"

"I don't know what you're implying. I had my coat on because I was coming from somewhere else."

David could see from Silas's expression that he didn't believe him. He jumped to his feet. Simultaneously Silas's arm shot out and gripped David's wrist, clamping it with surprising force.

He looked Silas in the eye. "Why did you refuse to do the book event with me when I won the award, Silas? Why? I idolized you."

"Why? Because you're nothing! *You're nothing!* You don't belong on a stage with me! I was only your hero because you thought that would make you a hero!"

David tried to pull his wrist away. "You're a monster! Bonnie saw it right away, and I should have listened. The devil who tears people down until they fall apart, piece by piece, before blaming them for weakness."

"You killed Van Knox!" Silas wailed, the words echoing off the walls. "You did it!"

"No!" David was trembling, losing his balance. As they struggled, the contents of the table slid around. "Let go!"

Silas's face was beet red. Suddenly he resembled his drunk son Markus on the night of the party. "How dare you! Another cockroach, another rat, begging me for secondhand scraps of dignity, trying to nibble out a survival from my successes, from the genius that I've lavished onto the world! Embarrassing! You'd let my life go down the sewer you crawled out of!"

Silas's grip tightened. David stretched his free arm toward the door, which was too far to reach.

With his other hand, Silas slapped David across the face. Then Silas wrapped both hands around his neck.

"You're nothing, Trent! A fraud and a failure underfoot real men! I'll crush you!" Silas was spitting, his eyes bulging.

"Silas!" David hissed with sputtering breath. He tried kicking the door behind him but couldn't reach it with his shoe. "Stop!"

His throat burned. Silas's fingers felt like a thousand little knives piercing his skin. Suddenly the fingertips softened a little, then some more, until they slid off his neck.

Freed, David gasped and wheezed.

Silas's face had grown redder than his uniform. He clutched his chest with one hand, and gestured desperately with his other. He had flipped from being in a rage to being in a medical crisis. He needed help.

Regaining his breath, David swerved to the door, then stopped, looking back at Silas, who was silently beseeching him for mercy.

All he saw was a monster. Silas might not have killed Van Knox, no—but he demeaned Van Knox, like he did David, like he did everyone to serve his ego. Silas had never deserved the praise and love he received from the world, and it was impossible to avoid an ugly thought: this crimson-faced beast, who consumed anyone less fortunate around him, however brilliant, deserved death.

David scanned the table for the Post-it notes Silas had been writing at the end of their conversation, but everything was in disarray, and most of the papers had fallen.

Silas, helpless and weak, was jabbing a finger toward the door, indicating he needed urgent help. His eyes begged.

David decided Silas deserved a chance. He would count to thirty. He counted in his head. Realizing David was standing there, not moving, Silas shook his head weakly. Pleading. Ten. Eleven. Twelve. Silas dropped to his knees, both hands now clasping his chest. Sixteen. Seventeen. Eighteen. Silas collapsed to one side. His eyes landed on a call button at one end of the table. He began an excruciating attempt to push himself up from the floor, reaching. Twenty-two, twenty-three . . .

When David got to thirty in his silent count, he unhurriedly walked over to the door, glanced once more at Silas, then pressed the button for the guard. David thought about Silas's hypertension, about the pill bottle he had seen in his study, and the fact that it might help a medic to know his prescription, but he blocked that from his thoughts. He opened the door, screaming, his call echoing through the hall. "Help! Someone help! He needs a doctor now!"

12

SOMETIMES DAVID WOULD PICK UP the paperback edition of *The Crises*, holding it at arm's length as though seeing it for the first time. He would run his fingers along the embossed circular emblem in the upper corner that read WINNER, then below it BEST FIRST NOVEL AWARD BLS. The emblem matched a physical bronze medallion the Boston Literary Society had given him, engraved with his name. Parable had redesigned the cover for the paperback release, now depicting a stylized tunnel of neurons and synapses from inside a human brain. He was happier with this than the prairie sunset on the original hardcover. Like the cover, Parable's attitude improved with the award, becoming noticeably more supportive. The award had prompted new reviews, including a brief but glowing paragraph in a roundup of new paperbacks that ended up syndicated in a dozen newspapers around the country. Parable arranged a series of readings at bookstores and added David to a program they'd recently initiated that matched book clubs with authors able to participate via speakerphone. The publisher's marketing executive explained to him in a conference call with his editor and agent how book clubs could become a force multiplier for a book's journey, with five to ten book purchases at a time, and frequent recommendations from one book club to another. David's calendar gradually filled with visits to schools and literary fundraisers and auctions.

It was his favorite time of year, which made all of this even more enjoyable. To live in Cambridge in autumn was to walk through a painting, the air busy with scattered leaves and slow breezes.

"When I first published my book," he would tell audiences, "I went to sign a book at the bookstore, and the employee asked to see my ID."

This would get a laugh as a relatable moment, and would make David feel good about himself, since the subtext could now be interpreted as: Who would ask *me* for ID?

The line got such a good response that he started ad-libbing on it. "I took out my ID and asked, 'Do you have a rash of people trying to sign books that aren't theirs?' The clerk said, 'Yes, we had that problem with some Virginia Woolf books lately.'" More laughter.

Occasionally someone at his events mentioned Silas Hale. But it did not come from any knowledge of a connection between David and Silas. At events for *any* local novelist, someone was bound to ask how that author felt about what happened to Silas because it was the talk of the literary community. David's visit to the jail had ended with Silas carried out, lifeless, on a stretcher, as David and others were herded out of the way. The morning after that, David had received a call from Rebecca Hale.

"David, this is Rebecca Hale, Silas Hale's wife. You lived above us."

How strange that she would think he had to be reminded.

"Rebecca," said David. "I'm so sorry to be speaking under these circumstances. How are you?"

"We're told you visited Silas when . . . it happened."

"That's right, I was there. I didn't know if I should contact you to—I guess I'm still in shock, honestly. He had asked me to visit earlier, but I had been out of state."

"I hope you'll be praying with us for his recovery."

David paused, shocked that Silas was alive. "How is he?"

"He hasn't regained consciousness. They've induced a coma and . . . upsetting, it's all so upsetting."

"He's strong. I know he'll pull through."

After that, David hungered for updates. Three days later, Christine Horvack called from the district attorney's office.

"I'm sorry to have to be calling you," she said.

"Please," he said, hardly able to get words out. "Go ahead."

"As you probably know, Mr. Hale was placed in a medically induced coma. He regained consciousness this morning in the hospital."

David could have fallen over backward. "Wow. That's unbelievable news. Is he talking?"

"Not anymore."

"I don't understand."

"When he woke, he was beginning to scream and shout. Something about taking his revenge. A slurred mixture of incoherent tirades, according to those present, that went on about ninety seconds. His son thought he might have been quoting lines about vengeance from one of his books, though he said he never read his father's books, so he wasn't sure. The outburst was just long enough to trigger another heart episode, this time fatal. He died at 9:09 this morning."

David swallowed hard. "I can't believe it."

"As a courtesy, we've been reaching out to those we interviewed for the case with the update. I'm sorry, I know you were a neighbor and had a collegial friendship with him, no matter what happened between him and Mr. Van Knox. This isn't easy to hear. For the record, did you notice anything unusual when you saw Mr. Hale?"

"He was in a state, I guess. Very agitated toward the jail and toward you—the prosecutors, I mean. He thought everyone was against him."

He had never been as relieved as when he hung up the phone a few minutes later. Now, four and a half months later, when the topic of Silas came up at speaking events for the paperback edition of his novel, David had several rote responses ready to deploy. "I don't think the level of sadness can be measured over such a loss to literature," he'd say, sometimes adding, "W. H. Auden wrote of Yeats, 'The day of his death was a dark cold day.'" That received nods and murmurs of agreement from his audiences, which had gradually been growing larger.

The continuous stress David had experienced from the end-of-the-year party in December until the visit to the jail in early June had taken a toll long afterward. He lost weight and that summer came down with pneumonia, which seemed to go away and then recurred, necessitating a repetitive cycle of doctors' appointments and X-ray sessions. The silver lining came when Bonnie heard about his health through mutual friends, upon which her fierce compassion kicked in. She checked in on him, first by phone and then in person. Before falling ill, he had tried to reconnect multiple times without success. But his convalescence, which lasted nearly a month, brought her back to him. He apologized at length, told her how much he had missed her, and acknowledged he had gone through low points that he had inexcusably allowed to warp their relationship. She admitted to missing him, too, and her confusion at his behavior actually allowed her to begin to accept it as an anomaly, one that was a product of a time and place that had passed, rather than a character flaw. He promised to work on his communication, and they committed to building the relationship back to where it had been.

One day he got a call from his publicist at Parable, which in itself was a cause for excitement.

"I have good news for you, David," the publicist said. "Very good news, in fact. *Vanity Fair* wants to do a profile of you."

"No. *Vanity*—No! *Vanity Fair*. Really?"

"*Vanity Fair*."

"Really?"

"Their demographics have aged up, so their book editor is expanding their coverage of younger, up-and-coming writers. Your award must have put you on their radar, especially considering that a few other literary prizes shuttered in the past year and a half for lack of funds, so there was a smaller playing field. As I've told you, timing can be all the difference between something and nothing."

David had only spoken to the publicist a few times, and he was sure she had never told him that. "That's amazing. I'm grateful they'd even think of me."

"It's unusual, to be honest, for a first-time novelist. I suspect you have a big fan there who lit a fire under the editor. I'll be in touch with details once I know them. Probably a sit-down interview or two first, then maybe they'll send a photographer. Shall I tell them yes?"

"Yes, of course, absolutely I'm in! A photo shoot, too?"

"Maybe."

"You think so?"

"It will mean national exposure, a huge boost for awareness and sales, and likely other publicity that we can piggyback onto, plus an internal bump in marketing budget for your title."

By the time he received this news, he was subletting an apartment in an extension of the Charles Hotel, a busy complex at the hub of Cambridge, overlooking the river, using the award money and royalties from the paperback. Bonnie remained in her place in Brookline. They were taking their reconciliation seriously but slowly, not wanting to invite setbacks.

The award had also brought invitations to gatherings that included some highly established writers in Boston, a few of whom had their own publicists, mainly to get them into new restaurants and onto the society pages of the glossies. They considered themselves brands, not writers, and needed to constantly bring fresh blood into their circles to look in touch with the literary vibes. These social circles expanded outward, somewhat peculiarly, to food critics, relationship columnists, and a television meteorologist. He was invited to dinners and drinks. Even when someone else paid for these, the outing would involve other stops, and buying rounds of drinks. That could add up to hundreds of dollars, which David worried about, though none of the other people present seemed to.

Each day passed with one thing on his mind. The only thing he wanted was to be given a date when he'd sit down with the *Vanity Fair* reporter, and the longer he waited, the more worried he became that the magazine's editors had lost interest or changed their minds. Then, with two days' notice, his publicist texted an address in downtown Boston where he would meet the reporter for lunch. To be taken out for lunch by *Vanity Fair* was a dream he hadn't even known he had. He couldn't believe it was happening. In typical fashion, when Bonnie heard, she insisted they have their own lunch out to celebrate his upcoming lunch with the journalist.

When the day came for the interview, David vowed not to arrive too early, but since he was terrified of showing up late, he ended up downtown a half hour early in spite of himself. After wasting some time, he allowed himself to arrive just a few minutes early at the address, which turned out to be the Harvard Club of Boston, the entrance essentially unmarked except by two flags, one American and one with the Harvard emblem. Entering, he found himself stopped by a uniformed guard at the front desk. Only members were allowed to go past his desk, the guard explained.

"My name is David Trent. I'm meeting a writer from *Vanity Fair* here at the restaurant. For lunch." That last part was superfluous, he realized as he said it.

The guard found his name on a list and asked him to wait. There was nowhere to sit, so he stood around awkwardly, feeling as if he was making a delivery rather than waiting to attend the most important interview of his career.

The guard returned and indicated where David should go, toward the main dining section of the club.

David made a right turn into a bar with red leather booths and dark wood tables. It was still early for lunch, and only a few tables were occupied. Past this area was the larger dining room. Barnaby Masters sat alone at one of the tables in the dining room.

"David!" Barnaby stood up and gave him a friendly wave.

David flinched at the coincidence, then noticed a copy of *The Crises* on Barnaby's table. Only then did it dawn on him why Barnaby was there.

"How long has it been?" Barnaby asked. "I would have dropped you a line myself but didn't have your contact info, so I let the magazine handle everything with your publicist. Come on, sit down, brother, sit down. How have you been these days?"

"It's been a while," David answered the first question, his thoughts miles behind.

"Sorry to hear about your fiancée."

"What?"

"Oh, none of my business, apologies. Brandi told me you and your fiancée—Bonnie, was it?—had split up."

"No. I mean, yes, we took time apart. I was under some stress. Things are better now, actually. We're giving it a shot."

"Glad to hear it. Nothing like a soulmate. By the way, excuse the bumptious locale," he said, waving at their surroundings. "I thought it would have some special meaning. Anyway, I've freelanced a few times before for *Vanity Fair*, and I can't tell you how glad I am this worked out. I've been looking forward to it immensely. Especially given our shared connection."

David stared at him, dumbfounded.

"Our affection for Silas Hale," Barnaby clarified, as though it was too obvious to have to articulate. "It's a beautiful thing to get to write this profile with that link between us. And to be completely candid with a fellow scribbler, it has all but unmoored my own fiction writing."

"What has?"

"The loss of Silas. He was a north star for me, a beacon at sea. To know he's not here in this world anymore—that pains me each day. I really only understood the meaning of mentorship once he was gone. Each of my short stories I was crafting to perfection, word by word. On the strength of the buzz about my collection, I was finally going to get my fiction in the *Paris Review*, in the *New Yorker*, the last obstacles I still faced. Did you know Vladimir Nabokov didn't get a story into the *New Yorker* until he was forty-six? But I couldn't meet my publisher's deadlines anymore. I didn't trust my instincts without Silas. That's why I thought it was apt to meet up here, to commune in these hallowed environs, to remind us of where it started with Silas at Harvard."

"I didn't go to Harvard, Barnaby."

Barnaby took this in for a moment, then decided to ignore it. "Was just thinking of my experiences with Silas there. I just want that spirit infused in the profile, kind of to marinate in it, if that makes sense."

"I'm honored that we can do this together."

"No. I'm grateful to you, brother, that I have this opportunity." Barnaby took off his glasses, looking squarely into David's face. "In my rut, I need these gigs to fuel the tank. As I say, he was my mentor, and my inner compass feels shattered, its gears leaking all over the ground."

David gave a pained smile in reply. He sympathized with Barnaby's grief, but didn't want to lose sight of why he was there. "Barnaby, I have no experience with this. So how . . ."

"Worry not. You're in my hands. Let's order some grub on Condé Nast's tab and roll up our sleeves."

David exhaled. The tension passed pretty quickly, all things considered, so now he could enjoy the experience as planned. "I'm incredibly excited about this, Barnaby."

The conversation flowed much more easily than he would have expected, given Barnaby's personality, David jumping around from his writing routines to his childhood to the relationships that shaped him, extolling Bonnie for her nonprofit work with at-risk families, which provided perspective when he felt mired in creative problems. They laughed like old friends about the pros and cons of different Cambridge coffee shops and cafés, and David gave his rundown of favorites and his preferred times to frequent them. When interrupted by the servers, David was very careful about what he should order, knowing magazine profiles often detailed a subject's dining preferences. Philip Roth once commanded a *Vanity Fair* reporter not to divulge what he ordered from the menu at their lunch for that very reason, but David had no such leverage. Barnaby recommended the cheeseburger, which David agreed to. He wanted a Greek salad, but worried how that might translate onto the page. Probably something along the lines of: "He ordered the salad, forgoing the more substantial choices that were savored at the table by those living in the moment."

In response to a question about where he sought inspiration, he showed Barnaby some photos on his phone of his favorite streets and vistas in Cambridge. David talked about how he had always liked to visit footbridges in Cambridge, looking for the one immortalized by William Faulkner in *The Sound and the Fury* as the place where Quentin Compson jumped to his death, becoming a patron saint (albeit a fictional one) to struggling writers. "There's a plaque on one bridge, but there are reasons to think that's not actually the one Faulkner intended. So I alternate visiting the bridges, and jot down the details.

One day, maybe I'll find the right one, although there's an appeal in never knowing."

This seemed to please Barnaby. "That's brilliant. Brilliant! We should walk around to some of the bridges sometime so you can show me!"

No one had ever taken an interest in that habit since David had moved to Cambridge, and for once Barnaby helped him feel seen. "You got a deal."

The topic finally shifted to *The Crises* itself. Barnaby tapped a finger onto his copy. "I've been reading!"

"That means the world," David said, laughing nervously.

"So, your protagonist follows the advice of an inspirational speaker, but his start-up still goes bankrupt, then he tracks down the inspirational speaker before finding him in a crisis he has to help him out of. I got to say, just speaking for myself, I don't quite get it."

"Which part?"

"Take the last paragraph, and your protagonist's ultimate emotional landing spot. 'It was too great a loss.' It's a weakness in you, a form of cowardice, that you need to leave the reader with a flimsy reservoir of hope. Your instincts are old-fashioned, like you have an unconscious fantasy about having been a writer in another era. Look at this—two pivotal scenes in your book have the characters inside train stations. How many people still experience important points in their lives in train stations?"

"I wouldn't say . . ." David stammered.

"Don't misunderstand me. There's nothing wrong with the book, not at all, David." Barnaby grinned with an open, friendly air. "But whatever it is, it's certainly not *award* material. 'I thought of him as I found him at the station.' What is that? How does that challenge the world and the social structure? It's so normal. So normal. I wonder if you even know why— You must realize how normal it is."

David's skin heated with embarrassment. Barnaby's expression remained fixed. The dining room was busier, and servers were rushing around them.

"Barnaby, what . . . why . . ."

"You're in good hands, I promise. I just want to get to know you for this piece, David, backward and forward. Everything about you. I want to scrape below that harmless exterior and reach the real David Trent. I'm planning on reaching out to writers you've known, charting your whole experience, three hundred and sixty degrees of David."

He tensed. "That sounds . . ." He didn't finish the sentence, didn't know how to respond, or even exactly what he was responding to. "Thank you, Barnaby."

"Profiles can be intense! I appreciate that, and I understand that you might consider backing out—this is of course totally your prerogative. No hard feelings either way. My advice, though, is that now that you've given your commitment to *Vanity Fair*, the last thing you want to do is withdraw and be blacklisted not just by *Vanity Fair*, but by every Condé Nast publication. Plus your publisher would be, frankly, apoplectic, and rightfully so. They'd probably drop you on the spot. So I just want to do the best job I can. To get to know you and your every secret better than anyone ever has before. I want this experience to be definitive, to surround you, to reach inside your brain and pull it out to examine it."

He was still tapping the cover of *The Crises*, a little more forcefully with every stab of his finger. This time around, Barnaby reminded David of someone. He couldn't place it at first, then it struck him: the voice rasping and trembling when speaking to the waitstaff, the head tilted backward in superiority as he listened impatiently, the tight-fitting shirt beneath the heavy sweater. Barnaby was becoming Silas Hale.

"You know what?" Barnaby said. "Before we go, let's have a moment of silence together for Silas. Can we?"

Barnaby cleaned his eyeglasses with the heavy cloth napkin before returning them to his face. He tossed the napkin on the floor, then trapped David's left hand with his right palm, a gesture of quasi-prayer for Silas.

David barely restrained himself from interrupting the moment to use his free hand to pick up Barnaby's napkin before a server had to. In fact, he had to concentrate so intensely on not reaching for it that his hand began to tremble. Barnaby watched David, as though daring him to do it. The stalemate lasted twenty or thirty seconds that felt like an eternity. Finally one of the older servers noticed and stopped, struggling to stoop down in his stiff uniform. He handed Barnaby a fresh one, folded into a perfect triangle.

13

DAVID WAS OUT OF BALANCE. Barnaby had made his malicious intent clear. Or had he? Taking a walk by the Charles River, David tried to remember verbatim what Barnaby said and convince himself that there were alternative interpretations, and that those interpretations could be perfectly harmless.

I want to get to know you for this piece, David, backward and forward. Everything about you.

Wasn't that true of all magazine profiles, really?

To know you and your every secret better than anyone ever has before.

Boiled down, the job of the writer of a profile. Didn't mean that Barnaby actually suspected David of hiding some dark secret.

I want this experience to be definitive, to surround you, to reach inside your brain and pull it out to examine it.

Quality journalism for a quality magazine feature, however hyperbolic.

Bonnie, who had a half day at her office, was waiting by his door when he got home, anxious to hear about the journalist and their conversation.

"I actually know him already," David said. "His name is Barnaby."

"That's even better! He's nice?"

David tried to be as open with Bonnie as possible since their reconciliation, but he also couldn't explain everything without pulling her into places he didn't want to go. "He really wants to do a good job with this one, I think."

David had received an email from his publicist, asking him to call to check in, and he excused himself from Bonnie to make the call from his balcony overlooking the river.

"How was lunch?" she asked.

"I think it went well. Hard to tell."

"You kept him hooked?"

He hesitated. "I think so."

"Our marketing team is really excited about *Vanity Fair*. In fact, the whole office is. Great work, David."

The whole office! It made him feel sick to think of it. He also received an unexpected email from Craig Stanton, one of his former MFA professors that he kept in touch with from time to time. Stanton had always been polite though never overly interested in David's writing.

Congrats about Vanity Fair doing a story! was the subject heading. David stared at this, trying to understand how Craig knew.

Opening the email, David discovered that Barnaby had reached out to interview Craig and, the email implied, several other faculty members. David typed a reply to Craig, asking if he knew anyone else Barnaby had interviewed, and insisting on knowing every question Barnaby had asked him. His mind raced in circles. Could looking into his experience at graduate school lead Barnaby to wonder about Melody Bradshaw's recommendation? But in an instant he convinced himself that he was making a dramatic leap. It was years ago now; nobody had any reason to remember one of his recommendations. Admissions was a separate department from the teaching faculty, and personnel in the admissions office had probably turned over two or three times in the years since he applied. David knew he had a habit of drawing attention to things he didn't want attention drawn to, with his tendency to ask questions.

David deleted his entire interrogatory email draft, instead writing in its place: Thanks, Craig! I'm excited and appreciate you helping out!

He had two other messages of note waiting for him. One was an email that came from Rebecca Hale, who seemed confused about how to use email. Is this your correct email address? she asked. She said it was important they speak in person. Then he received a text from Brandi, asking to meet for dinner. He couldn't guess what she wanted, but was content to arrange any kind of distraction. At her suggestion, they met in Harvard Square in a cavernous spot dotted with decorative casks, where diners sat at picnic-style tables. It was dark, and David was satisfied with feeling that he blended into the noisy crowd, just another mildly disaffected twentysomething in a fleece scarfing down truffle fries.

He couldn't remember Brandi ever being so friendly and complimentary. Though he had never thought that she harbored any romantic interest in him, for the first ten minutes he began to wonder. He was considering slipping into the conversation that he and Bonnie had patched things up when Brandi shifted gears.

"This reminds me of an Irish pub," she said. "Order another truffle fries, if you see the waiter? It's all comped. Hmm, I wish I were from Belfast. Don't you?"

"What?"

"You're from New Jersey, right?"

"No," he said, impatient. "Michigan."

She purred with fascination. "I always forget that about you. It's like being from nowhere, a bit."

"How?"

"What?"

"How is the food comped?"

"*Boston Magazine* is doing a write-up on the place as a new hot spot. They have a writer here somewhere."

"That gets us free food?"

"The manager wanted a lot of people here tonight so the magazine would do a good write-up about the vibes. I went to boarding school with her. She asked me to bring someone, and I thought of you." She sighed, annoyed at his confused expression. "Haven't we been friends for years?"

He wasn't entirely sure they had ever been more than acquaintances.

"Being profiled in *Vanity Fair* is a big deal, David," she said, adding her sly purr. "It doesn't hurt to be out there more in the public eye."

"How do you know about that? About the *Vanity Fair* profile?"

"Barnaby interviewed me."

"He did?"

"Does that surprise you that much?" She gave an offended huff. "He said he's interviewing everyone who knows you. Don't I count? And to think I introduced you to him, and you got him to profile you. You do remember it was me that connected the two of you, right?"

"Did he say I *convinced* him to get *Vanity Fair* to profile me?"

Brandi paused to think before answering. "No, I guess he didn't say that, come to think of it. He did say he pitched you to *Vanity Fair* when they put a call out to their freelancers to write about debut novelists. I just assumed you'd nudged him."

It threw every choice by Barnaby back into a potentially more sinister light. Barnaby hadn't been assigned to write about him; he had brought the idea to *Vanity Fair*. "No, Brandi," David said curtly. "I didn't nudge. I didn't know about it until I heard from my Parable publicist."

"Who cares, right?" Grabbing his arm turned into lightly punching it. She was looking around, maybe for truffle fries, maybe for the

Boston Magazine writer or photographer. "This may sound incoherent, and in a way it is, but with the right exposure, I wouldn't need to depend on audiences liking my plays. It's about me, not them—if it's about them, then it minimizes the art. Does that make sense? I've always worried that if the public enjoys something too much, maybe it means less."

"Did he say who he was interviewing?"

"What?"

"Barnaby. Did he say who else he was talking to for the profile?"

"No, not to me," she said, then seemed to reconsider. "Actually, he mentioned one name. Melody Bradshaw."

"What about her?"

"That he was talking to her about you. Can you stop thinking about yourself for a second, man?"

Brandi wanted to complain about her parents and to vent about other playwrights who had unfair advantages. David managed to appear to be listening. All the while, his mind reeled back to the disastrous end-of-the-year party, when he had stupidly bragged to Barnaby about knowing Melody. It was possible that Barnaby was just collecting quotes for the profile from writers who knew David. But the combination of Barnaby's questions to David's MFA professors and his reaching Melody gripped David's mind and made him want to get away from Brandi as soon as he could.

His thoughts balanced on a tightrope between being convinced that Barnaby was trying to sabotage him, and feeling reassured that he was just an extremely thorough journalist.

On Wednesday morning David entered Simon's Coffee Shop on Massachusetts Avenue. The café was the shape of a railroad car, and as David scoped out the choice of tables, there was Barnaby, sipping foam from an oversize mug. David could have collapsed on the spot. His routine. He had told Barnaby about his café rotation in detail, answering questions that anyone but a writer would find tedious but that David had thought were flattering, a reflection of the importance he had waited to reach his whole life.

Simon's hot oatmeal maple scone and London Fog, always picks me up midweek when things otherwise feel like a grind. David had said that, or something like it, as he'd rambled with unbridled self-importance at the Harvard Club. On Barnaby's table now was a pastry with a tan glaze that David would recognize anywhere: maple scone. Transfixed as he was, it took a moment before David realized that Barnaby's table was pushed together with another one. His companion's back was to David.

"Hi, can I help you?"

David shoved his gray wool baseball cap as far down on his face as possible, bending the brim to further block his face. He continued to stare across the café.

"Hello?" the barista tried again.

"Sorry, still deciding," David said, dropping into a chair where he sat sidesaddle, resting his head on his hand, his fingers splayed to partially block his face but still let him watch Barnaby. There were three small tables between him and Barnaby's table, allowing David to position himself behind enough obstructions to remain hidden.

Barnaby's raven-haired companion briefly swiveled to reach for something, and he could see her in profile. It was Leni from Silas's holiday party. Valentina Maldenado. She seemed to be doing the talking. Barnaby's expression and body language looked serious, even somber. Leni mirrored this back. David desperately wanted to get closer, to overhear even a snippet of what they were saying, but every moment he stayed increased the risk that one of them would spot him. He jumped out of his seat and, turning his back on the scene, slipped out the door between two customers who were entering.

Back at his apartment, David tried to recall everything he had said to Leni at the Hales' party, and vice versa, before Lee Van Knox had told him who Leni was and that he had brought her there to reveal to her that she was the rightful winner of the award. She had volunteered the fact that she had met Barnaby before—and that she despised him. What could they have been commiserating about at Simon's? If Barnaby was trying to plant ideas in Leni's head, who knew how quickly that would lead to questions about David's award, and then . . .

Everywhere he went, David expected Barnaby to show up. He tried telling himself that, like all the writers in the area, Barnaby had his own rotation of cafés, some of which overlapped with his, but he didn't believe that, certainly not after seeing him with Leni. He received an email from his publicist arranging a follow-up interview with Barnaby for two days later. David ignored it, prompting her to call.

"Didn't you get my email?" she asked. "We need to confirm the follow-up with the *Vanity Fair* writer."

"Is it necessary to meet again? I already talked to Barnaby for a pretty long time."

She gasped in horror. "David, what do you mean? It's great he wants to talk to you more. Why would you hesitate?"

"I guess I just want to refocus on my writing."

"If they need more material, it might become an even longer profile. Every inch of real estate in an issue of *Vanity Fair* is worth its weight in gold. You have your whole life ahead of you to disappear into your writing."

She gave him the details of where to meet Barnaby, which he pretended to jot down, though he remembered them from the email. By arranging the meeting through the publisher, Barnaby had made it impossible for David to duck the sit-down.

In the meantime, David decided to do some digging on Barnaby, hoping to find information that could keep him at bay. During his dinner with Brandi, he'd considered that she knew Barnaby better than him, and had squeezed in a few innocuous questions about him. Now he planted a seed with Jace to find out what he could about Barnaby from other writers Jace knew, using the excuse that he wanted to respond to questions in their interviews in ways that kept Barnaby's level of interest high. (Jace, for his part, complained that Barnaby had not asked to interview *him* about David.) In a few other conversations with local writers, David casually threw in a question or two about Barnaby, then feigned indifference to the answers.

He heard again and again that Barnaby was considered one of the most gifted and brilliant writers around Boston, that he was destined for fame, and of course that he was Silas Hale's protégé and heir apparent. He was also able to gradually piece together that Silas had been a kind of unofficial editor for Barnaby's short story manuscript, reading and commenting on the stories before they were sent to the publisher. After Silas's death, Barnaby apparently went into a creative tailspin, as he already had alluded to during the Harvard Club lunch. Before long, the publishing contract for the collection was canceled, and he was asked to pay back his advance.

Being asked to return an advance from a publisher was a writer's nightmare. When the scenario came up, a writer's voice would drop into a whisper, as if talking about a terminal diagnosis. But in reality it happened so rarely that it was largely a literary bogeyman. David wouldn't have believed it had happened to Barnaby had he not heard it from two informants.

When David next sorted through his mail, he found an envelope with a company on the return address that he didn't recognize. Opening this, he found a printed letter.

Hi David,
We met at Silas Hale's party. I would like to speak with you, if possible. Please stop by my office at your convenience, anytime during work hours. Address below.

The letter was signed "Leni (Valentina) Maldenado." Below, she had written in a hurried postscript.

P.S. Congratulations on the award

14

DAVID LIT THE CORNER OF the letter on the stovetop's blue-orange flame and watched in a daze as the words disappeared. He smothered the burning paper under his shoe.

With the incineration he'd intended to wipe Leni's request out of his mind, pretend he'd never seen it. The idea of going anywhere near her or her office horrified him. But he also had to cling to the hope that whatever Barnaby wanted from Leni, whatever Barnaby tried to convince her about him or the award, it could be reversed. If there was any window of time to sway her, he needed to try, no matter how objectionable the notion of facing her.

Arriving at a massive glass-and-concrete tower in the tangle of Boston's financial district, David felt small and gauche in his zip-up sweater and sneakers. He thought of himself as a stowaway whenever he entered a corporate setting. Even the air in the building seemed different, colder and purer, which must have galvanized some people but made him feel anxious and lost. He followed the directories on the wall and elevator banks to Colony Mutual, the company on the letterhead she had sent him, which was now ashes. He had to go in and then out of the elevator twice before he figured out that he had to select his destination on a screen outside the elevator, which then assigned him a specific elevator to ride up. Was the purpose efficiency, or intimidation?

At the Colony lobby, he was pointed toward a corridor lined with offices, and then a receptionist directed him to another door that was propped partially open. In a small room Leni, her hair tied up, tapped at her keyboard, pausing to roll her head backward in a neck stretch. She wore a crimson blazer. He stood for a moment watching her in stunned amazement, not at her but at himself, for coming this far. He knocked lightly.

"Just a second, please," she said without looking up, then held up one finger. "Let me get this email out." She finally looked up. "Yes?" For a moment she showed no recognition. "Oh, David! Your hair is longer, maybe? You got my note."

And burned it. "I did. Is this a good time?"

"Sorry, it's one of those days. You probably don't even remember me."

"Of course I do." Right away, he worried he'd spoken too emphatically, suggesting he had reasons to think about her. "I really enjoyed our chat that night. Should I . . ." He gestured to the door.

"Please," she said, signaling to close it, which made his heart skip. Whatever bomb she was going to drop, she wanted privacy. Was she recording the conversation? He couldn't ask, not without giving away how scared he was of what might be said. "Six years here and I've only had my own office for a year. My forays into writing fiction kept me sane for a while, though to be fair, some might debate whether that ever worked."

From the time he'd spent with Leni at the Hales' party, David remembered her sarcastic and personable demeanor, tinged with insecurity. She still seemed easy to talk to, but beyond the surface banter, she struck him as a little more distant. Perhaps that was a prelude to anger, or to whatever accusation had led her to ask him to come, or maybe it was nothing more than a reflection of the professional atmosphere of climate-controlled offices. He scanned the desk and shelves. Among the rows of reference books, there was a lonely copy of Leni's novel, *Crisis*, the estranged twin to his own novel. It leaned between a plain black binder labeled ANNUAL RATES and a book called *Concepts and Coverage: Risk Management.*

"You all right?" She glanced over her shoulder to follow his gaze at the shelves behind her.

He pretended to be looking elsewhere. "It's a great office."

"How is Bonnie?"

He was thrown.

"Sorry," she continued, "I remember everything I ever hear—it's a curse. You mentioned her when we met. Anyway, thank you for stopping by. Your name actually came up recently, a useful coincidence."

"Oh?" She didn't say who brought up his name, but he knew full well it was Barnaby.

"I should explain why I asked you to meet me." She laughed a sharp little laugh, nearly impaling him with suspense. "That would help, right? Silas Hale had a sizable life insurance policy through Colony Mutual. I've been assigned to the internal inquiry into his death."

"I don't understand. From what I know, he had hypertension and died of a heart attack. Why would there be an inquiry?"

"You're right. But our auditors concluded that his medical condition was partially caused by his incarceration. That's where things get a bit complicated. If Silas's death was facilitated by his incarceration, and his incarceration resulted from the commission of a crime, then our insurance will decline to pay his beneficiary." She leaned forward with a conspiratorial air. "Colony Mutual would love to save that chunk of change."

"That's too bad for the Hales."

"It's a downer. But it's not even so cut-and-dried. Because he died, the state's criminal case was never concluded in the courts. The case ended there, as far as the legal system is concerned, with no answers.

So Colony Mutual is left to determine for itself whether a preponderance of evidence available to us points to Silas Hale as being responsible for Lee Van Knox's death. If it does, then the company won't pay a dime to his family; if not, it will."

"So once he died, you and the insurance company became the cops and prosecutors rolled into one."

"In a nutshell," she said.

David's gaze shifted to a cardboard box on the floor, filled with file folders, labeled on the side with marker HALE, S.

She saw where he was looking. "The case documents."

His hands fidgeted as he stared at the box. He wondered what was in there about him, or what details could be connected to him if someone looked closely enough. A gratifying image came into his mind. He would grab the box and run out the door with it. Leni wasn't law enforcement; she couldn't arrest him. What could she do? The thrill produced by the scenario was fleeting, once its absurdity became clear.

"Are those files from the police investigation?" Even as he asked it, the question sounded clumsy, suspiciously prying even to his own ear. Was it normal that someone might ask her that? She didn't seem to wonder, thankfully.

"Police don't usually share their case files. Colony, like all insurance companies, actually, uses private investigators in these kinds of situations, to get their hands on what they can here and there. At the same time, our lawyers apply for access to various court records, which are easier to obtain than whatever the police compiled themselves."

Court records, at least, would have been focused on proving Silas's part in Lee Van Knox's death. David felt a fresh wave of relief that he had made himself so useless to the district attorney's office. It was possible that nothing inside that box referred to him at all, except perhaps in an ancillary way, since the police timeline had indicated that he was not even living at Observatory Hill at the time of the murder.

"I made the mistake of mentioning to my boss that I met Silas Hale," Leni continued. "As soon as the powers-that-be heard that, they assigned me the case. Even though my interaction with Silas was limited to him barking orders at us at that holiday party."

"That's not some kind of conflict of interest, that you met him?"

"No such thing as recusals in insurance investigations." She rolled her eyes. "Maybe they also thought that because I wrote my little novel in my previous life and taught a few writing classes as an adjunct professor, I would have some insight into writers. As I mentioned, when your name came up recently, it was brought to my mind that you lived in the Hales' household for a time. While you were writing your book, right?"

"I lived above them, actually. The top floor is a unit that gets rented out. Someone else owned that part of the house. We lived there for a while, a bit less than a year and a half. My novel"—he froze up momentarily, wishing he could talk about anything in the world other than his book to her—"was really mostly finished by the time we moved in."

"You knew Lee Van Knox?"

"Casually."

She seemed to be waiting for more, then nodded. "Same. I met him a few times at writers' conferences. He was actually the one to invite me to the Hales' party. I ran into him outside—he was arriving as I left. Really surreal. I sometimes think about that."

The way she stretched out her last sentence made it sound meaningful, a lingering sentiment in quest of resolution.

Fearing the silence, David jumped in with, "He seemed nice," then regretted it. "Like you said."

She hadn't said that, but she nodded in agreement. The point seemed to make her think about her writing days. "He told me he was a fan of my writing. I think if you really admire someone's writing, you should make sure to avoid meeting them. Which reminds me, I need to pick a chapter." She glanced at her novel on the shelf, then noticed David's look of confusion. "Sorry! Ignore me, I'm just talking to myself."

"A chapter of your novel?"

"It's nothing. Eight or nine months ago a friend of mine started planning a series of readings in a bar in Newton, and I made the mistake of agreeing to be one of her guinea pigs and read a chapter out loud. She's calling her series Pages in a Pub, or something god-awful like that. It seemed impossibly far away, but now it's coming up. Not sure if you'd have any interest in coming . . ."

"Oh."

"Sorry, that was pushy. Crowds make me vomit, so it would be nice to have friendly faces. No pressure, of course."

"Not at all, that sounds great," he said, feeling a twinge in the pit of his stomach, though at least the topic seemed to have migrated further away from Silas and Van Knox.

Her jaw tensed for a moment. "I'm curious about something, David, if you don't mind. What's your opinion of when Lee Van Knox's death occurred? I'm guessing you followed the story in the news. Do you think it really happened almost a month after we saw Lee at the party?"

He paused so that he would appear to be mulling this over. "I never stopped to think about it much. That's what the police figured out, wasn't it? I have to be honest, I'm feeling pretty worthless to you right about now. I wish I could be helpful."

She shook her head. "It's not your responsibility. I just started thinking that some of the writers who knew Silas, like you and Barnaby Masters, might have insights that have been missed before."

"Did Barnaby Masters contact you?"

She seemed thrown by the question. "Contact me? No, no. The

other way around. I needed to talk to him about this, so I asked to meet with him. Silas Hale was Barnaby's mentor, after all, so his name cropped up on these lists of people to chat with. Funny, I remember Barnaby wouldn't give me the time of day at that party."

"Mentor," David couldn't stop himself from muttering resentfully. Leni looked back at him with a quizzical expression, but he piled on to it quickly, trying to test her opinion without incriminating himself. "Barnaby can be a handful."

She ignored the bait. "When I met him recently, he mentioned he was writing an article about you. And that your novel has been getting attention since winning your award? Congrats, again!"

He felt his face burn, imagining it bright red, before pivoting to check the time. "Speaking of writing . . ."

"Of course! I should let you get back to it."

Another round of small talk closed their conversation, as if they had never been speaking about anything morbid. But emblazoned in his thoughts was that one word, *when*, and her preoccupation with the timeline of Van Knox's death. It had been fleeting, but the single word had gravitational pull. He couldn't stop thinking it ironic that if Leni's writing career had succeeded, she might have left her insurance company job, and wouldn't be inquiring into the death of Silas Van Knox, which in turn was jeopardizing David's future. She could destroy him.

The day approached for the next Barnaby meeting. David contemplated not showing up, claiming a last-minute illness, which Parable certainly couldn't blame him for. But that would do nothing to prevent further conversation between Leni and Barnaby, and the more the two of them compared notes about Silas, or about him, the higher the risk that one of them could pull a thread that unraveled everything. He knew that this time he would have to confront Barnaby and demand to know the real intention of writing his profile.

As he descended into the cramped, dimly lit brick basement of Grendel's Den, Barnaby rose from a table and waved him over. "Thanks for doing this, David, I have more questions and thought it would be easier to sit down in person again instead of asking by email or on the phone."

"I have questions of my own this time, Barnaby."

"Get off your feet, brother, please. I already ordered the loaded nachos, I thought you wouldn't mind. Did you know this little place used to have a whole floor above this? Down here people hid from themselves or someone else, while the people above thought they were the ones who deserved the light. But the place shrank down to its rightful form, a dark corner where man takes shelter from the universe."

David resisted even considering whether these observations might be insightful. "I'm not in the mood, Barnaby."

"Menu?" Barnaby asked. They were each ignoring what the other was saying.

"Thanks, not hungry."

"I received something very interesting from your MFA program. Between you and me, the schools aren't really supposed to share these things, but some of those administrators at writing programs are writers themselves. I find writers can be corrupted in return for the smallest favors."

Barnaby had a pile of manila file folders on the table, which he fanned out like a Vegas dealer. One folder was labeled MFA. Others that David could make out were OBSERVATORY HILL and THE CRISES. While David was trying to scan the folders, he also noticed that there were three table settings. They could have been there before they came, he told himself. But then he realized that there were three glasses filled with water.

Barnaby continued opening and closing folders. "I have to stay more organized when I'm reporting than I do with my fiction."

The Award

David rose to his feet, poised to leave.

Barnaby looked up, but not at David. "Ah, here she is."

Melody Bradshaw was hurrying in, a whirlwind with two silk scarves flowing around her. "So sorry to be late. You have to tell me something is starting forty minutes earlier, Barn, otherwise I'm bound to be the last to stumble in, like Chelone."

"David," Barnaby said, "you're familiar with Chelone, the Greek goddess of hesitation and tardiness?"

Melody interrupted Barnaby's chance to lecture him about antiquity by kissing him on the cheek, then turned to David with a big, bright smile and gave him an even bigger, more enthusiastic kiss.

"You!" she said with the first kiss, and then again with the second. "Two of my favorite writers, what a treat." She sat, forcing David to return to his seat. "What an occasion."

David raised his eyebrows, prompting her to clarify.

"A *Vanity Fair* profile! Incredibly exciting, David. That's career-defining, my dear. If I had that at your age, but how old are—no, don't tell me, I'll become lightheaded!"

Barnaby slapped the table. "I love it, love this energy. Isn't this great to have Melody with us, David?"

David swallowed hard, taking a sip of water to hide his nerves and his rage at Barnaby. "Incredible."

"I'll cut to the chase," Barnaby jumped in. "I really want to get under David's skin for the piece, really say to the world, 'This is the David Trent you never knew, and after reading this, you'll never forget him.'"

"Love that," Melody said. "What we need as we all cope with Silas's loss is to cherish each other and celebrate and lift up the writers around us."

"Couldn't agree more. I've been talking to the writers who had influence on David, and you were on the top of the list, Melody."

"I'm honored," Melody said.

"I wanted some insights into the strengths you saw in him so early on. I understand you worked with him at a few conferences back in the day, and wrote a recommendation, and I'm hoping there are memories to extract."

She nodded enthusiastically at the mention of the conferences, then stopped, tilting her head a little. "Recommendation?"

"See, I'm chronicling David's journey to his MFA program. What I noticed was that his cohort's admission cycle happened right around the time of your back-to-back fellowships in Prague and Florence, Melody. I can only imagine what a blur that period was, and wonder how you managed to fit in anything else."

Melody seemed lost, her cheeks coloring.

"Anyhow," Barnaby went on with increasing animation, "I was fortunate enough to connect with some of David's MFA faculty. It's not Iowa, but they're punching above their weight. They're excited for exposure for David as a success story for their little program. In fact, one of the junior faculty was kind enough to bend the rules and send me parts of David's application for admission. Just a real treasure trove of insight into your mental space, brother."

David jumped in: "I really don't want to spend Melody's time on these minutia, Barnaby—"

Barnaby spoke over him. "Here's what I thought would be great. Melody, I want to get your impressions when you look back at your recommendation for David years later, and then I can record what it brings to mind. No objections?" He indicated his portable digital recorder, and lightly tapped a red button with obvious relish.

"Really, Melody, Barnaby and I never discussed whether you'd be up for all this," David said. "It's an imposition." The red light on the recorder took on a demonic hue.

"It's for the best, brother," Barnaby said. "And for this exercise, it's best if you stay . . . invisible."

The Award

Barnaby slid a document from his MFA folder across the table to Melody. She stared down at it for a moment, her eyes narrowing. One hand on the folder, she slid it closer to her, then flipped the cover open, staring down.

"This is—"

Barnaby was giddy, delighting in what he had to say, which he seemed to have practiced beforehand in a mirror. "That's your recommendation for David."

She pushed the folder and paper back toward Barnaby by a few inches. "Hold on." She dug through her purse.

Barnaby watched David squirm. All the while, David tried to incline his head imperceptibly to see if the printout of the recommendation included the fake email address that David had used, which would have spelled the end of the charade as soon as she looked down. He didn't spot one, but he couldn't be sure.

"I need my other glasses for this. I'm not as young as my author photo." Melody swapped her glasses, though the prescription seemed wrong or outdated, as she had to move the page farther and then closer before she finally started to read.

Time stood still for David. Melody's face, usually a constant flow of expressions, seemed to freeze up entirely as she read. She paused at several points in order to read a phrase or two out loud. "Impressed with his ability to convey passion through prose," she read. "Sparkles with erudite storytelling." It went on to discuss some detailed points about a short story of David's, insights David had taken from Melody's actual evaluation for the story at a conference. ". . . A tendency toward dogmatic ideas around literary style." David had remembered that when they talked at the writing conference, Melody had said she detested the use of towards instead of toward, even though both were technically correct. Now as she read it, that word *toward* stuck in his ear. Had she stalled, reading that word?

Could David have had it backward years ago—could she have detested the word *toward* and insisted on using *towards*? Had that one letter had just exposed him?

When she finished reading, she removed her reading glasses with a sharp, sweeping gesture. The restaurant seemed to go silent. "Barnaby, if you don't mind, I just . . ." She took a long, deep breath, then turned away from the paper and looked right at David. "I need to say something to you," she said, her voice unsteady. Then she choked back a sob. "This makes me so happy."

"What?"

"I'm so glad I helped even in this small way to boost a young writer's voice."

"But this recommendation . . ." Barnaby started. "You were abroad, and I had heard you were totally off grid during that period."

"This is off the record, Barnaby, my love. But I was such a mess at that time in my life. I had overcommitted myself to travel and teaching, I had contracts with two different publishers that weren't supposed to overlap but did, my marriage was falling apart before my eyes, I was robbing Peter to pay Paul, creatively and emotionally speaking, and on a bad mixture of antidepressants that wasn't exactly kosher. I barely knew up from down for two years. I just thank heavens I was even able to find time to get things done for other people when so much fell through the cracks. That makes my heart sing, and I thank you for digging that up, Barnaby. I've done so many recommendations for students and writers in my career, and reading this reminds me of my thoughts from first discovering David's fiction at those conferences."

She grabbed David's hand across the table. "I knew you when, buddy. You better remember that!"

He reinflated. He could see that Barnaby was not convinced. Still, for the first time since Barnaby had invaded his life, David had managed to block his move, to knock him down on his face, and he basked in the immensity of his satisfaction. Barnaby was stuck. David could seize control over his life again.

"Melody," he said, warmly gripping her hand in return, "your mentorship always meant the world to me."

Now her sobs took over. David got up and hugged her, holding a staredown with Barnaby over her shoulder as she wept.

15

THE VICTORY REVITALIZED DAVID'S DAILY routine, as his fears that Barnaby would be lurking around corners everywhere in Cambridge dissipated. He phoned in to a scheduled radio interview about his novel for a small market in Wisconsin. It went well, as though he knew every question before the slow-speaking host finished asking. Radio bookers tended to copy each other, and several other radio interviews followed over the next few days.

After some thought, David decided to attend Leni's reading at the bar in Newton; avoiding it could make him conspicuous. He was one of a dozen or so friends and acquaintances of Leni and the other three readers to show up. The bar was too spacious to make for a good reading space, since only those sitting in a section off to the side would see the event. Leni's former college roommate, the host, gave long, disorganized introductions before each reader took a stool and read an excerpt. David noticed the command Leni had, even sitting sidesaddle on a wobbly stool in this dimly lit room better made for any other purpose. She exhibited no sense of self-importance, nor was she apologetic for using anyone's time, as one of the other writers was. She opened *Crisis* to a dog-eared page—what writers dog-eared their own books? Most treated them like sacred objects—

and began reading with a steady, startling intimacy. Everything else fell away as he listened.

Leni read: "It is generous to call it a plan. Call it what it is, a long shout into the darkness. She remembers a Christmas Eve childhood conversation with her sister verbatim, or at least she thinks she remembers it that well, every word and mutual shriek. Something in those giggling talks under a blanket fort, she wants to believe, will tell her where to find Sissy today. The people who say Sissy went missing do not understand. They cannot close their eyes and see her, so real, three inches from their face, her breath a peppermint cloud that never fades. Anything but missing."

Leni read for just over fifteen minutes, and David could have listened for another hour. When she was finished, Leni said, "That's all for my reading—actually that's all I'll be writing."

David gasped, and wondered if anyone had heard him. He could not trust himself after that. He quivered slightly from the emotion in Leni's voice and her words. When the next writer started reading, David pretended he had to be somewhere else, catching Leni's eye and pointing to a nonexistent wristwatch while waving. She mouthed *Thank you* and waved goodbye with both hands.

DAVID JUDGED IT PLAUSIBLE THAT Barnaby had decided to back off altogether after their evening underground at Grendel's Den. Bonnie was spending a couple nights every week at David's place in Cambridge, and he insisted on going to her apartment in Brookline on other nights so they could spend more time together without her feeling inconvenienced.

She came home with an especially bright smile and immediately kissed him, which qualified as an unusual rush toward affection, considering that their dynamic was still being rebuilt. He beamed.

"Well, good news," she said with pride.

"Tell me!"

"I did it."

"Great. What did you do?"

"I took care of it!"

The comment sank in slowly before striking him as strange and possibly important.

"Sorry, Bon, you've lost me. What did you take care of?"

"Barnaby."

His voice cracked when he repeated the name. "Barnaby?"

She nodded solemnly. She explained that Barnaby Masters had contacted her to tell her that his editor at *Vanity Fair* might pull the plug on the whole profile unless he quickly whipped up some more personal angles about David.

How did he get her number? The question rumbled in his head before he remembered handing his phone to Barnaby at the Harvard Club, letting him swipe through his photos and take notes on places that gave David his inspiration.

"He said you had given him my number. I called you a couple times right after he called me to see what you'd want me to say, but you didn't answer, and he said his schedule was tight. That it was now or never."

David forgot he'd turned his phone off during another radio interview call-in earlier in the day.

"You shouldn't have—"

"I was about to apologize and tell him that I couldn't do anything without speaking to you."

He sighed with relief.

"David, don't worry. I realized I could not jeopardize *Vanity Fair*. So I said yes. I was able to leave work early and stop at the coffee shop where he said to meet him. It was no problem, and it went really well. I was thrilled to help."

He couldn't believe what he was hearing. "What personal angle was Barnaby talking about?"

She blinked at him, surprised at his worried expression. "He wanted to know a little more about our life at home when you were finishing your novel. About our time staying at Observatory Hill. He was interested in how the Hales treated us, and how you overcame difficulties."

"What did you tell him?" In his head, he screamed the question, but caught himself and somehow managed to sound calm.

"Just the truth. I told him they refused to put on the heat in the winter, and that despite it becoming virtually unlivable, you never let it throw off your writing and publishing plans. It's a testament to you. David, no matter what came between us back then, I never stopped admiring how you wouldn't waver about chasing your dreams. You know that?"

"What did he say?"

"About what?"

"The heat, the house. What did Barnaby say about any of it?" He fumbled his determination to control his tone, his voice beginning to hint at his internal hysteria.

"He said in reporting the story, he had to gather even seemingly minor details, so I went over some of the temperatures I recorded. . . . I'd remind you, David, that we're talking about Silas Hale. Rest in peace, but he was a murderer!"

"Was he?" he blurted out.

"You're right, he never had his day in court. Not for us to pass judgment. Still, come on, we don't have to pull punches. Our heating is a pretty small matter compared to homicide, but it shows strength of character that you never used that as an excuse, never abandoned your goals during a critical time, even when I couldn't handle it. David, I never mentioned our rocky period, if you're worried about that. Are you upset?"

He had leaped to his feet and paced in front of her. Then he took her by the shoulders. "Of course not." He hugged her. "Thank you so much for jumping in with no notice. I'm just sorry you were inconvenienced."

She drew her hand across his forehead. "You're sweating."

"I'm nervous about the article."

"You told me Barnaby was doing a good job," she said, still trying to feel out his reaction.

"Right. He is. I'm glad you got to meet him. He can just be intense."

"I noticed that. But think about it from his side. This article obviously means a lot to him, too. And for you, this is what we've been waiting to happen for you for so long, you are not letting it slip away. Don't think for a second I'd let that happen."

She hugged him again, and David realized in that moment that despite Bonnie's always accommodating and sunny exterior, she could not be crossed. A person who believed in innate goodness could not forgive someone who failed that test. All along, she had needed to feel a sense of justice about the heating situation, which she still vaguely blamed for breaking their engagement. Indirectly, by sitting down with Barnaby, she had taken her revenge on Silas.

How would she feel about David if she found out what he had done?

When they were embracing, at least, Bonnie couldn't see the panic on his face. She couldn't understand, of course, anything about how Barnaby had used her against him. Even David couldn't quite assess the damage or guess precisely what Barnaby was after. It was dizzying. Bonnie had an early day the next morning, so she planned to stay the night at her own place. David managed to be cheerful until she made her way out.

He also had not had the heart yet to tell Bonnie about the state of his finances. He didn't want her to volunteer to help him. Between his lifestyle in the months after receiving the award, and paying Cambridge rent on his own, plus using all his energies toward trying to block Barnaby's moves, leaving no time to track his overall budget, he was sinking into the red fast. He had to take money out of a small retirement account that he had opened when he worked at the marketing start-up. He would have to leave his apartment within months, if not weeks.

What he feared most was that whatever unknown details Barnaby discovered or thought he'd discovered, he had been sharing them with Leni. David was startled but hardly shocked, then, when Leni sent a text asking if he could meet her in the early evening outside an Indian restaurant twenty minutes' walk from Harvard Square.

He had no choice but to go. He paused in front of the restaurant to steel himself before entering. For a fleeting moment, he decided to leave, to just stand her up and deal with the aftermath. He turned to go at the same moment Leni appeared on the sidewalk.

"Did today suddenly get much colder, or is it me?" she asked. "We all love putting on our coats in October, and then soon enough autumn laughs at you for forgetting what's coming. Slaps you in the face."

"Leni. Good to see you. Want to go inside?"

"Actually, sorry, I didn't have a chance to explain, David. I didn't want to get into it over text, but I was hoping you'd come to my office with me. We could order food there. There's some sensitive things I wanted to show you, so I thought it would be better to do it on a weekend, after hours."

He looked around, still wondering if he might be better off to walk away. "Into Boston?"

"I know it's a pain. But if you don't mind, T fare is on me."

Now he understood she had asked to meet outside the Indian place, not to eat there, but because it was near an entrance to a T station, part of the scattershot system of Boston-area subway lines.

They walked to the entrance and then together descended a steep escalator that seemed to never end. Between the two escalators was a sculptural installation of bronze work gloves tumbling down the length of the ride. Some people had left their own work gloves on the sculpture, either as a tribute to it or to mock it.

Inside the dark station, David and Leni found they had just missed a train, its rear light dimming and fading down the black tunnel. An announcement soon came on that their T line was experiencing delays, and there would be an extended wait.

The suspense he felt about what Leni was going to tell him became excruciating. If Barnaby had already shared with her the new information that he had extracted from Bonnie, she could have connected new dots using that big box of court files she kept in her office.

"I feel bad to stretch this out," she said, her meaning hanging for him ominously in the air. "It's like waiting for water to boil, isn't it? Looking for that train light to come through a tunnel."

He was lightheaded, imagining what he would feel when he finally found out what was in store. Despair, dread, regret, probably. It was appropriate, somehow, that Leni was the one who would pull that final lever to seal his fate, a writer with the natural abilities, the special qualities, the creative poise, he'd wished for.

"I'm getting off my feet," he said, taking a seat on the bench by the wall, set back several feet from the platform.

"I'll look out for the train. Thanks for being such a good sport, David."

A computer-generated voice emitted another announcement about the delay, prompting the last few passengers waiting to give up and leave, leaving the section of the station desolate, somehow managing to match David's emotional state. Leni stood by the tracks, stubbornly, impatiently fixated on one end of the tunnel.

He closed his eyes. He considered all the possible outcomes of Leni bringing him after hours to the office. She might have wanted to give him one last chance to explain what she had finally realized, after her immersion in the records, was the truth. But he had trouble believing that, and he also had trouble convincing himself it was worth the risk to try to sway her. Barnaby's discovery must have added to her earlier suspicions about the timeline of Van Knox's death, which could only mean one thing. There were no ways left to stop what was coming.

He rose to his feet and took a few slow, measured steps toward her and the tracks, a macabre march upon the platform that vibrated slightly underfoot.

"So sorry about this, David," she called back to him without looking. "I feel terrible to pop up out of the blue, then make you wait this long. Don't hate me."

"I don't," he said, probably too quietly for her to hear. She looked striking, her red coat floating back toward him as the faintest recessed lights from above caught gold highlights in her hair that he hadn't noticed before.

"I think I see our train finally, at least!" she called out.

The horn of the oncoming train, which was between the previous station and theirs, rang out to announce its approach. He scanned the still empty station, left and right.

"Leni, about that night. The night of the party. I have to admit something about it."

She turned to glance at him, her eyes widened. "Please. Let's wait until we're alone."

"We are." He stepped closer to her, raising his voice as the volume of the train's rumbling increased. "Really. I want to—to get everything off my chest about that night."

"Not now. Not here—"

"Yes."

"You already know," she said, gasping, then blocking her face with the side of her hand.

"What? What're you——"

She shook her head back and forth in a furious motion. "I'm sorry. It's my fault. It's all my fault."

Caught off guard, David stumbled backward as the noxious gust of air from the approaching train surrounded them. Trembling, she had wobbled toward the tracks, and he grabbed her by the coat with his already outstretched hand, pulling her to him, away from the danger of the ledge. She fell into his body and stayed there, curling into his shoulder for a moment and clenching her fists.

The train screeched to a stop, emitting a long exhale before the doors creaked open. Inside the train, they sat together. She didn't want to talk more on the ride, drained by her outburst of emotion.

By the time they were in her office, she had collected herself. She poured a full glass of water, gulping it down. She apologized for her behavior for a fifth time, before starting in. "I needed someone to speak to, someone who could understand the situation. I couldn't keep it bottled up longer, you know?"

"I understand, of course." In fact, he could only deal with problems by bottling them up.

"I'm just going to say it, David. I'm going to come out and say it. Lee Van Knox's death was my fault. I mentioned to you that he reached out and invited me to the party. He was very mysterious about the whole thing, implying there was a reason but not telling me what it was. I had crossed paths briefly with him before. I thought maybe he had read and liked some of my short stories. I don't know what I thought, exactly. But once he arrived at Silas Hale's house, he just seemed to avoid me! It occurred to me that he wanted me there for some other reason. Maybe he thought I was personally interested in him, and when I didn't show that kind of interest, he decided to ignore me. I still don't know."

David nodded, encouraging her to continue.

"I told you I only saw him outside, but that wasn't true. I got waylaid before I could make my way out. I behaved immaturely. I was just so annoyed. Really annoyed! I had been so nervous, about being in a crowd, about what Lee wanted from me, and I had arrived so early that Silas Hale ended up putting me to work next to his housekeeper of fifteen years, whose name I'm not even sure Silas or his wife knew. You knew some of that, obviously, because that's when I met you. Then, standing there in their kitchen, it hit me: Did Lee Van Knox just ask me to come there so I could do menial chores for Silas Hale for free? The thought inflamed me. That he used me to please some overstuffed literary god. When Lee arrived, he and Silas were arguing, and Silas, maybe thinking he just wanted to calm Lee down, demanded that Lee try one of his homemade champagnes, and listed the flavors—blood orange, apple kiwi, strawberry cream, white raspberry. God, I'll never forget that list. Anyway, Lee asked for raspberry. I was still trying to leave when Silas found me and asked me to get Lee a glass. I noticed that Lee winced at the mention of kiwi, so what did I do? I decided to get him the kiwi champagne, right before I finally slipped out."

David waited for more. "Is that it?"

"I lied to you about something else, David. Colony Mutual didn't ask me to take the Silas Hale case because I had met him, or because I published a novel. When I heard the case was Colony's, I requested the assignment so that I could look through the files, because I was scared to death what it might say about me in them. There's a photo in the district attorney's files in which Lee was tagged, weeks after the party. I studied it closely. Very closely. I don't think it's him, and it began to become clear to me that he really might have died the night of the party. That night when we were there! From the investigation files Colony obtained, I could see a list of allergies Lee had, a long list, and as a kid he had been closely monitored, that's how he became obsessed with his health, running, cycling, all that. Usually kiwi intolerance is harmless, but serious allergies to it can be deadly. I believe he became sick from that stupid drink I gave him out of spite, and that he wandered somewhere in the house, where he died later. I think Silas might have panicked, maybe thought it was his fault for some reason, or his son's fault because he was intoxicated, and hid his body in his crawl space. I've been using my interviews with witnesses from the party, you and Barnaby included, deceptively, to try to find out if anyone suspected he might have died that night, because if they did, that could lead police to me! I'm sorry I couldn't explain why I wanted to come here, but you see why I couldn't risk talking in the T station or in a restaurant where someone might hear. My whole future could rest on one stupid mistake!"

"Calm down, Leni. What about the medical examiner's report? I thought it was definitive about the timeline."

She shook her head, then pulled documents out from the cardboard box, passing them to him.

"I shouldn't even show you any of this," she said, "but take a look and you'll see the postmortem report is a mess because of the rats." And the cold, he thought, though she didn't seem to know about the lack of heat. She continued: "They couldn't do an accurate analysis of what was in his system, but did find elevated immunoglobulin E in his blood—that's what certain fruits produce when digested. When I interviewed Barnaby at Simon's coffee shop, it became clear he had been obsessing over what happened between Silas and Lee—I mean, really obsessing. I asked around, and before Barnaby was working on this *Vanity Fair* profile of you, he had convinced the *Globe* to let him do an article about Silas, but the *Globe* editors dropped it when it became clear that Barnaby was being reckless with his reporting, trying to prove Silas had been innocent all along. He worshipped Silas Hale and won't accept that Silas was responsible for Lee's death. Barnaby gives me the creeps, and the more he seems to be investigating that night, the creepier he is. You seemed to know—I mean, to think, that Barnaby is a malicious person. I liked you from the first time we met, David, and I have a good instinct for people. I need someone I can trust, who can understand my predicament. I need your advice. I need an objective opinion from someone who knew the people involved. What do I do?"

"First of all, you can't blame yourself. You don't know what happened." He paused for effect. "None of us can know what happened. Not even the police."

"All it would take is one person to notice the detail about Lee's allergies, and to work backward to someone who saw me pour his drink. I can't live like this, waiting for Barnaby or someone like him to drop the hammer. I'm going to go to the police. I'll show them the misidentified cyclist. Then they could throw out their timeline, and I'll explain that I think he died the night of the party, and that it was my fault."

"No," David blurted out. "You can't do that."

She squinted.

He went on. "Your whole life would be turned upside down for something you don't know had anything to do with it!"

She sank into a contemplative expression. "I'd lose my job if I did it, that's for sure," she said, shaking her head. "My bosses would realize I manipulated them to get my hands on these files. And that would just be a start. But what am I supposed to do? I can't sleep, I can barely eat, I'm just waiting for things to fall apart. Why did I do it? Why?"

"Listen, anyone could give the wrong drink to someone by accident."

"But it wasn't an accident."

"It could have been, though, easily."

She glared at David for a moment with slight confusion at his rationale, then shrugged. "Thanks for trying to make me feel better. But I know the truth. It was a mistake, a terrible choice that arose out of base irritation, but not an accident."

David tried again. "I lived with Silas Hale. I saw a different side of him. He had a rage churning inside him all the time, and who knows what could have happened between him and Van Knox?"

"You're right. I know. But even if it wasn't my drink that caused the death, Barnaby's digging will lead to me sooner or later. If I go to the police, at least I could explain my side, and whatever happens, I'll just be ready to handle it out in the open the best I can."

If she succeeded in convincing the police that Van Knox died on the night of the party, the case would be reopened, and the first thing they'd do was dissect that night again minute by minute, at which point it was certain they'd land on David, far more certain, at least, than bothering with Leni. What he couldn't tell her was that Barnaby wasn't trying to dig into her life at all, but rather into his.

"What if you didn't have to worry about Barnaby?" he asked. "Would that change anything?"

"Sure. But how——"

"Let me talk to him," he said, interrupting. "He's interviewing me for the magazine, right? I can use that opportunity to turn the tables on him without him realizing it, to try to pick his brain. Let me try to figure out what he's really thinking."

She seemed open to this, then appeared worried about David. "Would you do that? Couldn't that backfire? If he catches on, he could cancel your profile. It's *Vanity Fair*——"

"Who cares? We're not going to let him hurt you."

She gave another slight shrug and shook her head, still unsure.

"Hey, Leni, we're not. Right?"

"Thanks, David," she said, cracking a small, self-pitying smile. "I'm lucky I met you."

To his surprise, she stood up and threw her arms over his shoulders, holding him tight.

16

WITH SO MANY UNCONTROLLED FORCES to keep in check, David did not want to risk stringing along Rebecca Hale, which might prompt her to ask around about him. So far, he had replied to her email asking to sit down together with a noncommittal placeholder. Now, he forced himself to call her to arrange a time to visit, which she suggested he do the same day. When he went to 6 Observatory Hill Road, David found himself more moved than he thought he would be. The first time he had laid eyes on this house, he had so many ambitions that had seemed unobtainable. Some of those ambitions—a good number of them—had come to pass, despite so many who had tried to rip them away and others who were still attempting to do so. This house, orange like the autumn sun, had been his castle, his fortress, a bastion to battle back against the poachers who wanted to massacre his dreams.

The door was opened by Markus Hale, which surprised and then worried David.

"Mom!" he called out.

Markus looked more like a football linebacker than David had realized the first time they met. He hardly seemed to care about David's presence.

"How have you been, Markus?" David said, making conversation while he waited for Rebecca.

"We've met?"

David thought about Markus pounding on his door, asking him to join the snowball fight, then recalled how Markus had been drinking the night of the party.

He smiled. "My mistake."

Rebecca invited him in, and they sat at the kitchen table, where he could visualize her preparing vegetables on the night of Van Knox's death.

"Thanks for coming, David," she said.

"How are things here?" he asked.

Her head rocked in a pendulum motion, then the word she chose surprised him. "Peaceful. Strangely so."

"Is there anything I can help with?"

"Maybe," she said. Her voice was stuck in one register, a blunt monotone that gave no clues about her emotions. "First, I want to know what happened. What *really* happened."

David fidgeted under the table. "What do you mean?"

"When you visited him at the jail. I think you might be keeping something from me. Trying to be sensitive to my feelings. Everyone is, and it makes me angry. What set my husband off, David?"

He almost said, "It really wasn't my fault," before realizing she had not suggested that he was to blame for anything, and that it would sound definitively like something was his fault if he said that. He wanted to say, "I did everything I could," but it sounded like a lie even in his mind.

Finally, he said: "Honestly, Rebecca, he was ranting so much against his lawyers, the police, the prosecutors, blaming them for everything, it was hard to get a sense of his state of mind. When I realized he was having a medical crisis, I called the guards in for help. I told them about his hypertension, which he had mentioned to me before."

She nodded gravely. "People were dazzled by his intellect from the time he was young. As a graduate student, he'd speed around on a motorcycle and quote John Donne on demand and wrap people around his finger. But nobody could be half as dazzled by Silas as Silas was, and that's what would get him into trouble."

He couldn't understand how that connected with his description of meeting with Silas at the jail. But it gave him permission to stray from the topic, too. "I'm sure you miss him."

Her eyes roamed around the room filled with memories. "We kept a one-bedroom apartment in downtown Boston. He convinced me it would be a change of scenery, that we could use it all the time whenever we went to the theater or symphony, but for the most part we never used it, except when he stayed there after being at a library late or a book conference. Now I may have to live alone in that empty, hollow place."

"You're selling this house?"

"I might have no choice. Silas spent money we didn't have. I still haven't been able to trace all that he squandered. Once upon a time, on the floor above us, long before you lived there, there was a very old man named Ed, a former astronaut, of all things—one of those early ones, the Apollo missions. Imagine splitting your time between outer space and Observatory Hill. Silas wanted to buy the top floor from Ed, but Ed didn't want to sell, and Silas made the man's life miserable. This man had survived going to the moon, but down here, he was harassed by Silas to the point of a mental breakdown. It was a match to the death, quite literally, as the old man wouldn't budge until his corpse was taken out on a gurney. By then, Silas had drained our accounts again. Investments that Silas thought he could profit off of by being the smartest man in every room. What I do from this point on will depend mostly on the conclusion of the insurance investigation, on whether they pay the policy out. If they determine that Silas was culpable for Lee Van Knox's death, they'll pay me nothing, unless I take Colony Mutual—our insurer—to court, which would bankrupt me to try. I barely knew Lee Van Knox, but apparently Silas hated him. So what does that mean? He despised people. He would say, 'The worst thing about writing is having readers.' His readers, who loved him, worshipped him! He'd say he'd pull their strings like a puppet master, and that he could whip their emotions around for kicks. You could say I spent our marriage avoiding being another marionette."

David became restless, searching for something acceptable in response. He thought back to the party, trying to remember if Rebecca could have noticed Silas introducing him to Markus, who now had gone into another room and was playing a video game that filled the hallway with the sounds of explosions and shrieks. "I wish I could do something more. That's your son in the other room?"

"Yes, that's Markus who let you in. Silas could never quite see himself in him."

"I had some experience with that with my father. He wasn't openly hostile about what I wanted to do, but I wished he could understand writing, could understand why I need it."

"How sad it is. You might have traded places with Markus, and maybe he would have been happier with your father. I'm sorry you were subjected to the kind of anger in Silas that you witnessed at the jail. Tell me, David, if you don't mind, what was the last thing he talked to you about during your visit?"

"The last thing?"

"He held on for days in the hospital after you saw him, but never spoke again, not much that we could understand, at least, other than incoherent rants. You alone likely heard his last words. His last meaningful words, anyway. Don't spare me, no matter how harsh a light they put him in."

"I'd have to really think about it."

She waited, not planning on closing the conversation without the answer.

"Actually, he had calmed down before I realized he needed medical help. He had just started talking about my novel, *The Crises*. He had found it at the jail library." He added quietly: "He said he read it."

"Oh? That's remarkable."

"He said he thought it was beautiful. He said he saw his own writing embedded in mine, that I was carrying on his voice. That I was a successor and he was my literary ancestor. 'A beautiful thing,' he said. As I think about it, those were the last words I heard."

"'A beautiful thing.'" She seemed content with this. "That makes sense. One of the few words we could hear when he was slurring words in intensive care before he passed was 'David.' A few times: David, David, David. It's nice to know he was thinking clearly at times in those last weeks. He was obsessively writing notes arguing for his innocence on Post-its."

"I noticed that," David said nervously, thinking of the Post-it with the words *phone*, *Van Knox*, and then a string of *Davids* written on it.

She shook her head, shrugging the thought away. "It's been so overwhelming lately, we couldn't even pick up all that detritus of his raging mind. He was lost already, in a way, before his collapse."

"The detritus. You mean his notes?"

"Um-hm. All that scribbling he was doing in his cell. There was a limited window of time to collect it all, but apparently the deadline passed a couple of days ago. When you don't get back there on time, they discard all of it. They make you crawl on your hands and knees between a labyrinth of bureaucratic buildings and kiss the disgusting ground they walk on, and if you miss your chance to reclaim property, private detectives are there like vultures to collect everything."

He sat up at attention. "Private detectives?"

"The PIs know the wardens' schedules, when things get thrown into dumpsters by the boxful, and they scoop them up."

"Who do they work for?"

"Who knows?" Rebecca said, sighing, thankfully not registering his heightened interest. "Vultures."

David knew who had private investigators gathering material on Silas—Colony Mutual.

Rebecca took a deep breath, interpreting David's silence to indicate that he, too, was contemplating the unknowns of her new life. "There's a freedom in all of this for me, if you can understand that. It's hard to explain. Hopefully the insurance investigation will take a turn for the better, and I'll never have to deal with that fetid apartment in Boston, and we can all move on."

17

ON HIS WAY OUT OF Observatory Hill, David immediately called Leni, hanging up when he heard her voicemail prompt. He started composing a text to her, but she called back before he finished.

"Leni. Did the private investigators bring in more papers on the case in the last day or two?"

"Why?"

"Hard to explain on the phone. It's important for what we've talked about."

"I don't know. I'm actually in Des Moines."

"Iowa?"

"It's an insurance hub, for your information. Let me check back in the office. Call you back."

David waited. He appreciated Leni's confidential tone of voice, which reassured him that they were acting as a team. His phone rang fifteen minutes later.

"Yes, I can confirm that a new box was delivered for me yesterday, but I was already out of the office," she reported.

The Post-its written by Silas in that box could include details of David coming back to Silas's part of the house and taking the coat, and elsewhere likely indicate that a cell phone was ringing. Sure, it might take some time to decipher the scribbling, but once Leni looked at these, once she figured them out, they could open her eyes to new facts, and if she turned on David, the rest of the dominoes would fall. He imagined her studying the last thing Silas wrote before his collapse. *DavidDavidDavidDavidItwasDavid* . . .

"You still there?" she asked.

"Yes."

"What's wrong?"

"When will you be back?"

"Tomorrow."

He didn't have a lot of time. "Leni, I have to get into your office now."

"What? David, whatever it's about, I promise I'll handle it tomorrow."

"It's not soon enough. I'll explain more later. I can't say too much on the phone. But Barnaby is on his way to Colony Mutual."

"David, what are you talking about? How do you know?"

He came up with a full-blown story on the spot. He said that he'd been told by a mutual friend of Barnaby's that Barnaby was going to Colony Mutual's office to conduct interviews. "He's meeting with some public relations person. I don't remember the name."

"Jack? Or Mei?"

David picked Jack, though said he couldn't be sure, just to be safe.

"I don't know him. He's pretty high up." She sounded worried.

"I have reason to think he's just using the meeting with public relations as a ruse," David said. "I think he found out about the documents coming in from the private investigators and he thinks there's something about you in them. Leni, we have to stop him from seeing them!"

"I'll call security."

"No. Don't do that. It will only call attention to it. We have to keep this as quiet as possible, so no one else thinks to look through the material first. Barnaby is from a wealthy family and could pay someone off. My friend said Barnaby could be there in the next hour. I'll get over there and head him off from finding anything."

"Are you sure? I don't want to get you more mixed up than you are, David. Not for my sake."

"Just get me inside, I'll do the rest."

DAVID REGRETTED HOW DISHEVELED HE looked as he passed a wall of mirrors surrounding the elevator bank before he reached the reception desk for Colony Mutual.

"David Trent," he identified himself to the receptionist. "I believe Valentina Maldenado left word that I was stopping by. I'm picking something up from her office."

The receptionist tapped something into her computer, then nodded a dispassionate confirmation. "Sign in, please," she said, indicating a sheet on a clipboard.

David picked up the clipboard and angled it toward his body so she wouldn't see. He found space between the names of visitors to squeeze in the words "Barnaby Masters," then an illegible name for someone Barnaby was purportedly there to see, with a time of arrival about half an hour earlier. Then he added his own name to another line.

The receptionist, not noticing that two new signatures had been added instead of one, appeared finished with him, so he went into the hallway and began walking.

"I'm here," he said quietly. The Bluetooth earpiece was connected to a call with Leni in Des Moines. He had rushed to meet up with Jace, who had been practicing Ultimate Frisbee in the park with a team he recently joined. Jace set up the device to be used with David's cell while explaining how to use it and droning on about the advantages of his Nokia over the top competitor, Motorola, most of which David could hardly follow.

As David set off down the hall of Colony Mutual, he made sure his hair was falling loosely over his ear to cover up the device. He continued to Leni: "Barnaby is already somewhere inside."

Her panicked voice came from his earpiece: "You saw him?"

"Only his name on the sign-in sheet. I don't think he's been here long."

"You remember how to get to my office?"

"Remind me." In fact, every excruciating detail of his two visits was imprinted in his mind, but he let her relay meticulous directions to keep her engaged. At her office door, she fed him the code for a keypad. The door floated open.

"Do you see it?"

David looked everywhere. "I only see the same box that was here last time."

"Damn. The PI must have deposited the new one with the library because I'm out of town."

"There's a library?"

"Not the good kind with books that anyone would want to read. An insurance library—files, rules, lists of case precedents, anything that hasn't been or can't be digitized. This is good, actually. This is fine. You can get out of there and go home."

"What do you mean? I haven't found anything."

"If the box is in the library, Barnaby won't be able to access it. I'll get to it tomorrow when I'm back."

David stewed. "Excellent," he said. "Stay on with me for a minute to make sure I find my way out, will you?"

He revised his plan. He stepped out of her office, then stood still for a few beats.

He lowered his voice into a whisper. "Hold on."

"What? David?" Her concerned voice became louder as his hushed. "What's wrong?"

He waited a little longer before answering, as though he was watching something unfold. "It's Barnaby. I was about to head out and saw him passing near the reception desk with some guy."

"Jack? Was it Jack? Did he have a dark mustache?"

David avoided the question. "Barnaby was asking him about seeing the library, and the guy said he'd take him there after lunch."

"What? Do you think . . . Did he see you?"

"No, I don't think so. Quick. How do I get into the library before he does, Leni?"

"Let me think, let me think."

Leni had an idea. She explained that she had a part-time administrative assistant who came once a week, and Leni kept a badge for her in a drawer in her desk. Retrieving this from her office, David followed her directions to an elevator that took him to a different floor, then to a room the size of a decent public library reading room, with high ceilings and picture windows. The windows looked out over an atrium that housed the company dining hall.

"About to go in. Will they examine the badge?"

"It's an insurance firm, not the CIA. No. But you can't take any boxes without them checking them out and scanning them into their system with the badge. You don't look much like Sienna, my assistant, so that could be a problem."

The badge opened the door to the library, and he entered.

"Okay," Leni said, "do you see the shelves on the back wall to your right?"

"Yep," he whispered. He headed for a row of shelves with boxes on them. Following her directions, he found the shelf for M. There was a box labeled with Leni's name.

"Take it to the librarian and ask for it to be put into storage."

"Why?"

"They have a back room for papers that they think aren't going to be used for a while. This way no one will even know it's there, Barnaby won't be able to see it if he goes there, and I'll grab it as soon as I'm back."

David cringed. "Got it." Heaving the box, he walked back toward the shelves. He pretended to be looking down at the atrium, then waited. He brought the box to a table.

"What's going on? I couldn't hear anything. Did you hand in the box?"

"Leni, I see Barnaby through the window. He's finishing up in the dining hall."

"Already?"

"I think he's rushing Jack to finish a coffee."

"Get rid of the box then!" she urged.

"I can't," he said in a whisper, looking at the librarian, who was sitting, flipping through a magazine in a haze of boredom. "The librarian is helping someone else, and there's another person waiting."

"It's usually empty in there! What do we do?"

"Don't worry. I'll go through it now," David said. "If there's anything incriminating about you, I'll take care of it." He sat down with the box and dug into its contents.

"Are you nervous?"

"What?"

"When I get nervous, I sing Adele to myself. Do you know her album? Her lyrics soothe me, I don't know why."

"I've heard some of it," David said.

"I'm not a great singer, but just hang in there and I'll help you through it."

"What do you mean?"

She started singing Adele's "Chasing Pavements," and whether it really was the lyrics or just the idea that someone was singing in his ear, it settled him down. He was touched. Putting his end of the call on mute, he found himself whispering to her while she sang. "Leni, this is all my fault, not yours. I'm sorry. I'm sorry you've been living with this." She kept singing, not hearing a word he said, of course, but he felt an irrational relief as the truth spilled out. "I did this, only me, not you."

The spell of his confession was broken when he found stacks of Post-it notes and an assortment of notebooks. On the Post-its, between almost illegible notes about the detectives and prosecutors, there were details of the case that Silas listed as needing to be examined or re-examined. He found items about the coats, a ringing cell phone, and then about David coming back to get a coat. He dogeared each.

He unmuted himself. "The librarian is glaring at me," he said. "I'll call you back." He hung up the call, then tore off the earpiece, which had become heavy and hot.

He waited until the librarian turned a page, which made a slight noise as she kept her eyes downward, then tore off the section in question, crumbling it into a ball and placing it in his mouth. The paper tasted like glue and dust. It was a tedious and unpleasant process, but still highly gratifying. Finally he found the notes Silas took in front of him at the jail, including the one that read *DavidDavidDavidDavidItwasDavid*.

All in all, seven balls of paper ended up in his mouth. He deposited the box back on the shelf. Once he returned to the hall, he spit the paper balls out into his hand and stuffed them into his pocket.

For most of the way back on the train, the cell signal was lost. He was irked, when he finally had a signal, to see that Leni had called three times and left a voicemail. Anything they had to say to each other shouldn't have been recorded in a voicemail, and the fact that she would leave a message made him concerned that she was becoming incautious.

When he climbed back onto the sidewalk from the train station, he listened to the voicemail.

"It's Leni! Call me when you can. Thank you for what you did today. But I can't ask you to keep putting yourself on the line. This was more proof that Barnaby is out of control. For him to show up in my office, I can't believe . . ." She didn't finish the sentence. "I created a monster by talking with him. When I get back tomorrow, I'm going to put an end to this. I'm going right to the police!"

18

BARNABY HAD EMAILED DAVID THAT he had a few last questions for the profile, suggesting again that they take a walk around some of the footbridges David had mentioned visiting. David didn't reply. Barnaby emailed again, insisting on a wrap-up conversation.

When David got ahold of Leni after hearing her voicemail, he was able to make a dent in her determination about the police, but stalling her return from Iowa would do more to ensure she wouldn't act rashly. When he was inside her office he had been able to find some personal information that could come in handy, including her flight information and confirmation numbers. That night, he called the airline.

The next day he received a text from Leni: The airline screwed up and moved me to a return flight a day later. At least I got them to upgrade me to have more legroom! And Colony got me a company phone, my first smartphone, so I have time to learn to use it. Another day in glamorous Des Moines.

Great about extra legroom seats, he wrote back. Make 'em pay!

Between Leni's agitation about Barnaby's invented visit to her office, and Barnaby actually crossing the line of decency by involving Bonnie, David's choices were running out.

David emailed him: Hey Barnaby, sorry for the delay, happy to meet again.

It was time for the next step, as Barnaby wished. The final step.

He continued: I agree w the idea of choosing one of the bridges. In fact, I think I've identified the actual bridge that Faulkner wrote into Sound and the Fury! Happy to meet there and show you, if you keep which bridge it is between us. I want to claim the literary glory (ha) of discovering it.

David remembered reading over the years about a few unexpected instances of deaths from jumping or diving from some of the lesser-known, deceptively harmless-looking bridges on the Charles River. The height of these bridges and level of the river would combine to generate blunt force trauma when jumpers hit the water, the equivalent of being hit by a car, while in other cases the shock of the experience or of the cold temperatures led to quick drowning. One particular bridge, a hundred and fifty years old, was set apart from busier areas and had needed repairs for more than a decade, but it was not frequented enough for authorities to devote funds to a restoration. It was a hazard for reckless or drunk students, or anyone who might be taken by surprise while on it.

How about tomorrow morning, 10:30? I have to run errands during the day.

That would be low tide, which he looked up, when the distance was greatest between bridge and water. Nearby college students who hadn't already left town for Thanksgiving break would be at classes or still asleep, so the area should be even quieter. Meanwhile, after pushing Barnaby off the bridge, David would be the perfect witness to the fatal accident. It was Barnaby, after all, who had originally asked to meet at a bridge; he had proof of that. David merely chose which one. And the loss of Barnaby would undeniably harm David as much as or more than that of anyone in the world; he needed Barnaby to be alive and well to finish the *Vanity Fair* article, arguably marking the peak of David's career. It would be viewed as a sad turn of events for all involved, including David. Especially David! On an ethical level, if anyone was culpable, it would be Barnaby, for his monomaniacal quest to bully and break him down.

Great, see you there! Barnaby replied, as if they were buddies. **The secrets of the bridge are safe with me, brother.**

Looking forward! David wrote back, pal to pal, brother to brother.

He prepared. He went to the T station where he had seen discarded pairs of actual gloves alongside the glove sculpture, pocketing a pair in weathered but decent shape when nobody was looking. He also walked to the chosen footbridge several times to study every inch of it.

He slept well that night, and woke up to a wonderful feeling that he would be moving on, completely clear of Barnaby's deviousness and free to pursue life again. His primary concern was that Barnaby might sense something amiss and cancel the rendezvous. His phone rang twice in the morning, and the ring of a phone had never been so ear-piercing. The first time was from a doctor's office, confirming an upcoming checkup he had meant to cancel. The second was from a number he didn't recognize, and he almost didn't pick up, then worried that not answering could leave some unknown loose end, but it turned out to be a recorded solicitation for a car warranty.

When the time came to leave his apartment, he felt dizzy, sickened. There was no way he was steady enough to do what had to be done. He emailed Barnaby that they'd have to meet later.

What time, David? Barnaby wrote back. **I'm on deadline and have to close this up to make the April issue.**

Hours went by. **Might change to a different day,** he emailed Barnaby.

Need to meet TODAY, Barnaby insisted.

Barnaby was more right than he could have known, and his messages only helped generate the record that he needed to show that the meeting had happened on Barnaby's insistence, not his own. If Barnaby was overworked, overtired, lost his balance on a dilapidated bridge, that would be Barnaby's fault. It all had to be done, in any case, before Leni was back from Des Moines, and before Barnaby managed to warp David's world beyond repair.

David replied: **Understood. On my way to bridge.**

The skyline and the Charles River were lit burnt orange by the lowering sun. Approaching the spot in question, David slowed his step. Though they were meeting so much later than he had originally planned, the area was as deserted as he could have hoped. The sloping, grassy banks on either side were overgrown, discouraging anyone who might otherwise sit and watch the river. He spotted a man in a hoodie and overcoat wandering aimlessly, possibly one of the many who lived on the streets in Cambridge, but the wanderer made his way in another direction.

"Don't get shy now," Barnaby called out. He was already there, standing in the middle of the bridge, where the arch was highest, a messenger bag on his shoulder.

David put his hand in the inside pocket of his pea jacket, feeling the beat-up leather where he had stowed the gloves. His sweater vibrated with his heartbeat, and he pushed his hand against his chest as though that could steady it. He stepped onto the bridge and, without saying a word, began moving closer to Barnaby.

"Apologies for haranguing you about meeting," Barnaby said. "I hope I didn't come off as unfeeling."

"Not a problem." David had expected to be remorseful in advance of what he had to do, but the smug expression on Barnaby's face made him hate him and everything he stood for, more than he already had. Barnaby had never earned his opportunities, and never fought for them. He had merely mastered being at the right place at the right time.

"See," Barnaby continued, "it wasn't just our schedules I had to manage."

"You're ready for me?" Behind Barnaby came a younger man with close-shaved hair and a dangling earring, weighed down by equipment around his neck, including a camera with a long lens.

"I asked that you keep the location of this bridge to yourself—"

"Finn doesn't care about *The Sound and the Fury* or Faulkner. He doesn't care about you, either. Trust me. We need photos for the piece. That's why a bridge was such a good idea. Perfect setting, beautiful lighting this time of day, so this all worked out."

David followed instructions to stand at different points on the bridge, staring down at the water, glancing across at the sunset. The photographer took light readings. David desperately hoped the photographer was just going to snap a few pictures and leave, but as a quarter of an hour ticked away, then another, he resigned himself to the fact that the photographer would not be leaving before Barnaby, and certainly not going anywhere far enough for what David came to do. Teams of rowers periodically streamed by in shells. The coaches, in their launches, called out instructions. He watched this, wistful at the sight.

"You seem distracted today," Barnaby said at one point.

"No."

"Good. I think we need some photos from the bank below, looking up."

The photographer climbed down from the bridge. As soon as he was out of earshot, Barnaby moved close enough to speak without being heard by their third wheel, but not so close as to be in the frame of the photos.

"I want him to capture some shots of you as your life changes forever," Barnaby said, his face fixing itself in a sneer.

In that moment, David found himself scrutinizing Barnaby's messenger bag. Was it similar to the one worn by the man who had a couple years earlier barged through the line where David stood at the sandwich shop, smashing the door against a baby stroller like some kind of madman? *Move!* he had screamed, shoving them all aside. At one point he had thought that could have been Lee Van Knox, but might it have been Barnaby, instead? Was that who Barnaby had been all along, a marauder, a screamer, a pusher, a man who valued a sandwich over the safety of a child?

"I haven't figured every detail out. I'll freely admit that, Trent. But I know it was you. I know it was you, not Silas, who killed Lee Van Knox."

David swallowed. "What are you babbling about, Barnaby?"

"I knew the moment I opened your novel and began to realize it would never have won an award. There's some glimmer of substance in there you might take pride in. But it was far too ordinary to win that award. An award, as I happened to remember from an otherwise dull chat I once had at a literary marketplace conference, that Lee Van Knox administered. So I had to know: What connected the fact that Lee Van Knox's body was found inside that house, and the fact that you lived there beforehand? It hit me altogether. It was the award. When you spotted Van Knox at the party, you went white as a sheet."

The photographer wanted a wide shot, and he was walking even farther away along the bank. David kept his voice down, but he knew the photographer could not hear any of it, anyway.

"I have no idea what—this is insane. Goodbye. I'm leaving, Barnaby." He turned and started walking.

"Didn't you wonder why I pitched doing a feature about you to my *Vanity Fair* editor in the first place? Took some convincing to get them to bite, too, but I'm pretty good at being convincing, and once I got the assignment, I had my runway to find everything I needed about you. In fact, you were spoonfeeding it to me!"

David slowed down and then came to a stop.

Barnaby went on. "Then some nervous wannabe writer who works in insurance asked to have coffee with me, and she asked, as if an afterthought, what I believed about the timeline of Van Knox's death, which made me wonder: Could Van Knox possibly have died sooner than they said? But the key to it all came from your gracious Bonnie, thinking she was helping you by proving to me how cruel Silas was when he refused to heat the house. She even recorded the temperatures, and sent me photos of the thermometer! That third floor was so cold, the body nestled right below it was preserved longer than anyone would have expected. The death happened long before anyone realized. But of course, you know that already—firsthand."

Barnaby held up a business card. It belonged to Christine Horvack, the assistant district attorney.

"You spoke to her?" David asked quietly.

"You did, too, I assume? They debriefed all the people they could find who knew Silas and might have seen him with Van Knox."

"You told her this nonsense."

"They will be very interested, don't you think? But not yet. Call me selfish. I want this to break in my *Vanity Fair* piece. As I say, I haven't figured out where every puzzle piece goes, haven't exactly figured out why you descended to this pathetic nadir, like Dante chased down into hell by beasts."

Barnaby laid out one of his theories, which suggested that he had cycled through others before arriving at a grand conclusion. David had met Van Knox somewhere, he said, and stumbled on something incriminating about him. When he found out that Van Knox was in charge of the award committee for the Boston Literary Society, David blackmailed him into rigging the Best First Novel Award to go to him. David thought people would see him differently, but they still saw him for what he was. The night of the party, something changed. Maybe by that point Van Knox had found a spine and regretted letting David force his hand, or maybe David got greedy and demanded something more from Van Knox. Then, Van Knox confronted him.

"And either way you killed him—premeditated or no, who knows, maybe you don't even know—and then sat back to let Silas take the fall."

The flash sparked from the photographer's camera far off on the grassy bank, illuminating an expression on David's face that wavered between horror and defiance. The photographer, bored and oblivious to the life-changing conversation, must have been content with the shots he had taken, as he wandered off to shoot the skyline. David couldn't imagine how the moment would come out in the photo, maybe as a blur. He managed to hold back almost any emotion or reaction from his face. "I thought coming up with a plot was beneath your artistry as a writer, Barnaby. Do you really believe a single word of what you're saying?"

Barnaby's scratchy laugh returned, triumphant. "I'm holding your life in my hands, brother! I have your death sentence in my back pocket and, hand to God, I'm relishing it. The feeling, I can't even describe it! I'm a demigod watching you from Olympus, deciding how your fate will unfold. This won't be a profile, it will be an exposé of a grifter, a portrait of a fraud right before his life is over, a Judgment Day. It will go down in history."

"What is it about me that bothers you so much?"

"I was Silas Hale's literary heir. You were a dust mite on his shoe! I should have been walking in his footsteps. I should have a feature being written about me in *Vanity Fair*! But you wormed your way into Silas's life. When Silas died, everything fell apart for me. At one point I cursed out the president of the imprint that was planning to publish my book. They dropped me flat, emptying my pockets on my way down, to be vindictive. Well, I'm getting it back, brother, all of it. You were responsible, and you're going to be my comeback."

Darkness had spread around them. The photographer was now in the distance, sitting on the grass, watching Barnaby for the sign that they could leave.

David took a few steps closer to Barnaby. He reached back into his inside coat pocket and pulled out the gloves.

Barnaby frowned, squinting at the gloves. "You cold, Trent?"

David glanced over at the photographer, then back at Barnaby. He tossed the gloves over the side.

He watched for a moment while the gloves floated, barely rippling the water, the empty fingers caressing the surface. He turned once again, then walked away across the bridge, not looking back at Barnaby this time.

DAVID SAW A CALL COMING in from Leni. He let it go to voicemail. She was back in Boston, calling as soon as she landed at Logan Airport.

I'm going to be off grid for a while, David texted, but don't worry about Barnaby. Can't go into details now, but he won't be bothering you! Which he believed was true.

Leni would know everything soon enough, but he didn't have the heart to be the one to tell her or Bonnie or his parents or anyone else. He wasn't brave enough. Maybe it had been inevitable. Even if Barnaby hadn't come for him. Maybe it had been a matter of time before something inside him forced him to confess. Maybe he would even feel a sense of freedom at the truth coming out. Maybe he could be grateful that Barnaby would tell the story before he would, exempting him from the pain of that first admission, and allowing him to dispute whatever specific parts Barnaby got incorrect, as though that would matter much to anyone but David.

19

HE HAD BEGUN TO WONDER, almost as a neutral observer who was merely curious about the whole situation might have done, how his demise would unfold once the profile was published. Maybe it wouldn't be quick at all, not a gunshot but a gradual disassembling of his life, limb by limb. He couldn't say which he'd prefer. Why draw it out? The *Vanity Fair* article, from what Barnaby had revealed and what David could find out from his publicist, was assigned to the April 2011 issue. He wished he never had to see the article at all, and at the same time he waited for it every waking moment. He imagined some compelling ledes for the article, including: *By the time he was finished wreaking havoc, David Trent stood over two dead people who had influenced his literary career.*

He wished he could determine which day the guillotine would fall, at least. Glossy monthlies would come out roughly a week before the beginning of the month listed on the cover, so the April issue would be available at the end of March—it was usually released on either the first or second weekday of the week before the first of the next month, but sometimes delayed or accelerated for logistical reasons. No wonder print journalism was on shaky ground—people didn't even know when to look for a new issue when their life depended on it. The online versions of the print issue's various articles, meanwhile, were rolled out in a staggered, unpredictable fashion, with even more complicated access on proliferating e-readers and apps for tablets and some phones. All he could do was wait, never knowing when the death blow would fall.

In March, David told Bonnie he would be out of town for two weeks on a trip Parable had arranged for him, which would feature some speaking events at corporate book clubs. It wasn't true, but these kinds of events usually weren't listed publicly, so nobody could check on him. At least Bonnie wouldn't have to see his face when the issue came out, and she could quickly and quietly break their engagement and cut ties while he was gone, without fuss and with minimal embarrassment. To find out that someone she believed in, much less a man she'd planned to marry, was deceitful would be a big blow to Bonnie at the best of times. Using the last of his award money, he took some aimless detours, staying with a friend who was teaching a writing course in Rhode Island and then at a short-term rental in New York City before he decided to go to Canada at the start of the week in question. He didn't think being out of the country would necessarily help his situation, but perhaps it would slow down whatever hell was to come.

There was a Montreal-bound train that Monday from New York. He was never in a rush, not these days. Twelve hours of travel—really thirteen or fourteen hours, with the usual delays—meant no more to him than a five-minute walk around the block. Something about the unhurried monotony of a train ride, the patient repetition, fit the general somnolence that had descended upon him. He no longer felt pressure from the outside world, only responded to or even read messages when absolutely necessary. He stared at walls or windows for hours in his wait for fate to reach him. He saw no reason to struggle or put up a fight, and felt it was making him a different and more accepting person, though there would be no particular benefit to a metamorphosis, not at this point.

On the train, he noticed passengers on devices grappling with the spotty cellular and wireless service that Amtrak had started a few months earlier on this route. Served them right for trying to—well, trying to do anything, as far as he was concerned. He was content to roll up his jacket on the window and lean his head on it. When the conductors checked the tickets, they also passed out Canadian immigration forms, explaining that they might be needed upon arrival. He dug out a pen from his bag and started to fill his form out, but felt depleted at the idea of giving his personal data to strangers. He scribbled on the margins for a while, then stuck the form in the seat pocket. It wouldn't be needed for hours, in any case, and the way the conductor said "might" suggested a formality they were obliged to mention but would be overlooked.

David was distracted and a little amused by a conflict between two riders separated by four or five rows. One was trying to talk on her phone, battling the frequent drops in service and shouting into the void to test whether the person on the other end still heard her. The second rider was turning around to shoot dirty looks toward the first, sometimes emitting a shushing sound. Both were equally in the wrong, David decided; as the caller spoke too loudly in a bizarre attempt to overcome the poor reception, and the shusher should have chosen the Quiet Car, which was elsewhere on the train. Both, it seemed, had tied themselves to cosmically hopeless causes, and as punishment they would both be forever unsatisfied, stuck with each other until the end.

His jacket slipped, and the side of his head came to rest on the cool glass of the window. He only realized he had been asleep after he awoke, face to glass, to the feeling of vibration from his phone, signaling a new message. Turned out he had been sleeping for hours.

The text read: I saw Vanity Fair!

His eyes unblurred, and he stared. Then the screen blinked to black. In his general state of malaise, he had forgotten to charge his phone the night before, and after boarding the train he forgot that he forgot. He dug through his bag for his charger, fumbling to get it plugged into the seat's wall outlet. By the time the phone had enough power to turn on again, its signal strength was too weak to receive or send texts. He looked around the train, as though someone nearby might know something about his ruination before he did.

After a few minutes, he heard the loud talker start another cell conversation and knew there had to be a signal again. He immediately checked his phone, which had inched up in battery power. He powered up his laptop, clicking over to the *Vanity Fair* website and the sleek font of the headline: "David Trent's Way." But it was one of the articles kept behind a firewall that required a subscription, meaning that the editors thought it juicy enough that people would pay to read it. He tried to go to the subscription page, but the Wi-Fi gave out again. Besides, he couldn't subscribe to the magazine that was tearing his life down.

The train seemed to be under a bridge or inside a tunnel every three or four minutes now, cutting out any connection. The original text message had come from a gossipy cousin whose only contact with David seemed to happen when something appeared about his book in the media, or when a relative died. In desperation, David wrote back to him: **What did it say?** But after an agonizing wait, that text failed to go through. Even when service improved and the message was sent, there was no reply. The text's wording could mean anything. The exclamation point could be interpreted with polar opposite significances. Meanwhile the headline, "David Trent's Way," stubbornly gave away nothing.

Two Canadian officers wobbled their way through the train car, stopping to speak to passengers who were continuing all the way to Montreal. They requested the previously distributed immigration cards, and sometimes asked stock questions, such as "Why are you coming to Canada?" They appeared largely uninterested in the responses. Were they even listening to the passengers? Or were they actually looking for someone specific, and the questions were merely distractions, a ruse? Could the wheels of justice possibly spin so quickly, and could Massachusetts law enforcement have already mobilized the Canadian railroad police, now headed straight for him?

He was in the middle of the train car, and the immigration officers were slowly getting closer, one from the front, one from the back. David pulled out his immigration card that he still hadn't filled out beyond his name, which might be damning enough. He crumpled it up. The voice on the intercom announced a stop at Saratoga Springs, which was in upstate New York.

He gathered his belongings. As he was making his way through the aisle, one of the officers took the ticket stub from above the seat David had just abandoned.

"Going to Montreal? This is Saratoga Springs. Sir? Sir?"

David pretended he didn't hear. A split second later the door rattled open, and he practically leaped onto the platform, hit by a rush of biting air. He only looked back once, to see if either of the officers was following.

He hustled from the platform into the small brick building that comprised the station. More messages were accumulating on his phone. **WOW** was from one friend. Jace wrote—David could tell he typed it out with one finger, as he had seen him do a thousand times—**saw VF call me**. The small newsstand in the station did not carry *Vanity Fair*. The cashier gave him directions to two places that might. In town, he approached the magazine section of a larger newsstand. He spotted *Vanity Fair* on a display rack. A police officer was standing to one side of the section, speaking to someone David couldn't see from where he stood. His phone was pinging from his pocket, one message after the other. He hesitated, planning on just turning around and exiting, looking for the magazine elsewhere, but then at the last moment he charged right up to the magazine and, when he was close enough, threw it down onto the counter in front of the cashier. The police officer never looked in his direction.

As soon as David got outside, he tore through the magazine until his thumb landed on the article, anchored by a photo of him gazing down from the footbridge at the Charles. He first scanned that page and the next ones for Silas Hale's name. He only found one mention in a paragraph about David's literary influences. Then he searched for the name Lee Van Knox—nothing at all. Lost in confusion, he read the whole profile twice before he could believe what he was seeing. It was a fairly conventional, arguably glowing profile of David and his novel. He could not fathom that this was the article—he must have been trapped in the cruelest dream. Perhaps at the last minute Barnaby had worried about how the legal department of Condé Nast would view accusations of murder and cover-up in a literary profile, although that hardly provided an explanation for him writing something celebratory.

Emails and texts of congratulations flooded his phone throughout the day, so many he couldn't keep up. One stood out for being unusual. It was a curt message from the usually loquacious Brandi, asking to see him as soon as possible.

Having lost his seat on the train to Canada, David stayed overnight at the first bed-and-breakfast in upstate New York he could locate, then made the reverse trip. Back in Cambridge, he arranged to meet Brandi at the theater where she was rehearsing the new two-act play she had written, which was about a fictional theater company discovering a lost Shakespeare play. She led him to a balcony, where she could watch the rehearsal from a dark spot while they spoke privately.

"This director doesn't understand my vision," she said. "How did I get stuck with her? We couldn't afford someone better, that's how. Who said, 'There are the rich and the poor, and everyone else is embarrassed'? Who said that?"

"I'm not sure, Brandi."

"No use. Why are you always no use, David? Anyway, Barnaby asked that I talk to you."

David felt uneasy. "Barnaby did?"

She gave an annoyed purr. "Look, David, I'll be honest, I don't have time for this. You see I don't have time! But Barnaby implied he'd review my play in the *Globe* if I did him this favor and spoke to you for him. He wants to know if you saw the article."

David stared at her.

"I guess you saw it," she said. "He wants to know if you were happy with it."

What could he say? He answered what should have been obvious. "Very."

"He hopes that he can count on you."

"Sorry?"

She sighed. "He said he knows, and wants to know he can count on you."

"Count on me," he echoed back, further confused by everything she said, but getting the feeling that he should do whatever it took not to let her know.

"He hopes the *Vanity Fair* article is a peace offering. That's all he told me, David!"

He tried to read her face, but she genuinely seemed to know nothing more, and not to care about it beyond priming Barnaby to do a favor by passing along his message. Finally, he nodded solemnly. "Absolutely, Brandi. Of course I understand, and I appreciate you talking to me."

"Fiction writers! That's where the drama is."

When he got home, he combed through the messages that had piled up. There was a voicemail from Rebecca Hale. He thought that was notable enough that he called her back first.

"Sorry for the delay, Rebecca. I've been traveling."

"Congratulations, David," was the first thing she said, but she wasn't talking about *Vanity Fair*.

She explained that the brain trust at the *New Yorker*, in filling Silas's position as fiction editor at large, had asked Rebecca whom she thought Silas would select, and without hesitation she had told them David. "Even with my endorsement, they had more experienced names in mind," she continued. "But it's mostly honorary. And between my recommendation and your award, and hearing that *Vanity Fair* was profiling you on top of it, they agreed."

"I don't know what to say. I'm shocked and flattered, Rebecca. Thank you."

"When you told me what Silas said before his collapse, it was clear you were the only choice."

"What he said . . ."

"His last words, at least his last words in his right mind. About your book, that you were carrying his voice forward? 'A beautiful thing.' Wasn't that it? When he said your name to us in the hospital, he must have been trying to tell us that, too, but didn't have the strength. You'll find there's a very comfortable annual salary, without much work involved, a couple roles on panels and occasionally serving as a contest judge. Plus, the ability to place two or three fiction pieces a year by writers of your choice without any interference. I think you'll be pleased, and I know Silas would have been happy for it to be you."

In his overstuffed inbox, there was an email waiting from a name he hadn't recognized. It was from an executive at Condé Nast sharing the legal terms of the editorial role, which had been renamed the Silas Hale Fiction Editor at Large. Strangely, Silas's literary status had not been noticeably tarnished by the charges against him and his death. If anything, his legend had grown, and his apparent murder of Lee Van Knox, over time, was seen as some kind of unfortunate extension of a fiery mind. Van Knox was the collateral damage of genius.

David was invited to attend a literary gala at the American Museum of Natural History in New York City, where all the *New Yorker* editors would amass, a kind of coming-out for David that coincided with a more public announcement of his position with the magazine. He noted the difference between the New York literary scene and the one in Boston—in New York, writers could pass for actors or models, while in less polished Boston oddity was a commodity. From the vestibule where he and Bonnie checked in with gala staff, it was only a few steps later, through a corridor of elaborately designed vistas of various natural terrains, that they were surrounded by hundreds of contented literary powerhouses in gowns and tuxedos. They were all seemingly oblivious to the hundred-foot blue whale suspended from the domed glass ceiling above them. David couldn't stop looking up.

THE WORLD OF SUCCESSFUL WRITERS stretched out before his eyes. Writers as acclaimed, or more, as Silas Hale. They all seemed so happy and carefree. They wore smiles and produced regular fits of laughter for each other's benefit, and it seemed as though all their warmth at once welcomed him into their sphere. Inspired by their company, he could hardly have called to mind everything that had happened with Silas even if he wanted to. Memories seemed to dissolve. Deep down, he knew that in other contexts these same writers and editors might have looked askew at him or at each other as possible threats, but by an unspoken silent accord, being at the gala meant you belonged.

Writers and editors introduced themselves to David. He met publicists from Parable and *Vanity Fair* that he had spoken to and emailed with before. Even meeting in person, though, everyone still seemed to be just names, floating personae who were not seeing each other, not really. David breezily agreed to contribute a chapter to a book on fiction writing—why not?—and to give a paid talk to a creative writing class at Bard College. He wanted to stay at this gala and in this museum forever, but it also felt alarming. Listening to the speeches made him dizzy.

At one point Bonnie excused herself to the bathroom, and David took a walk through the exhibits, as guests were encouraged to do, although most declined. He reached a chamber where African elephants, frozen in time, were marching toward him.

"Looking good, Trent."

From behind him came Barnaby, grinning, wearing an immaculate black tuxedo.

Even though he wasn't entirely surprised, David shuddered.

"What are you doing here, Barnaby?"

"Covering the gala for *GQ*. The brass at Condé Nast were happy with my profile of you."

David didn't comment. Barnaby turned angry.

"Aren't you still pleased with it, brother?"

"What do you want?"

"It's been my dream for my fiction to appear in the pages of the *New Yorker* since I was ten. I could reach one brass ring after the other, every other magazine under the sun, but I still got steady rejections from the *New Yorker*, even once Silas came into my life. Time and again, Silas promised he'd publish one of my stories there. It would come up at least once a year, then the idea would vanish, and if I ever brought it up, he would rip into me about how I was a climber, a striver. He played with my heart, brother, and the more he did, the more he made sure he kept that grip. A week or so before the deadline for me to turn in your profile, I heard. I didn't believe it at first—I couldn't believe you were to succeed Silas. But then I heard it from a second source. And then again. So I threw my lot in with you, brother. I wonder, could I count on you to give my submission a fair chance?"

If he published Barnaby, David knew he could never come forward with a negative word about him. Technically, Barnaby might still be able to destroy him. But if he let the world know that Barnaby got into the *New Yorker* by blackmailing him, Barnaby would never recover his reputation. Mutually assured destruction.

"Is that all you want, Barnaby?"

"'Silhouettes against the Dimming Eden,'" Barnaby replied. "That's the story I have in mind, and I think it'll move you. Yes, this is what I want. Very much."

Barnaby believed that David had done horrible things, arguably even more terrible than what had actually happened. Yet he was willing to let him get away with all of it, just to see his name in the pages of the *New Yorker*, because he had longed for that, and longed for others to see that, and he could never shake that longing. David hated that he understood Barnaby so well. He wished he was incapable of making sense of him.

"What if I had done everything you said I did?" David asked. "Would you still accept my help?"

"What's in the past can't help either of us." Barnaby stared at him, picking up on his dissatisfaction. "I wonder if you're happy being a writer, Trent. Sometimes you seem more like a kind of mathematician of ethics, inventing formulas that add up to what is moral, what is just."

David was transfixed again by the elephants, who now did not seem to be marching, but stampeding. As if he remained another minute, he would be flattened, and they would run wild through the rest of the museum, killing every writer inside in their fancy outfits. He walked back to his table, but stopped at a distance, filled with pleasure as he watched Bonnie talking to new acquaintances about their upcoming wedding, glowing with pride in him and contentment with their relationship. He was here, where he needed to be. Everyone here was bulletproof, no matter what they had done in their lives, and what they would do in the future; they were part of a club that could never really be touched. At the same time, he felt a pang inside, a nagging feeling of things left undone, things that one day would seize him completely, like the moment after waking from a nightmare, when a terror is never more real or unavoidable.

AT THE END OF SUMMER David took a walk through Observatory Hill. He was meeting up with Jace for lunch at an Indian restaurant and took a detour to see the house. Sometimes he was aware of a somber feeling that came over him, when moments from the past would cut through to the front of his consciousness, but mostly he managed to distract himself before they took hold. Still, sometimes he would be struck by a flood of those feelings, and they would be harder to shake off.

As he neared the house, he knew he wouldn't ring the Hales' door, or at least he didn't think he would, but dug his hands in his pockets to ensure he wasn't tempted. When he got close, he saw a bouquet of helium balloons tied together, with the number 7 on the balloon in front. Behind the fence rose an inflatable bouncy house, with the happy shouts of children colliding coming from inside. He peered up at the third floor but couldn't make out anything.

Across the street, there were candles in Antoinette's windows, but they were not lit. Maybe she was mourning the loss of Silas Hale from the neighborhood, dimming the brightness of reflected light she felt shining on her literary salon. Perhaps she even regretted David's departure from the street, even if she never forgave him for keeping her out of the party.

DAVID REACHED OUT TO LENI. She wrote him back, apologizing for being an absentee correspondent, having been tied up with work-related matters, and asked if he could meet her next weekend, as she was leaving town the following week.

When the chosen time came, he walked up the two flights to her Back Bay apartment on Dartmouth Street. Prepared to knock, he found the door already open. The place was almost empty. There was a folded-up area rug in front of him, which brought to mind the memory of Silas watching him roll up the rug that covered the trapdoor.

"David?"

He snapped out of his reverie. Leni was staring at him with bewilderment.

"Leni. You're leaving?"

"I swear I've been meaning to tell you, but I've been crazed. I'm a terrible friend, I know. I'm moving to Des Moines."

"Des Moines?"

"Yep. I told you—"

"Insurance hub, right."

"A headhunter recruited me. A headhunter! I'm in demand."

"Of course you are, Leni, and should be. Congratulations." He hesitated. "What about Colony Mutual?"

"More money, more responsibility at the new place. Colony Mutual is too top-heavy for me to ever really move up the ladder. They barely flinched when I put in my notice."

"What did they decide to do with the Hale case?"

"The company went to arbitration with Rebecca Hale, and settled on a reasonable amount of money to pay out. I heard she still had so much debt she sold the house, moved to the suburbs. The investigation is officially closed, anyway." She was flitting around the apartment, organizing boxes.

"Leni, I can help get your writing out there again. Even in the *New Yorker*."

"You know what their original motto was?"

"Whose?"

"The *New Yorker*. I wrote a paper once in college about their history. Their original ads before their first issue proclaimed that the *New Yorker* will be 'the magazine which is not edited for the old lady in Dubuque.' It was meant to keep people away, to say we're better than you because of where you live or where you learned. Now I'll just be that lady in Dubuque—well, Des Moines."

"I can change that."

"How?" She gave a little laugh. "I don't write anymore, David."

"You could if you wanted to—your writing is incredible. You're incredible. You're born to do it. It's not right."

"Does it matter? There's no morality in it, David. Isn't that what we write about, one way or the other, when we write fiction? Characters groping for any sign of morality amid one cataclysm after another."

David sighed, frustrated. "Lee Van Knox invited you to that party at the Hales', yes?"

She was thrown by the comment, or maybe by the fact that he wanted to talk about it, about the dead man who had caused so much consternation. "And?"

"One of his roles was to organize the awards committees for the Boston Literary Society. I got to thinking recently. Maybe he wanted to put your novel up for another award? Or maybe you had won one that got overlooked, that he wanted to tell you about?"

She thought about this. "I guess it's . . . possible. But then why wouldn't he just have told me then?"

David shrugged. "Who knows? Something came up. He got distracted."

"Well, that's a theory, all right!" She laughed.

He couldn't grasp her flippant reaction. "What if you were meant to get an award for your novel, too, Leni?"

"I'm confused. What do you mean?"

"What if that novel was just the beginning for you? You didn't have to give up your writing and be in Des Moines."

"It's really nice there, David. People are friendly—they're welcoming, they're not trying to get something from you." Her usually grim but patient expression became just grim. "When Lee Van Knox invited me to that party, I had already been doing everything I could to get out of that world."

"I know, I know," he said, nervously laughing. "You never met so many sociopaths as you did when you started hanging out with writers."

She didn't return the smile. "People who rationalize that any harm they are doing is for some higher creative or moral good they've designed in their heads."

"Come on, Leni! You don't mean it."

"I know I can write. I knew that from the time I was ten! It was like music that flowed out of me. But . . ." She paused to consider the effect of her next words on him. "No offense, really. I don't want to live in fear of someone crushing me for their amusement. Awards or no awards, I'm lucky I escaped! The people I dealt with—well, let's say people are usually disappointing. The writers I got to know were either born corrupted or were corrupted the moment they published. That second category, they're the disease. They're werewolves, cannibals. They're everywhere. Then you're left with bad people being rewarded and acclaimed, with arrogance expected and emboldened—isn't that what drove you crazy about Barnaby?"

"No. No! I mean, yes. But it doesn't have to be like that."

"Some people have the stomach for it—you do, and I admire that more than I could tell you. The Lee Van Knox situation simply pulled me back where I didn't want to go. I never want to look back."

"Leni, really . . ."

She checked the time. "I really have to get a deposit dropped off with the movers. I'm going to lose my slot to get out of here."

She gave him a hug that was so sudden and tight it terrified him a little.

"I guess I won't see you for a while, Leni." He felt as if this empty apartment was his own, as if he had lived there amid all its nothingness and would never be able to leave, as if he would spend his days here, or somewhere like it, abandoned and alone.

She suddenly smiled, as though she'd just remembered a joke she'd saved to tell him. "I almost forgot!" She went to a bag and fished through it. "Don't make fun of me. I got a copy of your book. So funny—*Crisis*. *The Crises*. Great minds." She handed him the book and then found a pen.

"Great minds."

"Would you sign it for me before I go?"

He opened his book and it flipped right to the title page. What was she thinking as she watched him? Could she see through to his thoughts and fears that he might have done everything that anyone could accuse him of? And that he would always dread that the next Barnaby was waiting for him behind the next door?

"Leni," he said, "nothing would make me happier."

END

Acknowledgments

FOR A NOVEL ABOUT WRITERS not treating each other well, I am lucky to know so many on the other end of the spectrum, whose generosity sharing razor-sharp ideas at the manuscript stage made this book better: Eric Bennett, Gabriella Gage, Joseph Gangemi, Patrick McCullough, Cynthia Siegel, and Scott Weinger. My stellar publishing team bolstered the novel with their wholehearted faith and patiently crafted notes, led by my agent Suzanne Gluck and my editor Sara Nelson, with invigorating support from colleagues Lane Kizziah, Liv Guion, and Tracey Thompson at WME, and Jonathan Burnham, Edie Astley, Miranda Ottewell, Lindsay Prevette, and Becca Putman at HarperCollins. Thanks to my family support system in Susan and Warren Pearl and Marsha Selley, and for the steady encouragement of Kevin Birmingham, Ben Cavell, Jon Housman, and Greg Nichols. Thank you to my very first reader as always, Tobey, who gave me the confidence I needed for a story that had snuck up on me, and to Cooper, Graham, and Lulu, who sometimes believe me that I have writing I have to do.

About the Author

MATTHEW PEARL's books have been international and *New York Times* bestsellers and have been translated into more than thirty languages. His nonfiction writing has appeared in the *New York Times*, the *Boston Globe*, *Vanity Fair*, and *Slate*, and he edits *Truly*Adventurous* magazine. He has been chosen as Best Author in *Boston* magazine's "Best of Boston" issue and received the Massachusetts Book Award for Fiction.